THE COUNT
OF MONTE CRISTO
VOL V.

BY

ALEXANDRE DUMAS

British Library Cataloguing-in-Publication Data
A catalogue record for this book is available from the
British Library

Contents

Alexandre Dumas

Alexandre Dumas was born in Villers-Cotterêts, France in 1802. His parents were poor, but their heritage and good reputation – Alexandre's father had been a general in Napoleon's army – provided Alexandre with opportunities for good employment. In 1822, Dumas moved to Paris to work for future king Louis Philippe I in the Palais Royal. It was here that he began to write for magazines and the theatre.

In 1829 and 1830 respectively, Dumas produced the plays *Henry III and His Court* and *Christine,* both of which met with critical acclaim and financial success. As a result, he was able to commit himself full-time to writing. Despite the turbulent economic times which followed the Revolution of 1830, Dumas turned out to have something of an entrepreneurial streak, and did well for himself in this decade. He founded a production studio that turned out hundreds of stories under his creative direction, and began to produce serialised novels for newspapers which were widely read by the French public. It was over the next two decades, as a now famous and much loved author of romantic and adventuring sagas, that Dumas produced his best-known works – the D'Artagnan romances, including

The Three Musketeers, in 1844, and *The Count of Monte Cristo*, in 1846.

Dumas made a lot of money from his writing, but he was almost constantly penniless as a result of his extravagant lifestyle and love of women. In 1851 he fled his creditors to Belgium, and then Russia, and then Italy, not returning to Paris until 1864. Dumas died in Puys, France, in 1870, at the age of 68. He is now enshrined in the Panthéon of Paris alongside fellow authors Victor Hugo and Emile Zola. Since his death, his fiction has been translated into almost a hundred languages, and has formed the basis for more than 200 motion pictures.

CHAPTER 96.
THE CONTRACT.

Three days after the scene we have just described, namely towards five o'clock in the afternoon of the day fixed for the signature of the contract between Mademoiselle Eugenie Danglars and Andrea Cavalcanti,—whom the banker persisted in calling prince,—a fresh breeze was stirring the leaves in the little garden in front of the Count of Monte Cristo's house, and the count was preparing to go out. While his horses were impatiently pawing the ground,—held in by the coachman, who had been seated a quarter of an hour on his box,—the elegant phaeton with which we are familiar rapidly turned the angle of the entrance-gate, and cast out on the doorsteps M. Andrea Cavalcanti, as decked up and gay as if he were going to marry a princess. He inquired after the count with his usual familiarity, and ascending lightly to the second story met him at the top of the stairs. The count stopped on seeing the young man. As for Andrea, he was launched, and when he was once launched nothing stopped him. "Ah, good morning, my dear count," said he. "Ah, M. Andrea," said the latter, with his half-jesting tone; "how do you do."

"Charmingly, as you see. I am come to talk to you about a thousand things; but, first tell me, were you going out or just returned?"

"I was going out, sir."

"Then, in order not to hinder you, I will get up with you if you please in your carriage, and Tom shall follow with my phaeton in tow."

"No," said the count, with an imperceptible smile of contempt, for he had no wish to be seen in the young man's society,—"no; I prefer listening to you here, my dear M. Andrea; we can chat better in-doors, and there is no coachman to overhear our conversation." The count returned to a small drawing-room on the first floor, sat down, and crossing his legs motioned to the young man to take a seat also. Andrea assumed his gayest manner. "You know, my dear count," said he, "the ceremony is to take place this evening. At nine o'clock the contract is to be signed at my father-in-law's."

"Ah, indeed?" said Monte Cristo.

"What; is it news to you? Has not M. Danglars informed you of the ceremony?"

"Oh, yes," said the count; "I received a letter from him yesterday, but I do not think the hour was mentioned."

"Possibly my father-in-law trusted to its general notoriety."

"Well," said Monte Cristo, "you are fortunate, M. Cavalcanti; it is a most suitable alliance you are contracting, and Mademoiselle Danglars is a handsome girl."

"Yes, indeed she is," replied Cavalcanti, in a very modest tone.

"Above all, she is very rich,—at least, I believe so," said Monte Cristo.

"Very rich, do you think?" replied the young man.

"Doubtless; it is said M. Danglars conceals at least half of his fortune."

"And he acknowledges fifteen or twenty millions," said Andrea with a look sparkling with joy.

"Without reckoning," added Monte Cristo, "that he is on the eve of entering into a sort of speculation already in vogue in the United States and in England, but quite novel in France."

"Yes, yes, I know what you mean,—the railway, of which he has obtained the grant, is it not?"

"Precisely; it is generally believed he will gain ten millions by that affair."

"Ten millions! Do you think so? It is magnificent!" said Cavalcanti, who was quite confounded at the metallic sound of these golden words. "Without reckoning," replied Monte Cristo, "that all his fortune will come to you, and justly too, since Mademoiselle Danglars is an only daughter. Besides, your own fortune, as your father assured me, is almost equal to that of your betrothed. But enough of money matters. Do you know, M. Andrea, I think you have managed this affair rather skilfully?"

"Not badly, by any means," said the young man; "I was born for a diplomatist."

"Well, you must become a diplomatist; diplomacy, you know, is something that is not to be acquired; it is instinctive. Have you lost your heart?"

"Indeed, I fear it," replied Andrea, in the tone in which he had heard Dorante or Valere reply to Alceste [*] at the Theatre Francais.

"Is your love returned?"

* In Moliere's comedy, Le Misanthrope.

"I suppose so," said Andrea with a triumphant smile, "since I am accepted. But I must not forget one grand point."

"Which?"

"That I have been singularly assisted."

"Nonsense."

"I have, indeed."

"By circumstances?"

"No; by you."

"By me? Not at all, prince," said Monte Cristo laying a marked stress on the title, "what have I done for you? Are not your name, your social position, and your merit sufficient?"

"No," said Andrea,—"no; it is useless for you to say so, count. I maintain that the position of a man like you has done more than my name, my social position, and my merit."

"You are completely mistaken, sir," said Monte Cristo coldly, who felt the perfidious manoeuvre of the young man, and understood the bearing of his words; "you only acquired my protection after the influence and fortune of your father had been ascertained; for, after all, who procured for me, who had never seen either you or your illustrious father, the pleasure of your acquaintance?—two of my good friends, Lord Wilmore and the Abbe Busoni. What encouraged me not to become your surety, but to patronize you?—your father's name, so well known in Italy and so highly honored. Personally, I do not know you." This calm tone and perfect ease made Andrea feel that he was, for the moment, restrained by a more muscular hand than his own, and that the restraint could not be easily broken through.

"Oh, then my father has really a very large fortune, count?"

"It appears so, sir," replied Monte Cristo.

"Do you know if the marriage settlement he promised me has come?"

"I have been advised of it."

"But the three millions?"

"The three millions are probably on the road."

"Then I shall really have them?"

"Oh, well," said the count, "I do not think you have yet known the want of money." Andrea was so surprised that he pondered the matter for a moment. Then, arousing from his revery,—"Now, sir, I have one request to make to you, which you will understand, even if it should be disagreeable to you."

"Proceed," said Monte Cristo.

"I have formed an acquaintance, thanks to my good fortune, with many noted persons, and have, at least for the moment, a crowd of friends. But marrying, as I am about to do, before all Paris, I ought to be supported by an illustrious name, and in the absence of the paternal hand some powerful one ought to lead me to the altar; now, my father is not coming to Paris, is he? He is old, covered with wounds, and suffers dreadfully, he says, in travelling."

"Indeed?"

"Well, I am come to ask a favor of you."

"Of me?"

"Yes, of you."

"And pray what may it be?"

"Well, to take his part."

"Ah, my dear sir! What?—after the varied relations I have had the happiness to sustain towards you, can it be that you know me so little as to ask such a thing? Ask me to lend you half a million and, although such a loan is somewhat rare, on my honor, you would annoy me less! Know, then, what I thought I had already told you, that in participation in this world's affairs, more especially in their moral aspects, the Count of Monte Cristo has never ceased to entertain the scruples and even the superstitions of the East. I, who have a seraglio at Cairo, one at Smyrna, and one at Constantinople, preside at a wedding?—never!"

"Then you refuse me?"

"Decidedly; and were you my son or my brother I would refuse you in the same way."

"But what must be done?" said Andrea, disappointed.

"You said just now that you had a hundred friends."

"Very true, but you introduced me at M. Danglars'."

"Not at all! Let us recall the exact facts. You met him at a dinner party at my house, and you introduced yourself at his house; that is a totally different affair."

"Yes, but, by my marriage, you have forwarded that."

"I?—not in the least, I beg you to believe. Recollect what I told you when you asked me to propose you. 'Oh, I never make matches, my dear prince, it is my settled principle.'" Andrea bit his lips.

"But, at least, you will be there?"

"Will all Paris be there?"

"Oh, certainly."

"Well, like all Paris, I shall be there too," said the count.

"And will you sign the contract?"

"I see no objection to that; my scruples do not go thus far."

"Well, since you will grant me no more, I must be content with what you give me. But one word more, count."

"What is it?"

"Advice."

"Be careful; advice is worse than a service."

"Oh, you can give me this without compromising yourself."

"Tell me what it is."

"Is my wife's fortune five hundred thousand livres?"

"That is the sum M. Danglars himself announced."

"Must I receive it, or leave it in the hands of the notary?"

"This is the way such affairs are generally arranged when it is wished to do them stylishly: Your two solicitors appoint a meeting, when the contract is signed, for the next or the following day; then they exchange the two portions, for which they each give a receipt; then, when the marriage is celebrated, they place the amount at your disposal as the chief member of the alliance."

"Because," said Andrea, with a certain ill-concealed uneasiness, "I thought I heard my father-in-law say that he intended embarking our property in that famous railway affair of which you spoke just now."

"Well," replied Monte Cristo, "it will be the way, everybody says, of trebling your fortune in twelve months. Baron Danglars is a good father, and knows how to calculate."

"In that case," said Andrea, "everything is all right, excepting your refusal, which quite grieves me."

"You must attribute it only to natural scruples under similar circumstances."

"Well," said Andrea, "let it be as you wish. This evening, then, at nine o'clock."

"Adieu till then." Notwithstanding a slight resistance on the part of Monte Cristo, whose lips turned pale, but who preserved his ceremonious smile, Andrea seized the count's hand, pressed it, jumped into his phaeton, and disappeared.

The four or five remaining hours before nine o'clock arrived, Andrea employed in riding, paying visits,—designed to induce those of whom he had spoken to appear at the banker's in their gayest equipages,—dazzling them by promises of shares in schemes which have since turned every brain, and in which Danglars was just taking the initiative. In fact, at half-past eight in the evening the grand salon, the gallery adjoining, and the three other drawing-rooms on the same floor, were filled with a perfumed crowd, who sympathized but little in the event, but who all participated in that love of being present wherever there is anything fresh to be seen. An Academician would say that the entertainments of the fashionable world are collections of flowers which attract inconstant butterflies, famished bees, and buzzing drones.

No one could deny that the rooms were splendidly illuminated; the light streamed forth on the gilt mouldings and the silk hangings; and all the bad taste of decorations, which had only their richness to boast of, shone in its splendor. Mademoiselle Eugenie was dressed with elegant simplicity in a figured white silk dress, and a white rose half concealed in her jet black hair was her only ornament, unaccompanied by a single jewel. Her eyes, however, betrayed that perfect confidence which contradicted the girlish simplicity of this modest attire. Madame Danglars was chatting at a short distance with Debray, Beauchamp, and Chateau-Renaud.

Debray was admitted to the house for this grand ceremony, but on the same plane with every one else, and without any particular privilege. M. Danglars, surrounded by deputies and men connected with the revenue, was explaining a new theory of taxation which he intended to adopt when the course of events had compelled the government to call him into the ministry. Andrea, on whose arm hung one of the most consummate dandies of the opera, was explaining to him rather cleverly, since he was obliged to be bold to appear at ease, his future projects, and the new luxuries he meant to introduce to Parisian fashions with his hundred and seventy-five thousand livres per annum.

The crowd moved to and fro in the rooms like an ebb and flow of turquoises, rubies, emeralds, opals, and diamonds. As usual, the oldest women were the most decorated, and the ugliest the most conspicuous. If there was a beautiful lily, or a sweet rose, you had to search for it, concealed in some corner behind a mother with a turban, or an aunt with a bird of paradise.

At each moment, in the midst of the crowd, the buzzing, and the laughter, the door-keeper's voice was heard announcing some name well known in the financial department, respected in the army, or illustrious in the literary world, and which was acknowledged by a slight movement in the different groups. But for one whose privilege it was to agitate that ocean of human waves, how many were received with a look of indifference or a sneer of disdain! At the moment when the hand of the massive time-piece, representing Endymion asleep, pointed to nine on its golden face, and the hammer, the faithful type of mechanical thought, struck nine times, the name of the Count of Monte Cristo resounded in its turn, and as if by an electric shock all the assembly turned towards the door.

The count was dressed in black and with his habitual simplicity; his white waistcoat displayed his expansive noble chest and his black stock was singularly noticeable because of its contrast with the deadly paleness of his face. His only jewellery was a chain, so fine that the slender gold thread was scarcely perceptible on his white waistcoat. A circle was immediately formed around the door. The count perceived at one glance Madame Danglars at one end of the drawing-room, M. Danglars at the other, and Eugenie in front of him. He first advanced towards the baroness, who was chatting with Madame de Villefort, who had come alone, Valentine being still an invalid; and without turning aside, so clear was the road left for him, he passed from the baroness to Eugenie, whom he complimented in such rapid and measured terms, that the proud artist was quite struck. Near her was Mademoiselle Louise d'Armilly, who thanked the count for the letters of introduction he had so kindly given her for Italy, which she intended immediately to make use of. On leaving these ladies he found himself with Danglars, who had advanced to meet him.

Having accomplished these three social duties, Monte Cristo stopped, looking around him with that expression peculiar to a certain class, which seems to say, "I have done my duty, now let others do theirs." Andrea, who was in an adjoining room, had shared in the sensation caused by the arrival of Monte Cristo, and now came forward to pay his respects to the count. He found him completely surrounded; all were eager to speak to him, as is always the case with those whose words are few and weighty. The solicitors arrived at this moment and arranged their scrawled papers on the velvet cloth embroidered with gold which covered the table prepared for the signature; it was a gilt table supported on lions' claws. One of the notaries sat down, the other remained standing. They were about to proceed to the reading of the contract, which half Paris assembled was to sign. All took their places, or rather the ladies formed a circle, while the gentlemen (more indifferent to the restraints of what Boileau calls the "energetic style") commented on the feverish agitation of Andrea, on M. Danglars' riveted attention, Eugenie's composure, and the light and sprightly manner in which the baroness treated this important affair.

The contract was read during a profound silence. But as soon as it was finished, the buzz was redoubled through all the drawing-rooms; the brilliant sums, the rolling millions which were to be at the command of the two young people, and which crowned the display of the wedding presents and the young lady's diamonds, which had been made in a room entirely appropriated for that purpose, had exercised to the full their delusions over the envious assembly. Mademoiselle Danglars' charms were heightened in the opinion of the young men, and for the moment seemed to outvie the sun in splendor. As for the ladies, it is needless to say that while they coveted the millions, they thought they did not need them for themselves, as they were beautiful enough without them. Andrea, surrounded by his friends, complimented, flattered, beginning to believe in the reality of his dream, was almost bewildered. The notary solemnly took the pen, flourished it above his head, and said, "Gentlemen, we are about to sign the contract."

The baron was to sign first, then the representative of M. Cavalcanti, senior, then the baroness, afterwards the "future couple," as they are styled in the abominable phraseology of legal documents. The baron took the pen and signed, then the representative. The baroness approached, leaning on Madame de Villefort's arm. "My dear," said she, as she took the pen, "is it not vexatious? An unexpected incident, in the affair of murder and theft at the Count of Monte Cristo's, in which he nearly fell a victim, deprives us of the pleasure of seeing M. de Villefort."

"Indeed?" said M. Danglars, in the same tone in which he would have said, "Oh, well, what do I care?"

"As a matter of fact," said Monte Cristo, approaching, "I am much afraid that I am the involuntary cause of his absence."

"What, you, count?" said Madame Danglars, signing; "if you are, take care, for I shall never forgive you." Andrea pricked up his ears.

"But it is not my fault, as I shall endeavor to prove." Every one listened eagerly; Monte Cristo who so rarely opened his lips, was about to speak. "You remember," said the count, during the most profound silence, "that the unhappy wretch who came to rob me died at my house; the supposition is that he was stabbed by his accomplice, on attempting to leave it."

"Yes," said Danglars.

"In order that his wounds might be examined he was undressed, and his clothes were thrown into a corner, where the police picked them up, with the exception of the waistcoat, which they overlooked." Andrea turned pale, and drew towards the door; he saw a cloud rising in the horizon, which appeared to forebode a coming storm.

"Well, this waistcoat was discovered to-day, covered with blood, and with a hole over the heart." The ladies screamed, and two or three prepared to faint. "It was brought to me. No one could guess what the dirty rag could be; I alone suspected that it was the waistcoat of the murdered man. My valet, in examining this mournful relic, felt a paper in the pocket and drew it out; it was a letter addressed to you, baron."

"To me?" cried Danglars.

"Yes, indeed, to you; I succeeded in deciphering your name under the blood with which the letter was stained," replied Monte Cristo, amid the general outburst of amazement.

"But," asked Madame Danglars, looking at her husband with uneasiness, "how could that prevent M. de Villefort"—

"In this simple way, madame," replied Monte Cristo; "the waistcoat and the letter were both what is termed circumstantial evidence; I therefore sent them to the king's attorney. You understand, my dear baron, that legal methods are the safest in criminal cases; it was, perhaps, some plot against you." Andrea looked steadily at Monte Cristo and disappeared in the second drawing-room.

"Possibly," said Danglars; "was not this murdered man an old galley-slave?"

"Yes," replied the count; "a felon named Caderousse." Danglars turned slightly pale; Andrea reached the anteroom beyond the little drawing-room.

"But go on signing," said Monte Cristo; "I perceive that my story has caused a general emotion, and I beg to apologize to you, baroness, and to Mademoiselle Danglars." The baroness, who had signed, returned the pen to the notary. "Prince Cavalcanti," said the latter; "Prince Cavalcanti, where are you?"

"Andrea, Andrea," repeated several young people, who were already on sufficiently intimate terms with him to call him by his Christian name.

"Call the prince; inform him that it is his turn to sign," cried Danglars to one of the floorkeepers.

But at the same instant the crowd of guests rushed in alarm into the principal salon as if some frightful monster had entered the apartments, quaerens quem devoret.

There was, indeed, reason to retreat, to be alarmed, and to scream. An officer was placing two soldiers at the door of each drawing-room, and was advancing towards Danglars, preceded by a commissary of police, girded with his scarf. Madame Danglars uttered a scream and fainted. Danglars, who thought himself threatened (certain consciences are never calm),—Danglars even before his guests showed a countenance of abject terror.

"What is the matter, sir?" asked Monte Cristo, advancing to meet the commissioner.

"Which of you gentlemen," asked the magistrate, without replying to the count, "answers to the name of Andrea Cavalcanti?" A cry of astonishment was heard from all parts of the room. They searched; they questioned. "But who then is Andrea Cavalcanti?" asked Danglars in amazement.

"A galley-slave, escaped from confinement at Toulon."

"And what crime has he committed?"

"He is accused," said the commissary with his inflexible voice, "of having assassinated the man named Caderousse, his former companion in prison, at the moment he was making his escape from the house of the Count of Monte Cristo." Monte Cristo cast a rapid glance around him. Andrea was gone.

CHAPTER 97.
THE DEPARTURE FOR BELGIUM.

A few minutes after the scene of confusion produced in the salons of M. Danglars by the unexpected appearance of the brigade of soldiers, and by the disclosure which had followed, the mansion was deserted with as much rapidity as if a case of plague or of cholera morbus had broken out among the guests. In a few minutes, through all the doors, down all the staircases, by every exit, every one hastened to retire, or rather to fly; for it was a situation where the ordinary condolences,—which even the best friends are so eager to offer in great catastrophes,—were seen to be utterly futile. There remained in the banker's house only Danglars, closeted in his study, and making his statement to the officer of gendarmes; Madame Danglars, terrified, in the boudoir with which we are acquainted; and Eugenie, who with haughty air and disdainful lip had retired to her room with her inseparable companion, Mademoiselle Louise d'Armilly. As for the numerous servants (more numerous that evening than usual, for their number was augmented by cooks and butlers from the Cafe de Paris), venting on their employers their anger at what they termed the insult to which they had been subjected, they collected in groups in the hall, in the kitchens, or in their rooms, thinking very little of their duty, which was thus naturally interrupted. Of all this household, only two persons deserve our notice; these are Mademoiselle Eugenie Danglars and Mademoiselle Louise d'Armilly.

The betrothed had retired, as we said, with haughty air, disdainful lip, and the demeanor of an outraged queen, followed by her companion, who was paler and more disturbed than herself. On reaching her room Eugenie locked her door, while Louise fell on a chair. "Ah, what a dreadful thing," said the young musician; "who would have suspected it? M. Andrea Cavalcanti a murderer—a galley-slave escaped—a convict!" An ironical smile curled the lip of Eugenie. "In truth I was fated," said she. "I escaped the Morcerf only to fall into the Cavalcanti."

"Oh, do not confound the two, Eugenie."

"Hold your tongue! The men are all infamous, and I am happy to be able now to do more than detest them—I despise them."

"What shall we do?" asked Louise.

"What shall we do?"

"Yes."

"Why, the same we had intended doing three days since—set off."

"What?—although you are not now going to be married, you intend still"—

"Listen, Louise. I hate this life of the fashionable world, always ordered, measured, ruled, like our music-paper. What

I have always wished for, desired, and coveted, is the life of an artist, free and independent, relying only on my own resources, and accountable only to myself. Remain here? What for?—that they may try, a month hence, to marry me again; and to whom?—M. Debray, perhaps, as it was once proposed. No, Louise, no! This evening's adventure will serve for my excuse. I did not seek one, I did not ask for one. God sends me this, and I hail it joyfully!"

"How strong and courageous you are!" said the fair, frail girl to her brunette companion.

"Did you not yet know me? Come, Louise, let us talk of our affairs. The post-chaise"—

"Was happily bought three days since."

"Have you had it sent where we are to go for it?"

"Yes."

"Our passport?"

"Here it is."

And Eugenie, with her usual precision, opened a printed paper, and read,—

"M. Leon d'Armilly, twenty years of age; profession, artist; hair black, eyes black; travelling with his sister."

"Capital! How did you get this passport?"

"When I went to ask M. de Monte Cristo for letters to the directors of the theatres at Rome and Naples, I expressed my fears of travelling as a woman; he perfectly understood them, and undertook to procure for me a man's passport, and two days after I received this, to which I have added with my own hand, 'travelling with his sister.'"

"Well," said Eugenie cheerfully, "we have then only to pack up our trunks; we shall start the evening of the signing of the contract, instead of the evening of the wedding— that is all."

"But consider the matter seriously, Eugenie!"

"Oh, I am done with considering! I am tired of hearing only of market reports, of the end of the month, of the rise and fall of Spanish funds, of Haitian bonds. Instead of that, Louise—do you understand?—air, liberty, melody of birds, plains of Lombardy, Venetian canals, Roman palaces, the Bay of Naples. How much have we, Louise?" The young girl to whom this question was addressed drew from an inlaid secretary a small portfolio with a lock, in which she counted twenty-three bank-notes.

"Twenty-three thousand francs," said she.

"And as much, at least, in pearls, diamonds, and jewels," said Eugenie. "We are rich. With forty-five thousand francs we can live like princesses for two years, and comfortably for four; but before six months—you with your music, and I with my voice—we shall double our capital. Come, you shall take charge of the money, I of the jewel-box; so that if one of us had the misfortune to lose her treasure, the other would still have hers left. Now, the portmanteau—let us make haste—the portmanteau!"

"Stop!" said Louise, going to listen at Madame Danglars' door.

"What do you fear?"

"That we may be discovered."

"The door is locked."

"They may tell us to open it."

"They may if they like, but we will not."

"You are a perfect Amazon, Eugenie!" And the two young girls began to heap into a trunk all the things they thought they should require. "There now," said Eugenie, "while I change my costume do you lock the portmanteau." Louise pressed with all the strength of her little hands on the top of the portmanteau. "But I cannot," said she; "I am not strong enough; do you shut it."

"Ah, you do well to ask," said Eugenie, laughing; "I forgot that I was Hercules, and you only the pale Omphale!" And the young girl, kneeling on the top, pressed the two parts of the portmanteau together, and Mademoiselle d'Armilly passed the bolt of the padlock through. When this was done, Eugenie opened a drawer, of which she kept the key, and took from it a wadded violet silk travelling cloak. "Here," said she, "you see I have thought of everything; with this cloak you will not be cold."

"But you?"

"Oh, I am never cold, you know! Besides, with these men's clothes"—

"Will you dress here?"

"Certainly."

"Shall you have time?"

"Do not be uneasy, you little coward! All our servants are busy, discussing the grand affair. Besides, what is there astonishing, when you think of the grief I ought to be in, that I shut myself up?—tell me!"

"No, truly—you comfort me."

"Come and help me."

From the same drawer she took a man's complete costume, from the boots to the coat, and a provision of linen, where there was nothing superfluous, but every requisite. Then, with a promptitude which indicated that this was not the first time she had amused herself by adopting the garb of the opposite sex, Eugenie drew on the boots and pantaloons, tied her cravat, buttoned her waistcoat up to the throat, and put on a coat which admirably fitted her beautiful figure. "Oh, that is very good—indeed, it is very good!" said Louise, looking at her with admiration; "but that beautiful black hair, those magnificent braids, which made all the ladies sigh with envy,—will they go under a man's hat like the one I see down there?"

"You shall see," said Eugenie. And with her left hand seizing the thick mass, which her long fingers could scarcely grasp, she took in her right hand a pair of long scissors, and soon the steel met through the rich and splendid hair, which fell in a cluster at her feet as she leaned back to keep it from her coat. Then she grasped the front hair, which she also cut off, without expressing the least regret; on the contrary, her eyes sparkled with greater pleasure than usual under her ebony eyebrows. "Oh, the magnificent hair!" said Louise, with regret.

"And am I not a hundred times better thus?" cried Eugenie, smoothing the scattered curls of her hair, which had now quite a masculine appearance; "and do you not think me handsomer so?"

"Oh, you are beautiful—always beautiful!" cried Louise. "Now, where are you going?"

"To Brussels, if you like; it is the nearest frontier. We can go to Brussels, Liege, Aix-la-Chapelle; then up the Rhine to Strasburg. We will cross Switzerland, and go down into Italy by the Saint-Gothard. Will that do?"

"Yes."

"What are you looking at?"

"I am looking at you; indeed you are adorable like that! One would say you were carrying me off."

"And they would be right, pardieu!"

"Oh, I think you swore, Eugenie." And the two young girls, whom every one might have thought plunged in grief, the one on her own account, the other from interest in her friend, burst out laughing, as they cleared away every visible trace of the disorder which had naturally accompanied the preparations for their escape. Then, having blown out the lights, the two fugitives, looking and listening eagerly, with outstretched necks, opened the door of a dressing-room which led by a side staircase down to the yard,—Eugenie going first, and holding with one arm the portmanteau, which by the opposite handle Mademoiselle d'Armilly scarcely raised with both hands. The yard was empty; the clock was striking twelve. The porter was not yet gone to bed. Eugenie approached softly, and saw the old man sleeping soundly in an arm-chair in his lodge. She returned to Louise, took up the portmanteau, which she had placed for a moment on the ground, and they reached the archway under the shadow of the wall.

Eugenie concealed Louise in an angle of the gateway, so that if the porter chanced to awake he might see but one person. Then placing herself in the full light of the lamp which lit the yard,—"Gate!" cried she, with her finest contralto voice, and rapping at the window.

The porter got up as Eugenie expected, and even advanced some steps to recognize the person who was going out, but seeing a young man striking his boot impatiently with his riding-whip, he opened it immediately. Louise slid through the half-open gate like a snake, and bounded lightly forward. Eugenie, apparently calm, although in all probability her heart beat somewhat faster than usual, went out in her turn. A porter was passing and they gave him the portmanteau; then the two young girls, having told him to take it to No. 36, Rue de la Victoire, walked behind this man, whose presence comforted Louise. As for Eugenie, she was as strong as a Judith or a Delilah. They arrived at the appointed spot. Eugenie ordered the porter to put down the portmanteau, gave him some pieces of money, and having rapped at the shutter sent him away. The shutter where Eugenie had rapped was that of a little laundress, who had been previously warned, and was not yet gone to bed. She opened the door.

"Mademoiselle," said Eugenie, "let the porter get the post-chaise from the coach-house, and fetch some post-horses from the hotel. Here are five francs for his trouble."

"Indeed," said Louise, "I admire you, and I could almost say respect you." The laundress looked on in astonishment, but as she had been promised twenty louis, she made no remark.

In a quarter of an hour the porter returned with a post-boy and horses, which were harnessed, and put in the post-chaise in a minute, while the porter fastened the portmanteau on with the assistance of a cord and strap. "Here is the passport," said the postilion, "which way are we going, young gentleman?"

"To Fontainebleau," replied Eugenie with an almost masculine voice.

"What do you say?" said Louise.

"I am giving them the slip," said Eugenie; "this woman to whom we have given twenty louis may betray us for forty; we will soon alter our direction." And the young girl jumped into the britzska, which was admirably arranged for sleeping in, without scarcely touching the step. "You are always right," said the music teacher, seating herself by the side of her friend.

A quarter of an hour afterwards the postilion, having been put in the right road, passed with a crack of his whip through the gateway of the Barriere Saint-Martin. "Ah," said Louise, breathing freely, "here we are out of Paris."

"Yes, my dear, the abduction is an accomplished fact," replied Eugenie. "Yes, and without violence," said Louise.

"I shall bring that forward as an extenuating circumstance," replied Eugenie. These words were lost in the noise which the carriage made in rolling over the pavement of La Villette. M. Danglars no longer had a daughter.

CHAPTER 98.
THE BELL AND BOTTLE TAVERN.

And now let us leave Mademoiselle Danglars and her friend pursuing their way to Brussels, and return to poor Andrea Cavalcanti, so inopportunely interrupted in his rise to fortune. Notwithstanding his youth, Master Andrea was a very skilful and intelligent boy. We have seen that on the first rumor which reached the salon he had gradually approached the door, and crossing two or three rooms at last disappeared. But we have forgotten to mention one circumstance, which nevertheless ought not to be omitted; in one of the rooms he crossed, the trousseau of the bride-elect was on exhibition. There were caskets of diamonds, cashmere shawls, Valenciennes lace, English veilings, and in fact all the tempting things, the bare mention of which makes the hearts of young girls bound with joy, and which is called the "corbeille." [*] Now, in passing through this room, Andrea proved himself not only to be clever and intelligent, but also provident, for he helped himself to the most valuable of the ornaments before him.

* Literally, "the basket," because wedding gifts were originally brought in such a receptacle.

Furnished with this plunder, Andrea leaped with a lighter heart from the window, intending to slip through the hands of the gendarmes. Tall and well proportioned as an ancient gladiator, and muscular as a Spartan, he walked for a quarter of an hour without knowing where to direct his steps, actuated by the sole idea of getting away from the spot where if he lingered he knew that he would surely be taken. Having passed through the Rue Mont Blanc, guided by the instinct which leads thieves always to take the safest path, he found himself at the end of the Rue Lafayette. There he stopped, breathless and panting. He was quite alone; on one side was the vast wilderness of the Saint-Lazare, on the other, Paris enshrouded in darkness. "Am I to be captured?" he cried; "no, not if I can use more activity than my enemies. My safety is now a mere question of speed." At this moment he saw a cab at the top of the Faubourg Poissonniere. The dull driver, smoking his pipe, was plodding along toward the limits of the Faubourg Saint-Denis, where no doubt he ordinarily had his station. "Ho, friend!" said Benedetto.

"What do you want, sir?" asked the driver.

"Is your horse tired?"

"Tired? oh, yes, tired enough—he has done nothing the whole of this blessed day! Four wretched fares, and twenty sous over, making in all seven francs, are all that I have earned, and I ought to take ten to the owner."

"Will you add these twenty francs to the seven you have?"

"With pleasure, sir; twenty francs are not to be despised. Tell me what I am to do for this."

"A very easy thing, if your horse isn't tired."

"I tell you he'll go like the wind,—only tell me which way to drive."

"Towards the Louvres."

"Ah, I know the way—you get good sweetened rum over there."

"Exactly so; I merely wish to overtake one of my friends, with whom I am going to hunt to-morrow at Chapelle-en-Serval. He should have waited for me here with a cabriolet till half-past eleven; it is twelve, and, tired of waiting, he must have gone on."

"It is likely."

"Well, will you try and overtake him?"

"Nothing I should like better."

"If you do not overtake him before we reach Bourget you shall have twenty francs; if not before Louvres, thirty."

"And if we do overtake him?"

"Forty," said Andrea, after a moment's hesitation, at the end of which he remembered that he might safely promise. "That's all right," said the man; "hop in, and we're off! Who-o-o-p, la!"

Andrea got into the cab, which passed rapidly through the Faubourg Saint-Denis, along the Faubourg Saint-Martin, crossed the barrier, and threaded its way through the interminable Villette. They never overtook the chimerical friend, yet Andrea frequently inquired of people on foot whom he passed and at the inns which were not yet closed, for a green cabriolet and bay horse; and as there are a great many cabriolets to be seen on the road to the Low Countries, and as nine-tenths of them are green, the inquiries increased at every step. Every one had just seen it pass; it was only five hundred, two hundred, one hundred steps in advance; at length they reached it, but it was not the friend. Once the cab was also passed by a calash rapidly whirled along by two post-horses. "Ah," said Cavalcanti to himself, "if I only had that britzska, those two good post-horses, and above all the passport that carries them on!" And he sighed deeply. The calash contained Mademoiselle Danglars and Mademoiselle d'Armilly. "Hurry, hurry!" said Andrea, "we must overtake him soon." And the poor horse resumed the desperate gallop it had kept up since leaving the barrier, and arrived steaming at Louvres.

"Certainly," said Andrea, "I shall not overtake my friend, but I shall kill your horse, therefore I had better stop. Here are thirty francs; I will sleep at the Red Horse, and will secure a place in the first coach. Good-night, friend." And Andrea, after placing six pieces of five francs each in the man's hand, leaped lightly on to the pathway. The cabman joyfully pocketed the sum, and turned back on his road to Paris. Andrea pretended to go towards the Red Horse inn, but after leaning an instant against the door, and hearing the last sound of the cab, which was disappearing from view, he went on his road, and with a lusty stride soon traversed the space of two leagues. Then he rested; he must be near Chapelle-en-Serval, where he pretended to be going. It was not fatigue that stayed Andrea here; it was that he might form some resolution, adopt some plan. It would be impossible to make use of a diligence, equally so to engage post-horses; to travel either way a passport was necessary. It was still more impossible to remain in the department of the Oise, one of the most open and strictly guarded in France; this was quite out of the question, especially to a man like Andrea, perfectly conversant with criminal matters.

He sat down by the side of the moat, buried his face in his hands and reflected. Ten minutes after he raised his head; his resolution was made. He threw some dust over the topcoat, which he had found time to unhook from the ante-chamber and button over his ball costume, and going to Chapelle-en-Serval he knocked loudly at the door of the only inn in the place. The host opened. "My friend," said Andrea, "I was coming from Montefontaine to Senlis, when my horse, which is a troublesome creature, stumbled and threw me. I must reach Compiegne to-night, or I shall cause deep anxiety to my family. Could you let me hire a horse of you?"

An inn-keeper has always a horse to let, whether it be good or bad. The host called the stable-boy, and ordered him to saddle "Whitey," then he awoke his son, a child of seven years, whom he ordered to ride before the gentleman and bring back the horse. Andrea gave the inn-keeper twenty francs, and in taking them from his pocket dropped a visiting card. This belonged to one of his friends at the Cafe de Paris, so that the innkeeper, picking it up after Andrea had left, was convinced that he had let his horse to the Count of Mauleon, 25 Rue Saint-Dominique, that being the name and address on the card. "Whitey" was not a fast animal, but he kept up an easy, steady pace; in three hours and a half Andrea had traversed the nine leagues which separated him from Compiegne, and four o'clock struck as he reached the place where the coaches stop. There is an excellent tavern at Compiegne, well remembered by those who have ever been there. Andrea, who had often stayed there in his rides about Paris, recollected the Bell and Bottle inn; he turned around, saw the sign by the light of a reflected lamp, and having dismissed the child, giving him all the small coin he had about him, he began knocking at the door, very reasonably concluding that having now three or four hours before him he had best fortify himself against the fatigues of the morrow by a sound sleep and a good supper. A waiter opened the door.

"My friend," said Andrea, "I have been dining at Saint-Jean-au-Bois, and expected to catch the coach which passes by at midnight, but like a fool I have lost my way, and have been walking for the last four hours in the forest. Show me into one of those pretty little rooms which overlook the court, and bring me a cold fowl and a bottle of Bordeaux." The waiter had no suspicions; Andrea spoke with perfect composure, he had a cigar in his mouth, and his hands in the pocket of his top coat; his clothes were fashionably made, his chin smooth, his boots irreproachable; he looked merely as if he had stayed out very late, that was all. While the waiter was preparing his room, the hostess arose; Andrea assumed his most charming smile, and asked if he could have No. 3, which he had occupied on his last stay at Compiegne. Unfortunately, No. 3 was engaged by a young man who was travelling with his sister. Andrea appeared in despair, but consoled himself when the hostess assured him that No. 7, prepared for him, was situated precisely the same as No. 3, and while warming his feet and chatting about the last races at Chantilly, he waited until they announced his room to be ready.

Andrea had not spoken without cause of the pretty rooms looking out upon the court of the Bell Tavern, which with its triple galleries like those of a theatre, with the jessamine and clematis twining round the light columns, forms one of the prettiest entrances to an inn that you can imagine. The fowl was tender, the wine old, the fire clear and sparkling, and Andrea was surprised to find himself eating with as good an appetite as though nothing had happened. Then he went to bed and almost immediately fell into that deep sleep which is sure to visit men of twenty years of age, even when they are torn with remorse. Now, here we are obliged to own that Andrea ought to have felt remorse, but that he did not. This was the plan which had appealed to him to afford the best chance of his security. Before daybreak he would awake, leave the inn after rigorously paying his bill, and reaching the forest, he would, under pretence of making studies in painting, test the hospitality of some peasants, procure himself the dress of a woodcutter and a hatchet, casting off the lion's skin to assume that of the woodman; then, with his hands covered with dirt, his hair darkened by means of a leaden comb, his complexion embrowned with a preparation for which one of his old comrades had given him the recipe, he intended, by following the wooded districts, to reach the nearest frontier, walking by night and sleeping in the day in the forests and quarries, and only entering inhabited regions to buy a loaf from time to time.

Once past the frontier, Andrea proposed making money of his diamonds; and by uniting the proceeds to ten bank-notes he always carried about with him in case of accident, he would then find himself possessor of about 50,000 livres, which he philosophically considered as no very deplorable condition after all. Moreover, he reckoned much on the interest of the Danglars to hush up the rumor of their own misadventures. These were the reasons which, added to the fatigue, caused Andrea to sleep so soundly. In order that he might awaken early he did not close the shutters, but contented himself with bolting the door and placing on the table an unclasped and long-pointed knife, whose temper he well knew, and which was never absent from him. About seven in the morning Andrea was awakened by a ray of sunlight, which played, warm and brilliant, upon his face. In all well-organized brains, the predominating idea—and there always is one—is sure to be the last thought before sleeping, and the first upon waking in the morning. Andrea had scarcely opened his eyes when his predominating idea presented itself, and whispered in his ear that he had slept too long. He jumped out of bed and ran to the window. A gendarme was crossing the court. A gendarme is one of the most striking objects in the world, even to a man void of uneasiness; but for one who has a timid conscience, and with good cause too, the yellow, blue, and white uniform is really very alarming.

"Why is that gendarme there?" asked Andrea of himself. Then, all at once, he replied, with that logic which the reader has, doubtless, remarked in him, "There is nothing astonishing in seeing a gendarme at an inn; instead of being astonished, let me dress myself." And the youth dressed himself with a facility his valet de chambre had failed to rob him of during the two months of fashionable life he had led in Paris. "Now then," said Andrea, while dressing himself, "I'll wait till he leaves, and then I'll slip away." And, saying this, Andrea, who had now put on his boots and cravat, stole gently to the window, and a second time lifted up the muslin curtain. Not only was the first gendarme still there, but the young man now perceived a second yellow, blue, and white uniform at the foot of the staircase, the only one by which he could descend, while a third, on horseback, holding a musket in his fist, was posted as a sentinel at the great street door which alone afforded the means of egress.

The appearance of the third gendarme settled the matter, for a crowd of curious loungers was extended before him, effectually blocking the entrance to the hotel. "They're after me!" was Andrea's first thought. "The devil!" A pallor overspread the young man's forehead, and he looked around him with anxiety. His room, like all those on the same floor, had but one outlet to the gallery in the sight of everybody. "I am lost!" was his second thought; and, indeed, for a man in Andrea's situation, an arrest meant the assizes, trial, and death,—death without mercy or delay. For a moment he convulsively pressed his head within his hands, and during that brief period he became nearly mad with terror; but soon a ray of hope glimmered in the multitude of thoughts which bewildered his mind, and a faint smile played upon his white lips and pallid cheeks. He looked around and saw the objects of his search upon the chimney-piece; they were a pen, ink, and paper. With forced composure he dipped the pen in the ink, and wrote the following lines upon a sheet of paper:—

"I have no money to pay my bill, but I am not a dishonest man; I leave behind me as a pledge this pin, worth ten times the amount. I shall be excused for leaving at daybreak, for I was ashamed."

He then drew the pin from his cravat and placed it on the paper. This done, instead of leaving the door fastened, he drew back the bolts and even placed the door ajar, as though he had left the room, forgetting to close it, and slipping into the chimney like a man accustomed to that kind of gymnastic exercise, having effaced the marks of his feet upon the floor, he commenced climbing the only opening which afforded him the means of escape. At this precise time, the first gendarme Andrea had noticed walked up-stairs, preceded by the commissary of police, and supported by the second gendarme who guarded the staircase and was himself re-enforced by the one stationed at the door.

Andrea was indebted for this visit to the following circumstances. At daybreak, the telegraphs were set at work in all directions, and almost immediately the authorities in every district had exerted their utmost endeavors to arrest the murderer of Caderousse. Compiegne, that royal residence and fortified town, is well furnished with authorities, gendarmes, and commissaries of police; they therefore began operations as soon as the telegraphic despatch arrived, and the Bell and Bottle being the best-known hotel in the town, they had naturally directed their first inquiries there.

Now, besides the reports of the sentinels guarding the Hotel de Ville, which is next door to the Bell and Bottle, it had been stated by others that a number of travellers had arrived during the night. The sentinel who was relieved at six o'clock in the morning, remembered perfectly that just as he was taking his post a few minutes past four a young man arrived on horseback, with a little boy before him. The young man, having dismissed the boy and horse, knocked at the door of the hotel, which was opened, and again closed after his entrance. This late arrival had attracted much suspicion, and the young man being no other than Andrea, the commissary and gendarme, who was a brigadier, directed their steps towards his room.

They found the door ajar. "Oh, ho," said the brigadier, who thoroughly understood the trick; "a bad sign to find the door open! I would rather find it triply bolted." And, indeed, the little note and pin upon the table confirmed, or rather corroborated, the sad truth. Andrea had fled. We say corroborated, because the brigadier was too experienced to be convinced by a single proof. He glanced around, looked in the bed, shook the curtains, opened the closets, and finally stopped at the chimney. Andrea had taken the precaution to leave no traces of his feet in the ashes, but still it was an outlet, and in this light was not to be passed over without serious investigation.

The brigadier sent for some sticks and straw, and having filled the chimney with them, set a light to it. The fire crackled, and the smoke ascended like the dull vapor from a volcano; but still no prisoner fell down, as they expected. The fact was, that Andrea, at war with society ever since his youth, was quite as deep as a gendarme, even though he were advanced to the rank of brigadier, and quite prepared for the fire, he had climbed out on the roof and was crouching down against the chimney-pots. At one time he thought he was saved, for he heard the brigadier exclaim in a loud voice, to the two gendarmes, "He is not here!" But venturing to peep, he perceived that the latter, instead of retiring, as might have been reasonably expected upon this announcement, were watching with increased attention.

It was now his turn to look about him; the Hotel de Ville, a massive sixteenth century building, was on his right; any one could descend from the openings in the tower, and examine every corner of the roof below, and Andrea expected momentarily to see the head of a gendarme appear at one of these openings. If once discovered, he knew he would be lost, for the roof afforded no chance of escape; he therefore resolved to descend, not through the same chimney by which he had come up, but by a similar one conducting to another room. He looked around for a chimney from which no smoke issued, and having reached it, he disappeared through the orifice without being seen by any one. At the same minute, one of the little windows of the Hotel de Ville was thrown open, and the head of a gendarme appeared. For an instant it remained motionless as one of the stone decorations of the building, then after a long sigh of disappointment the head disappeared. The brigadier, calm and dignified as the law he represented, passed through the crowd, without answering the thousand questions addressed to him, and re-entered the hotel.

"Well?" asked the two gendarmes.

"Well, my boys," said the brigadier, "the brigand must really have escaped early this morning; but we will send to the Villers-Coterets and Noyon roads, and search the forest, when we shall catch him, no doubt." The honorable functionary had scarcely expressed himself thus, in that intonation which is peculiar to brigadiers of the gendarmerie, when a loud scream, accompanied by the violent ringing of a bell, resounded through the court of the hotel. "Ah, what is that?" cried the brigadier.

"Some traveller seems impatient," said the host. "What number was it that rang?"

"Number 3."

"Run, waiter!" At this moment the screams and ringing were redoubled. "Ah," said the brigadier, stopping the servant, "the person who is ringing appears to want something more than a waiter; we will attend upon him with a gendarme. Who occupies Number 3?"

"The little fellow who arrived last night in a post-chaise with his sister, and who asked for an apartment with two beds." The bell here rang for the third time, with another shriek of anguish.

"Follow me, Mr. Commissary!" said the brigadier; "tread in my steps."

"Wait an instant," said the host; "Number 3 has two staircases,—inside and outside."

"Good," said the brigadier. "I will take charge of the inside one. Are the carbines loaded?"

"Yes, brigadier."

"Well, you guard the exterior, and if he attempts to fly, fire upon him; he must be a great criminal, from what the telegraph says."

The brigadier, followed by the commissary, disappeared by the inside staircase, accompanied by the noise which his assertions respecting Andrea had excited in the crowd. This is what had happened. Andrea had very cleverly managed to descend two-thirds of the chimney, but then his foot slipped, and notwithstanding his endeavors, he came into the room with more speed and noise than he intended. It would have signified little had the room been empty, but unfortunately it was occupied. Two ladies, sleeping in one bed, were awakened by the noise, and fixing their eyes upon the spot whence the sound proceeded, they saw a man. One of these ladies, the fair one, uttered those terrible shrieks which resounded through the house, while the other, rushing to the bell-rope, rang with all her strength. Andrea, as we can see, was surrounded by misfortune.

"For pity's sake," he cried, pale and bewildered, without seeing whom he was addressing,—"for pity's sake do not call assistance! Save me!—I will not harm you."

"Andrea, the murderer!" cried one of the ladies.

"Eugenie! Mademoiselle Danglars!" exclaimed Andrea, stupefied.

"Help, help!" cried Mademoiselle d'Armilly, taking the bell from her companion's hand, and ringing it yet more violently. "Save me, I am pursued!" said Andrea, clasping his hands. "For pity, for mercy's sake do not deliver me up!"

"It is too late, they are coming," said Eugenie.

"Well, conceal me somewhere; you can say you were needlessly alarmed; you can turn their suspicions and save my life!"

The two ladies, pressing closely to one another, and drawing the bedclothes tightly around them, remained silent to this supplicating voice, repugnance and fear taking possession of their minds.

"Well, be it so," at length said Eugenie; "return by the same road you came, and we will say nothing about you, unhappy wretch."

"Here he is, here he is!" cried a voice from the landing; "here he is! I see him!" The brigadier had put his eye to the keyhole, and had discovered Andrea in a posture of entreaty. A violent blow from the butt end of the musket burst open the lock, two more forced out the bolts, and the broken door fell in. Andrea ran to the other door, leading to the gallery, ready to rush out; but he was stopped short, and he stood with his body a little thrown back, pale, and with the useless knife in his clinched hand.

"Fly, then!" cried Mademoiselle d'Armilly, whose pity returned as her fears diminished; "fly!"

"Or kill yourself!" said Eugenie (in a tone which a Vestal in the amphitheatre would have used, when urging the victorious gladiator to finish his vanquished adversary). Andrea shuddered, and looked on the young girl with an expression which proved how little he understood such ferocious honor. "Kill myself?" he cried, throwing down his knife; "why should I do so?"

"Why, you said," answered Mademoiselle Danglars, "that you would be condemned to die like the worst criminals."

"Bah," said Cavalcanti, crossing his arms, "one has friends."

The brigadier advanced to him, sword in hand. "Come, come," said Andrea, "sheathe your sword, my fine fellow; there is no occasion to make such a fuss, since I give myself up;" and he held out his hands to be manacled. The girls looked with horror upon this shameful metamorphosis, the man of the world shaking off his covering and appearing as a galley-slave. Andrea turned towards them, and with an impertinent smile asked,—"Have you any message for your father, Mademoiselle Danglars, for in all probability I shall return to Paris?"

Eugenie covered her face with her hands. "Oh, ho!" said Andrea, "you need not be ashamed, even though you did post after me. Was I not nearly your husband?"

And with this raillery Andrea went out, leaving the two girls a prey to their own feelings of shame, and to the comments of the crowd. An hour after they stepped into their calash, both dressed in feminine attire. The gate of the hotel had been closed to screen them from sight, but they were forced, when the door was open, to pass through a throng of curious glances and whispering voices. Eugenie closed her eyes; but though she could not see, she could hear, and the sneers of the crowd reached her in the carriage. "Oh, why is not the world a wilderness?" she exclaimed, throwing herself into the arms of Mademoiselle d'Armilly, her eyes sparkling with the same kind of rage which made Nero wish that the Roman world had but one neck, that he might sever it at a single blow. The next day they stopped at the Hotel de Flandre, at Brussels. The same evening Andrea was incarcerated in the Conciergerie.

CHAPTER 99.
THE LAW.

We have seen how quietly Mademoiselle Danglars and Mademoiselle d'Armilly accomplished their transformation and flight; the fact being that every one was too much occupied in his or her own affairs to think of theirs. We will leave the banker contemplating the enormous magnitude of his debt before the phantom of bankruptcy, and follow the baroness, who after being momentarily crushed under the weight of the blow which had struck her, had gone to seek her usual adviser, Lucien Debray. The baroness had looked forward to this marriage as a means of ridding her of a guardianship which, over a girl of Eugenie's character, could not fail to be rather a troublesome undertaking; for in the tacit relations which maintain the bond of family union, the mother, to maintain her ascendancy over her daughter, must never fail to be a model of wisdom and a type of perfection.

Now, Madame Danglars feared Eugenie's sagacity and the influence of Mademoiselle d'Armilly; she had frequently observed the contemptuous expression with which her daughter looked upon Debray,—an expression which seemed to imply that she understood all her mother's amorous and pecuniary relationships with the intimate secretary;

moreover, she saw that Eugenie detested Debray,—not only because he was a source of dissension and scandal under the paternal roof, but because she had at once classed him in that catalogue of bipeds whom Plato endeavors to withdraw from the appellation of men, and whom Diogenes designated as animals upon two legs without feathers.

Unfortunately, in this world of ours, each person views things through a certain medium, and so is prevented from seeing in the same light as others, and Madame Danglars, therefore, very much regretted that the marriage of Eugenie had not taken place, not only because the match was good, and likely to insure the happiness of her child, but because it would also set her at liberty. She ran therefore to Debray, who, after having like the rest of Paris witnessed the contract scene and the scandal attending it, had retired in haste to his club, where he was chatting with some friends upon the events which served as a subject of conversation for three-fourths of that city known as the capital of the world.

At the precise time when Madame Danglars, dressed in black and concealed in a long veil, was ascending the stairs leading to Debray's apartments,—notwithstanding the assurances of the concierge that the young man was not at home,—Debray was occupied in repelling the insinuations of a friend, who tried to persuade him that after the terrible scene which had just taken place he ought, as a friend of the family, to marry Mademoiselle Danglars and her two millions. Debray did not defend himself very warmly, for the idea had sometimes crossed his mind; still, when he recollected the independent, proud spirit of Eugenie, he positively rejected it as utterly impossible, though the same thought again continually recurred and found a resting-place in his heart. Tea, play, and the conversation, which had become interesting during the discussion of such serious affairs, lasted till one o'clock in the morning.

Meanwhile Madame Danglars, veiled and uneasy, awaited the return of Debray in the little green room, seated between two baskets of flowers, which she had that morning sent, and which, it must be confessed, Debray had himself arranged and watered with so much care that his absence was half excused in the eyes of the poor woman.

At twenty minutes of twelve, Madame Danglars, tired of waiting, returned home. Women of a certain grade are like prosperous grisettes in one respect, they seldom return home after twelve o'clock. The baroness returned to the hotel with as much caution as Eugenie used in leaving it; she ran lightly up-stairs, and with an aching heart entered her apartment, contiguous, as we know, to that of Eugenie. She was fearful of exciting any remark, and believed firmly in her daughter's innocence and fidelity to the paternal roof. She listened at Eugenie's door, and hearing no sound tried to enter, but the bolts were in place. Madame Danglars then concluded that the young girl had been overcome with the terrible excitement of the evening, and had gone to bed and to sleep. She called the maid and questioned her.

"Mademoiselle Eugenie," said the maid, "retired to her apartment with Mademoiselle d'Armilly; they then took tea together, after which they desired me to leave, saying that they needed me no longer." Since then the maid had been below, and like every one else she thought the young ladies were in their own room; Madame Danglars, therefore, went to bed without a shadow of suspicion, and began to muse over the recent events. In proportion as her memory became clearer, the occurrences of the evening were revealed in their true light; what she had taken for confusion was a tumult; what she had regarded as something distressing, was in reality a disgrace. And then the baroness remembered that she had felt no pity for poor Mercedes, who had been afflicted with as severe a blow through her husband and son.

"Eugenie," she said to herself, "is lost, and so are we. The affair, as it will be reported, will cover us with shame; for in a society such as ours satire inflicts a painful and incurable wound. How fortunate that Eugenie is possessed of that strange character which has so often made me tremble!" And her glance was turned towards heaven, where a mysterious providence disposes all things, and out of a fault, nay, even a vice, sometimes produces a blessing. And then her thoughts, cleaving through space like a bird in the air, rested on Cavalcanti. This Andrea was a wretch, a robber, an assassin, and yet his manners showed the effects of a sort of education, if not a complete one; he had been presented to the world with the appearance of an immense fortune, supported by an honorable name. How could she extricate herself from this labyrinth? To whom would she apply to help her out of this painful situation? Debray, to whom she had run, with the first instinct of a woman towards the man she loves, and who yet betrays her,—Debray could but give her advice, she must apply to some one more powerful than he.

The baroness then thought of M. de Villefort. It was M. de Villefort who had remorselessly brought misfortune into her family, as though they had been strangers. But, no; on reflection, the procureur was not a merciless man; and it was not the magistrate, slave to his duties, but the friend, the loyal friend, who roughly but firmly cut into the very core of the corruption; it was not the executioner, but the surgeon, who wished to withdraw the honor of Danglars from ignominious association with the disgraced young man they had presented to the world as their son-in-law. And since Villefort, the friend of Danglars, had acted in this way, no one could suppose that he had been previously acquainted with, or had lent himself to, any of Andrea's intrigues. Villefort's conduct, therefore, upon reflection, appeared to the baroness as if shaped for their mutual advantage. But the inflexibility of the procureur should stop there; she would see him the next day, and if she could not make him fail in his duties as a magistrate, she would, at least, obtain all the indulgence he could allow. She would invoke the past, recall old recollections; she would supplicate him by the remembrance of guilty, yet happy days. M. de Villefort would stifle the affair; he had only to turn his eyes on one side, and allow Andrea to fly, and follow up the crime under that shadow of guilt called contempt of court. And after this reasoning she slept easily.

At nine o'clock next morning she arose, and without ringing for her maid or giving the least sign of her activity, she dressed herself in the same simple style as on the previous night; then running down-stairs, she left the hotel, walked to the Rue de Provence, called a cab, and drove to M. de Villefort's house. For the last month this wretched house had presented the gloomy appearance of a lazaretto infected with the plague. Some of the apartments were closed within and without; the shutters were only opened to admit a minute's air, showing the scared face of a footman, and immediately afterwards the window would be closed, like a gravestone falling on a sepulchre, and the neighbors would say to each other in a low voice, "Will there be another funeral to-day at the procureur's house?" Madame Danglars involuntarily shuddered at the desolate aspect of the mansion; descending from the cab, she approached the door with trembling knees, and rang the bell. Three times did the bell ring with a dull, heavy sound, seeming to participate, in the general sadness, before the concierge appeared and peeped through the door, which he opened just wide enough to allow his words to be heard. He saw a lady, a fashionable, elegantly dressed lady, and yet the door remained almost closed.

"Do you intend opening the door?" said the baroness.

"First, madame, who are you?"

"Who am I? You know me well enough."

"We no longer know any one, madame."

"You must be mad, my friend," said the baroness.

"Where do you come from?"

"Oh, this is too much!"

"Madame, these are my orders; excuse me. Your name?"

"The baroness Danglars; you have seen me twenty times."

"Possibly, madame. And now, what do you want?"

"Oh, how extraordinary! I shall complain to M. de Villefort of the impertinence of his servants."

"Madame, this is precaution, not impertinence; no one enters here without an order from M. d'Avrigny, or without speaking to the procureur."

"Well, I have business with the procureur."

"Is it pressing business?"

"You can imagine so, since I have not even brought my carriage out yet. But enough of this—here is my card, take it to your master."

"Madame will await my return?"

"Yes; go." The concierge closed the door, leaving Madame Danglars in the street. She had not long to wait; directly afterwards the door was opened wide enough to admit her, and when she had passed through, it was again shut. Without losing sight of her for an instant, the concierge took a whistle from his pocket as soon as they entered the court, and blew it. The valet de chambre appeared on the door-steps. "You will excuse this poor fellow, madame," he said, as he preceded the baroness, "but his orders are precise, and M. de Villefort begged me to tell you that he could not act otherwise."

In the court showing his merchandise, was a tradesman who had been admitted with the same precautions. The baroness ascended the steps; she felt herself strongly infected with the sadness which seemed to magnify her own, and still guided by the valet de chambre, who never lost sight of her for an instant, she was introduced to the magistrate's study. Preoccupied as Madame Danglars had been with the object of her visit, the treatment she had received from these underlings appeared to her so insulting, that she began by complaining of it. But Villefort, raising his head, bowed down by grief, looked up at her with so sad a smile that her complaints died upon her lips. "Forgive my servants," he said, "for a terror I cannot blame them for; from being suspected they have become suspicious."

Madame Danglars had often heard of the terror to which the magistrate alluded, but without the evidence of her own eyesight she could never have believed that the sentiment had been carried so far. "You too, then, are unhappy?" she said. "Yes, madame," replied the magistrate.

"Then you pity me!"

"Sincerely, madame."

"And you understand what brings me here?"

"You wish to speak to me about the circumstance which has just happened?"

"Yes, sir,—a fearful misfortune."

"You mean a mischance."

"A mischance?" repeated the baroness.

"Alas, madame," said the procureur with his imperturbable calmness of manner, "I consider those alone misfortunes which are irreparable."

"And do you suppose this will be forgotten?"

"Everything will be forgotten, madame," said Villefort. "Your daughter will be married to-morrow, if not to-day—in a week, if not to-morrow; and I do not think you can regret the intended husband of your daughter."

Madame Danglars gazed on Villefort, stupefied to find him so almost insultingly calm. "Am I come to a friend?"

she asked in a tone full of mournful dignity. "You know that you are, madame," said Villefort, whose pale cheeks became slightly flushed as he gave her the assurance. And truly this assurance carried him back to different events from those now occupying the baroness and him. "Well, then, be more affectionate, my dear Villefort," said the baroness. "Speak to me not as a magistrate, but as a friend; and when I am in bitter anguish of spirit, do not tell me that I ought to be gay." Villefort bowed. "When I hear misfortunes named, madame," he said, "I have within the last few months contracted the bad habit of thinking of my own, and then I cannot help drawing up an egotistical parallel in my mind. That is the reason that by the side of my misfortunes yours appear to me mere mischances; that is why my dreadful position makes yours appear enviable. But this annoys you; let us change the subject. You were saying, madame"—

"I came to ask you, my friend," said the baroness, "what will be done with this impostor?"

"Impostor," repeated Villefort; "certainly, madame, you appear to extenuate some cases, and exaggerate others. Impostor, indeed!—M. Andrea Cavalcanti, or rather M. Benedetto, is nothing more nor less than an assassin!"

"Sir, I do not deny the justice of your correction, but the more severely you arm yourself against that unfortunate man, the more deeply will you strike our family. Come, forget him for a moment, and instead of pursuing him let him go."

"You are too late, madame; the orders are issued."

"Well, should he be arrested—do they think they will arrest him?"

"I hope so."

"If they should arrest him (I know that sometimes prisoners afford means of escape), will you leave him in prison?"—The procureur shook his head. "At least keep him there till my daughter be married."

"Impossible, madame; justice has its formalities."

"What, even for me?" said the baroness, half jesting, half in earnest. "For all, even for myself among the rest," replied Villefort.

"Ah," exclaimed the baroness, without expressing the ideas which the exclamation betrayed. Villefort looked at her with that piercing glance which reads the secrets of the heart. "Yes, I know what you mean," he said; "you refer to the terrible rumors spread abroad in the world, that the deaths which have kept me in mourning for the last three months, and from which Valentine has only escaped by a miracle, have not happened by natural means."

"I was not thinking of that," replied Madame Danglars quickly. "Yes, you were thinking of it, and with justice. You could not help thinking of it, and saying to yourself, 'you, who pursue crime so vindictively, answer now, why are there unpunished crimes in your dwelling?"' The baroness became pale. "You were saying this, were you not?"

"Well, I own it."

"I will answer you."

Villefort drew his armchair nearer to Madame Danglars; then resting both hands upon his desk he said in a voice more hollow than usual: "There are crimes which remain unpunished because the criminals are unknown, and we might strike the innocent instead of the guilty; but when the culprits are discovered" (Villefort here extended his hand toward a large crucifix placed opposite to his desk)—"when they are discovered, I swear to you, by all I hold most sacred, that whoever they may be they shall die. Now, after the oath I have just taken, and which I will keep, madame, dare you ask for mercy for that wretch!"

"But, sir, are you sure he is as guilty as they say?"

"Listen; this is his description: 'Benedetto, condemned, at the age of sixteen, for five years to the galleys for forgery.' He promised well, as you see—first a runaway, then an assassin."

"And who is this wretch?"

"Who can tell?—a vagabond, a Corsican."

"Has no one owned him?"

"No one; his parents are unknown."

"But who was the man who brought him from Lucca?"

"Another rascal like himself, perhaps his accomplice." The baroness clasped her hands. "Villefort," she exclaimed in her softest and most captivating manner.

"For heaven's sake, madame," said Villefort, with a firmness of expression not altogether free from harshness—"for heaven's sake, do not ask pardon of me for a guilty wretch! What am I?—the law. Has the law any eyes to witness your grief? Has the law ears to be melted by your sweet voice? Has the law a memory for all those soft recollections you endeavor to recall? No, madame; the law has commanded, and when it commands it strikes. You will tell me that I am a living being, and not a code—a man, and not a volume. Look at me, madame—look around me. Have mankind treated me as a brother? Have they loved me? Have they spared me? Has any one shown the mercy towards me that you now ask at my hands? No, madame, they struck me, always struck me!

"Woman, siren that you are, do you persist in fixing on me that fascinating eye, which reminds me that I ought to blush? Well, be it so; let me blush for the faults you know, and perhaps—perhaps for even more than those! But having sinned myself,—it may be more deeply than others,—I never rest till I have torn the disguises from my fellow-creatures, and found out their weaknesses. I have always found them; and more,—I repeat it with joy, with triumph,—I have always found some proof of human perversity or error.

Every criminal I condemn seems to me living evidence that I am not a hideous exception to the rest. Alas, alas, alas; all the world is wicked; let us therefore strike at wickedness!"

Villefort pronounced these last words with a feverish rage, which gave a ferocious eloquence to his words.

"But"" said Madame Danglars, resolving to make a last effort, "this young man, though a murderer, is an orphan, abandoned by everybody."

"So much the worse, or rather, so much the better; it has been so ordained that he may have none to weep his fate."

"But this is trampling on the weak, sir."

"The weakness of a murderer!"

"His dishonor reflects upon us."

"Is not death in my house?"

"Oh, sir," exclaimed the baroness, "you are without pity for others, well, then, I tell you they will have no mercy on you!"

"Be it so!" said Villefort, raising his arms to heaven.

"At least, delay the trial till the next assizes; we shall then have six months before us."

"No, madame," said Villefort; "instructions have been given. There are yet five days left; five days are more than I require. Do you not think that I also long for forgetfulness? While working night and day, I sometimes lose all recollection of the past, and then I experience the same sort of happiness I can imagine the dead feel; still, it is better than suffering."

"But, sir, he has fled; let him escape—inaction is a pardonable offence."

"I tell you it is too late; early this morning the telegraph was employed, and at this very minute"—

"Sir," said the valet de chambre, entering the room, "a dragoon has brought this despatch from the minister of the interior." Villefort seized the letter, and hastily broke the seal. Madame Danglars trembled with fear; Villefort started with joy. "Arrested!" he exclaimed; "he was taken at Compiegne, and all is over." Madame Danglars rose from her seat, pale and cold. "Adieu, sir," she said. "Adieu, madame," replied the king's attorney, as in an almost joyful manner he conducted her to the door. Then, turning to his desk, he said, striking the letter with the back of his right hand, "Come, I had a forgery, three robberies, and two cases of arson, I only wanted a murder, and here it is. It will be a splendid session!"

CHAPTER 100.
THE APPARITION.

As the procureur had told Madame Danglars, Valentine was not yet recovered. Bowed down with fatigue, she was indeed confined to her bed; and it was in her own room, and from the lips of Madame de Villefort, that she heard all the strange events we have related,—we mean the flight of Eugenie and the arrest of Andrea Cavalcanti, or rather Benedetto, together with the accusation of murder pronounced against him. But Valentine was so weak that this recital scarcely produced the same effect it would have done had she been in her usual state of health. Indeed, her brain was only the seat of vague ideas, and confused forms, mingled with strange fancies, alone presented themselves before her eyes.

During the daytime Valentine's perceptions remained tolerably clear, owing to the constant presence of M. Noirtier, who caused himself to be carried to his granddaughter's room, and watched her with his paternal tenderness; Villefort also, on his return from the law courts, frequently passed an hour or two with his father and child. At six o'clock Villefort retired to his study, at eight M. d'Avrigny himself arrived, bringing the night draught prepared for the young girl, and then M. Noirtier was carried away. A nurse of the doctor's choice succeeded them, and never left till about ten or eleven o'clock, when Valentine was asleep. As she went down-stairs she gave the keys of Valentine's room to M. de Villefort, so that no one could reach the sick-room excepting through that of Madame de Villefort and little Edward.

Every morning Morrel called on Noirtier to receive news of Valentine, and, extraordinary as it seemed, each day found him less uneasy. Certainly, though Valentine still labored under dreadful nervous excitement, she was better; and moreover, Monte Cristo had told him when, half distracted, he had rushed to the count's house, that if she were not dead in two hours she would be saved. Now four days had elapsed, and Valentine still lived.

The nervous excitement of which we speak pursued Valentine even in her sleep, or rather in that state of somnolence which succeeded her waking hours; it was then, in the silence of night, in the dim light shed from the alabaster lamp on the chimney-piece, that she saw the shadows pass and repass which hover over the bed of sickness, and fan the fever with their trembling wings. First she fancied she saw her stepmother threatening her, then Morrel stretched his arms towards her; sometimes mere strangers, like the Count of Monte Cristo came to visit her; even the very furniture, in these moments of delirium, seemed to move, and this state lasted till about three o'clock in the morning, when a deep, heavy slumber overcame the young girl, from which she did not awake till daylight. On the evening of the day on which Valentine had learned of the flight of Eugenie and the arrest of Benedetto,—Villefort having retired as well as Noirtier and d'Avrigny,—her thoughts wandered in a confused maze, alternately reviewing her own situation and the events she had just heard.

Eleven o'clock had struck. The nurse, having placed the beverage prepared by the doctor within reach of the patient, and locked the door, was listening with terror to the comments of the servants in the kitchen, and storing her memory with all the horrible stories which had for some months past amused the occupants of the ante-chambers in the house of the king's attorney. Meanwhile an unexpected scene was passing in the room which had been so carefully locked. Ten minutes had elapsed since the nurse had left; Valentine, who for the last hour had been suffering from the fever which returned nightly, incapable of controlling her ideas, was forced to yield to the excitement which exhausted itself in producing and reproducing a succession and recurrence of the same fancies and images. The night-lamp threw out countless rays, each resolving itself into some strange form to her disordered imagination, when suddenly by its flickering light Valentine thought she saw the door of her library, which was in the recess by the chimney-piece, open slowly, though she in vain listened for the sound of the hinges on which it turned.

At any other time Valentine would have seized the silken bell-pull and summoned assistance, but nothing astonished her in her present situation. Her reason told her that all the visions she beheld were but the children of her imagination, and the conviction was strengthened by the fact that in the morning no traces remained of the nocturnal phantoms, who disappeared with the coming of daylight. From behind the door a human figure appeared, but the girl was too familiar with such apparitions to be alarmed, and therefore only stared, hoping to recognize Morrel. The figure advanced towards the bed and appeared to listen with profound attention. At this moment a ray of light glanced across the face of the midnight visitor.

"It is not he," she murmured, and waited, in the assurance that this was but a dream, for the man to disappear or assume some other form. Still, she felt her pulse, and finding it throb violently she remembered that the best method of dispelling such illusions was to drink, for a draught of the beverage prepared by the doctor to allay her fever seemed to cause a reaction of the brain, and for a short time she suffered less. Valentine therefore reached her hand towards the glass, but as soon as her trembling arm left the bed the apparition advanced more quickly towards her, and approached the young girl so closely that she fancied she heard his breath, and felt the pressure of his hand.

This time the illusion, or rather the reality, surpassed anything Valentine had before experienced; she began to believe herself really alive and awake, and the belief that her reason was this time not deceived made her shudder. The pressure she felt was evidently intended to arrest her arm, and she slowly withdrew it. Then the figure, from whom she could not detach her eyes, and who appeared more protecting than menacing, took the glass, and walking towards the night-light held it up, as if to test its transparency. This did not seem sufficient; the man, or rather the ghost— for he trod so softly that no sound was heard—then poured out about a spoonful into the glass, and drank it. Valentine witnessed this scene with a sentiment of stupefaction. Every minute she had expected that it would vanish and give place to another vision; but the man, instead of dissolving like a shadow, again approached her, and said in an agitated voice, "Now you may drink."

Valentine shuddered. It was the first time one of these visions had ever addressed her in a living voice, and she was about to utter an exclamation. The man placed his finger on her lips. "The Count of Monte Cristo!" she murmured.

It was easy to see that no doubt now remained in the young girl's mind as to the reality of the scene; her eyes started with terror, her hands trembled, and she rapidly drew the bedclothes closer to her. Still, the presence of Monte Cristo at such an hour, his mysterious, fanciful, and extraordinary entrance into her room through the wall, might well seem impossibilities to her shattered reason. "Do not call any one—do not be alarmed," said the Count; "do not let a shade of suspicion or uneasiness remain in your breast; the man standing before you, Valentine (for this time it is no ghost), is nothing more than the tenderest father and the most respectful friend you could dream of."

Valentine could not reply; the voice which indicated the real presence of a being in the room, alarmed her so much that she feared to utter a syllable; still the expression of her eyes seemed to inquire, "If your intentions are pure, why are you here?" The count's marvellous sagacity understood all that was passing in the young girl's mind.

"Listen to me," he said, "or, rather, look upon me; look at my face, paler even than usual, and my eyes, red with weariness—for four days I have not closed them, for I have been constantly watching you, to protect and preserve you for Maximilian." The blood mounted rapidly to the cheeks of Valentine, for the name just announced by the count dispelled all the fear with which his presence had inspired her. "Maximilian!" she exclaimed, and so sweet did the sound appear to her, that she repeated it—"Maximilian!—has he then owned all to you?"

"Everything. He told me your life was his, and I have promised him that you shall live."

"You have promised him that I shall live?"

"Yes."

"But, sir, you spoke of vigilance and protection. Are you a doctor?"

"Yes; the best you could have at the present time, believe me."

"But you say you have watched?" said Valentine uneasily; "where have you been?—I have not seen you." The count extended his hand towards the library. "I was hidden behind that door," he said, "which leads into the next house, which I have rented." Valentine turned her eyes away, and, with an indignant expression of pride and modest fear, exclaimed: "Sir, I think you have been guilty of an unparalleled intrusion, and that what you call protection is more like an insult."

"Valentine," he answered, "during my long watch over you, all I have observed has been what people visited you, what nourishment was prepared, and what beverage was served; then, when the latter appeared dangerous to me, I entered, as I have now done, and substituted, in the place of the poison, a healthful draught; which, instead of producing the death intended, caused life to circulate in your veins."

"Poison—death!" exclaimed Valentine, half believing herself under the influence of some feverish hallucination; "what are you saying, sir?"

"Hush, my child," said Monte Cristo, again placing his finger upon her lips, "I did say poison and death. But drink some of this;" and the count took a bottle from his pocket, containing a red liquid, of which he poured a few drops into the glass. "Drink this, and then take nothing more to-night." Valentine stretched out her hand, but scarcely had she touched the glass when she drew back in fear. Monte Cristo took the glass, drank half its contents, and then presented it to Valentine, who smiled and swallowed the rest. "Oh, yes," she exclaimed, "I recognize the flavor of my nocturnal beverage which refreshed me so much, and seemed to ease my aching brain. Thank you, sir, thank you!"

"This is how you have lived during the last four nights, Valentine," said the count. "But, oh, how I passed that time! Oh, the wretched hours I have endured—the torture to which I have submitted when I saw the deadly poison poured into your glass, and how I trembled lest you should drink it before I could find time to throw it away!"

"Sir," said Valentine, at the height of her terror, "you say you endured tortures when you saw the deadly poison poured into my glass; but if you saw this, you must also have seen the person who poured it?"

"Yes." Valentine raised herself in bed, and drew over her chest, which appeared whiter than snow, the embroidered cambric, still moist with the cold dews of delirium, to which were now added those of terror. "You saw the person?" repeated the young girl. "Yes," repeated the count.

"What you tell me is horrible, sir. You wish to make me believe something too dreadful. What?—attempt to murder me in my father's house, in my room, on my bed of sickness? Oh, leave me, sir; you are tempting me—you make me doubt the goodness of providence—it is impossible, it cannot be!"

"Are you the first that this hand has stricken? Have you not seen M. de Saint-Meran, Madame de Saint-Meran, Barrois, all fall? Would not M. Noirtier also have fallen a victim, had not the treatment he has been pursuing for the last three years neutralized the effects of the poison?"

"Oh, heaven," said Valentine; "is this the reason why grandpapa has made me share all his beverages during the last month?"

"And have they all tasted of a slightly bitter flavor, like that of dried orange-peel?"

"Oh, yes, yes!"

"Then that explains all," said Monte Cristo. "Your grandfather knows, then, that a poisoner lives here; perhaps he even suspects the person. He has been fortifying you, his beloved child, against the fatal effects of the poison, which has failed because your system was already impregnated with it. But even this would have availed little against a more deadly medium of death employed four days ago, which is generally but too fatal."

"But who, then, is this assassin, this murderer?"

"Let me also ask you a question. Have you never seen any one enter your room at night?"

"Oh, yes; I have frequently seen shadows pass close to me, approach, and disappear; but I took them for visions raised by my feverish imagination, and indeed when you entered I thought I was under the influence of delirium."

"Then you do not know who it is that attempts your life?"

"No," said Valentine; "who could desire my death?"

"You shall know it now, then," said Monte Cristo, listening.

"How do you mean?" said Valentine, looking anxiously around.

"Because you are not feverish or delirious to-night, but thoroughly awake; midnight is striking, which is the hour murderers choose."

"Oh, heavens," exclaimed Valentine, wiping off the drops which ran down her forehead. Midnight struck slowly and sadly; every hour seemed to strike with leaden weight upon the heart of the poor girl. "Valentine," said the count, "summon up all your courage; still the beatings of your heart; do not let a sound escape you, and feign to be asleep; then you will see." Valentine seized the count's hand. "I think I hear a noise," she said; "leave me."

"Good-by, for the present," replied the count, walking upon tiptoe towards the library door, and smiling with an expression so sad and paternal that the young girl's heart was filled with gratitude. Before closing the door he turned around once more, and said, "Not a movement—not a word; let them think you asleep, or perhaps you may be killed before I have the power of helping you." And with this fearful injunction the count disappeared through the door, which noiselessly closed after him.

CHAPTER 101.
LOCUSTA.

Valentine was alone; two other clocks, slower than that of Saint-Philippe du Roule, struck the hour of midnight from different directions, and excepting the rumbling of a few carriages all was silent. Then Valentine's attention was engrossed by the clock in her room, which marked the seconds. She began counting them, remarking that they were much slower than the beatings of her heart; and still she doubted,—the inoffensive Valentine could not imagine that any one should desire her death. Why should they? To what end? What had she done to excite the malice of an enemy? There was no fear of her falling asleep. One terrible idea pressed upon her mind,—that some one existed in the world who had attempted to assassinate her, and who was about to endeavor to do so again. Supposing this person, wearied at the inefficacy of the poison, should, as Monte Cristo intimated, have recourse to steel!—What if the count should have no time to run to her rescue!—What if her last moments were approaching, and she should never again see Morrel! When this terrible chain of ideas presented itself, Valentine was nearly persuaded to ring the bell, and call for help. But through the door she fancied she saw the luminous eye of the count—that eye which lived in her memory, and

75

the recollection overwhelmed her with so much shame that she asked herself whether any amount of gratitude could ever repay his adventurous and devoted friendship.

Twenty minutes, twenty tedious minutes, passed thus, then ten more, and at last the clock struck the half-hour. Just then the sound of finger-nails slightly grating against the door of the library informed Valentine that the count was still watching, and recommended her to do the same; at the same time, on the opposite side, that is towards Edward's room, Valentine fancied that she heard the creaking of the floor; she listened attentively, holding her breath till she was nearly suffocated; the lock turned, and the door slowly opened. Valentine had raised herself upon her elbow, and had scarcely time to throw herself down on the bed and shade her eyes with her arm; then, trembling, agitated, and her heart beating with indescribable terror, she awaited the event.

Some one approached the bed and drew back the curtains. Valentine summoned every effort, and breathed with that regular respiration which announces tranquil sleep. "Valentine!" said a low voice. Still silent: Valentine had promised not to awake. Then everything was still, excepting that Valentine heard the almost noiseless sound of some liquid being poured into the glass she had just emptied. Then she ventured to open her eyelids, and glance over her extended arm. She saw a woman in a white dressing-gown pouring a liquor from a phial into her glass. During this short time Valentine must have held her breath, or moved in some slight degree, for the woman, disturbed, stopped and leaned over the bed, in order the better to ascertain whether Valentine slept—it was Madame de Villefort.

On recognizing her step-mother, Valentine could not repress a shudder, which caused a vibration in the bed. Madame de Villefort instantly stepped back close to the wall, and there, shaded by the bed-curtains, she silently and attentively watched the slightest movement of Valentine. The latter recollected the terrible caution of Monte Cristo; she fancied that the hand not holding the phial clasped a long sharp knife. Then collecting all her remaining strength, she forced herself to close her eyes; but this simple operation upon the most delicate organs of our frame, generally so easy to accomplish, became almost impossible at this moment, so much did curiosity struggle to retain the eyelid open and learn the truth. Madame de Villefort, however, reassured by the silence, which was alone disturbed by the regular breathing of Valentine, again extended her hand, and half hidden by the curtains succeeded in emptying the contents of the phial into the glass. Then she retired so gently that Valentine did not know she had left the room. She only witnessed the withdrawal of the arm—the fair round arm of a woman but twenty-five years old, and who yet spread death around her.

It is impossible to describe the sensations experienced by Valentine during the minute and a half Madame de Villefort remained in the room. The grating against the library-door aroused the young girl from the stupor in which she was plunged, and which almost amounted to insensibility. She raised her head with an effort. The noiseless door again turned on its hinges, and the Count of Monte Cristo reappeared. "Well," said he, "do you still doubt?"

"Oh," murmured the young girl.

"Have you seen?"

"Alas!"

"Did you recognize?" Valentine groaned. "Oh, yes;" she said, "I saw, but I cannot believe!"

"Would you rather die, then, and cause Maximilian's death?"

"Oh," repeated the young girl, almost bewildered, "can I not leave the house?—can I not escape?"

"Valentine, the hand which now threatens you will pursue you everywhere; your servants will be seduced with gold, and death will be offered to you disguised in every shape. You will find it in the water you drink from the spring, in the fruit you pluck from the tree."

"But did you not say that my kind grandfather's precaution had neutralized the poison?"

"Yes, but not against a strong dose; the poison will be changed, and the quantity increased." He took the glass and raised it to his lips. "It is already done," he said; "brucine is no longer employed, but a simple narcotic! I can recognize the flavor of the alcohol in which it has been dissolved. If you had taken what Madame de Villefort has poured into your glass, Valentine—Valentine—you would have been doomed!"

"But," exclaimed the young girl, "why am I thus pursued?"

"Why?—are you so kind—so good—so unsuspicious of ill, that you cannot understand, Valentine?"

"No, I have never injured her."

"But you are rich, Valentine; you have 200,000 livres a year, and you prevent her son from enjoying these 200,000. livres."

"How so? The fortune is not her gift, but is inherited from my relations."

"Certainly; and that is why M. and Madame de Saint-Meran have died; that is why M. Noirtier was sentenced the day he made you his heir; that is why you, in your turn, are to die—it is because your father would inherit your property, and your brother, his only son, succeed to his."

"Edward? Poor child! Are all these crimes committed on his account?"

"Ah, then you at length understand?"

"Heaven grant that this may not be visited upon him!"

"Valentine, you are an angel!"

"But why is my grandfather allowed to live?"

"It was considered, that you dead, the fortune would naturally revert to your brother, unless he were disinherited; and besides, the crime appearing useless, it would be folly to commit it."

"And is it possible that this frightful combination of crimes has been invented by a woman?"

"Do you recollect in the arbor of the Hotel des Postes, at Perugia, seeing a man in a brown cloak, whom your stepmother was questioning upon aqua tofana? Well, ever since then, the infernal project has been ripening in her brain."

"Ah, then, indeed, sir," said the sweet girl, bathed in tears, "I see that I am condemned to die!"

"No, Valentine, for I have foreseen all their plots; no, your enemy is conquered since we know her, and you will live, Valentine—live to be happy yourself, and to confer happiness upon a noble heart; but to insure this you must rely on me."

"Command me, sir—what am I to do?"

"You must blindly take what I give you."

"Alas, were it only for my own sake, I should prefer to die!"

"You must not confide in any one—not even in your father."

"My father is not engaged in this fearful plot, is he, sir?" asked Valentine, clasping her hands.

"No; and yet your father, a man accustomed to judicial accusations, ought to have known that all these deaths have not happened naturally; it is he who should have watched over you—he should have occupied my place—he should have emptied that glass—he should have risen against the assassin. Spectre against spectre!" he murmured in a low voice, as he concluded his sentence.

"Sir," said Valentine, "I will do all I can to live, for there are two beings whose existence depends upon mine—my grandfather and Maximilian."

"I will watch over them as I have over you."

"Well, sir, do as you will with me;" and then she added, in a low voice, "oh, heavens, what will befall me?"

"Whatever may happen, Valentine, do not be alarmed; though you suffer; though you lose sight, hearing, consciousness, fear nothing; though you should awake and be ignorant where you are, still do not fear; even though you should find yourself in a sepulchral vault or coffin. Reassure yourself, then, and say to yourself: 'At this moment, a friend, a father, who lives for my happiness and that of Maximilian, watches over me!'"

"Alas, alas, what a fearful extremity!"

"Valentine, would you rather denounce your stepmother?"

"I would rather die a hundred times—oh, yes, die!"

"No, you will not die; but will you promise me, whatever happens, that you will not complain, but hope?"

"I will think of Maximilian!"

"You are my own darling child, Valentine! I alone can save you, and I will." Valentine in the extremity of her terror joined her hands,—for she felt that the moment had arrived to ask for courage,—and began to pray, and while uttering little more than incoherent words, she forgot that her white shoulders had no other covering than her long hair, and that the pulsations of her heart could be seen through the lace of her nightdress. Monte Cristo gently laid his hand on the young girl's arm, drew the velvet coverlet close to her throat, and said with a paternal smile,—"My child, believe in my devotion to you as you believe in the goodness of providence and the love of Maximilian."

Then he drew from his waistcoat-pocket the little emerald box, raised the golden lid, and took from it a pastille about the size of a pea, which he placed in her hand. She took it, and looked attentively on the count; there was an expression on the face of her intrepid protector which commanded her veneration. She evidently interrogated him by her look. "Yes," said he. Valentine carried the pastille to her mouth, and swallowed it. "And now, my dear child, adieu for the present. I will try and gain a little sleep, for you are saved."

"Go," said Valentine, "whatever happens, I promise you not to fear."

Monte Cristo for some time kept his eyes fixed on the young girl, who gradually fell asleep, yielding to the effects of the narcotic the count had given her. Then he took the glass, emptied three parts of the contents in the fireplace, that it might be supposed Valentine had taken it, and replaced it on the table; then he disappeared, after throwing a farewell glance on Valentine, who slept with the confidence and innocence of an angel.

CHAPTER 102.
VALENTINE.

The night-light continued to burn on the chimney-piece, exhausting the last drops of oil which floated on the surface of the water. The globe of the lamp appeared of a reddish hue, and the flame, brightening before it expired, threw out the last flickerings which in an inanimate object have been so often compared with the convulsions of a human creature in its final agonies. A dull and dismal light was shed over the bedclothes and curtains surrounding the young girl. All noise in the streets had ceased, and the silence was frightful. It was then that the door of Edward's room opened, and a head we have before noticed appeared in the glass opposite; it was Madame de Villefort, who came to witness the effects of the drink she had prepared. She stopped in the doorway, listened for a moment to the flickering of the lamp, the only sound in that deserted room, and then advanced to the table to see if Valentine's glass were empty. It was still about a quarter full, as we before stated. Madame de Villefort emptied the contents into the ashes, which she disturbed that they might the more readily absorb the liquid; then she carefully rinsed the glass, and wiping it with her handkerchief replaced it on the table.

If any one could have looked into the room just then he would have noticed the hesitation with which Madame de Villefort approached the bed and looked fixedly on Valentine. The dim light, the profound silence, and the gloomy thoughts inspired by the hour, and still more by her own conscience, all combined to produce a sensation of fear; the poisoner was terrified at the contemplation of her own work. At length she rallied, drew aside the curtain, and leaning over the pillow gazed intently on Valentine. The young girl no longer breathed, no breath issued through the half-closed teeth; the white lips no longer quivered—the eyes were suffused with a bluish vapor, and the long black lashes rested on a cheek white as wax. Madame de Villefort gazed upon the face so expressive even in its stillness; then she ventured to raise the coverlet and press her hand upon the young girl's heart. It was cold and motionless. She only felt the pulsation in her own fingers, and withdrew her hand with a shudder. One arm was hanging out of the bed; from shoulder to elbow it was moulded after the arms of Germain Pillon's "Graces," [*] but the fore-arm seemed to be slightly distorted by convulsion, and the hand, so delicately formed, was resting with stiff outstretched fingers on the framework of the bed. The nails, too, were turning blue.

    * Germain Pillon was a famous French sculptor (1535-1598).

His best known work is "The Three Graces," now in the Louvre.

Madame de Villefort had no longer any doubt; all was over—she had consummated the last terrible work she had to accomplish. There was no more to do in the room, so the poisoner retired stealthily, as though fearing to hear the sound of her own footsteps; but as she withdrew she still held aside the curtain, absorbed in the irresistible attraction always exerted by the picture of death, so long as it is merely mysterious and does not excite disgust. Just then the lamp again flickered; the noise startled Madame de Villefort, who shuddered and dropped the curtain. Immediately afterwards the light expired, and the room was plunged in frightful obscurity, while the clock at that minute struck half-past four. Overpowered with agitation, the poisoner succeeded in groping her way to the door, and reached her room in an agony of fear.

The darkness lasted two hours longer; then by degrees a cold light crept through the Venetian blinds, until at length it revealed the objects in the room. About this time the nurse's cough was heard on the stairs and the woman entered the room with a cup in her hand. To the tender eye of a father or a lover, the first glance would have sufficed to reveal Valentine's condition; but to this hireling, Valentine only appeared to sleep. "Good," she exclaimed, approaching the table, "she has taken part of her draught; the glass is three-quarters empty."

Then she went to the fireplace and lit the fire, and although she had just left her bed, she could not resist the temptation offered by Valentine's sleep, so she threw herself into an arm-chair to snatch a little more rest. The clock striking eight awoke her. Astonished at the prolonged slumber of the patient, and frightened to see that the arm was still hanging out of the bed, she advanced towards Valentine, and for the first time noticed the white lips. She tried to replace the arm, but it moved with a frightful rigidity which could not deceive a sick-nurse. She screamed aloud; then running to the door exclaimed,—"Help, help!"

"What is the matter?" asked M. d'Avrigny, at the foot of the stairs, it being the hour he usually visited her.

"What is it?" asked Villefort, rushing from his room. "Doctor, do you hear them call for help?"

"Yes, yes; let us hasten up; it was in Valentine's room." But before the doctor and the father could reach the room, the servants who were on the same floor had entered, and seeing Valentine pale and motionless on her bed, they lifted up their hands towards heaven and stood transfixed, as though struck by lightening. "Call Madame de Villefort!— Wake Madame de Villefort!" cried the procureur from the door of his chamber, which apparently he scarcely dared to leave. But instead of obeying him, the servants stood watching M. d'Avrigny, who ran to Valentine, and raised her in his arms. "What?—this one, too?" he exclaimed. "Oh, where will be the end?" Villefort rushed into the room. "What are you saying, doctor?" he exclaimed, raising his hands to heaven.

"I say that Valentine is dead!" replied d'Avrigny, in a voice terrible in its solemn calm.

M. de Villefort staggered and buried his head in the bed. On the exclamation of the doctor and the cry of the father, the servants all fled with muttered imprecations; they were heard running down the stairs and through the long passages, then there was a rush in the court, afterwards all was still; they had, one and all, deserted the accursed house. Just then, Madame de Villefort, in the act of slipping on her dressing-gown, threw aside the drapery and for a moment stood motionless, as though interrogating the occupants of the room, while she endeavored to call up some rebellious tears. On a sudden she stepped, or rather bounded, with outstretched arms, towards the table. She saw d'Avrigny curiously examining the glass, which she felt certain of having emptied during the night. It was now a third full, just as it was when she threw the contents into the ashes. The spectre of Valentine rising before the poisoner would have alarmed her less. It was, indeed, the same color as the draught she had poured into the glass, and which Valentine had drunk}; it was indeed the poison, which could not deceive M. d'Avrigny, which he now examined so closely; it was doubtless a miracle from heaven, that, notwithstanding her precautions, there should be some trace, some proof remaining to reveal the crime. While Madame de Villefort remained rooted to the spot like a statue of terror, and Villefort, with his head hidden in the bedclothes, saw nothing around him, d'Avrigny approached the window, that he might the better examine the contents of the glass, and dipping the tip of his finger in, tasted it. "Ah," he exclaimed, "it is no longer brucine that is used; let me see what it is!"

Then he ran to one of the cupboards in Valentine's room, which had been transformed into a medicine closet, and taking from its silver case a small bottle of nitric acid, dropped a little of it into the liquor, which immediately changed to a blood-red color. "Ah," exclaimed d'Avrigny, in a voice in which the horror of a judge unveiling the truth was mingled with the delight of a student making a discovery. Madame de Villefort was overpowered, her eyes first flashed and then swam, she staggered towards the door and disappeared. Directly afterwards the distant sound of a heavy weight falling on the ground was heard, but no one paid any attention to it; the nurse was engaged in watching the chemical analysis, and Villefort was still absorbed in grief. M. d'Avrigny alone had followed Madame de Villefort with his eyes, and watched her hurried retreat. He lifted up the drapery over the entrance to Edward's room, and his eye reaching as far as Madame de Villefort's apartment, he beheld her extended lifeless on the floor. "Go to the assistance of Madame de Villefort," he said to the nurse. "Madame de Villefort is ill."

"But Mademoiselle de Villefort"—stammered the nurse.

"Mademoiselle de Villefort no longer requires help," said d'Avrigny, "since she is dead."

"Dead,—dead!" groaned forth Villefort, in a paroxysm of grief, which was the more terrible from the novelty of the sensation in the iron heart of that man.

"Dead!" repeated a third voice. "Who said Valentine was dead?"

The two men turned round, and saw Morrel standing at the door, pale and terror-stricken. This is what had happened. At the usual time, Morrel had presented himself at the little door leading to Noirtier's room. Contrary to custom, the door was open, and having no occasion to ring he entered. He waited for a moment in the hall and called for a servant to conduct him to M. Noirtier; but no one answered, the servants having, as we know, deserted the house. Morrel had no particular reason for uneasiness; Monte Cristo had promised him that Valentine should live, and so far he had always fulfilled his word. Every night the count had given him news, which was the next morning confirmed by Noirtier. Still this extraordinary silence appeared strange to him, and he called a second and third time; still no answer. Then he determined to go up. Noirtier's room was opened, like all the rest. The first thing he saw was the old man sitting in his arm-chair in his usual place, but his eyes expressed alarm, which was confirmed by the pallor which overspread his features.

"How are you, sir?" asked Morrel, with a sickness of heart.

"Well," answered the old man, by closing his eyes; but his appearance manifested increasing uneasiness.

"You are thoughtful, sir," continued Morrel; "you want something; shall I call one of the servants?"

"Yes," replied Noirtier.

Morrel pulled the bell, but though he nearly broke the cord no one answered. He turned towards Noirtier; the pallor and anguish expressed on his countenance momentarily increased.

"Oh," exclaimed Morrel, "why do they not come? Is any one ill in the house?" The eyes of Noirtier seemed as though they would start from their sockets. "What is the matter? You alarm me. Valentine? Valentine?"

"Yes, yes," signed Noirtier. Maximilian tried to speak, but he could articulate nothing; he staggered, and supported himself against the wainscot. Then he pointed to the door.

"Yes, yes, yes!" continued the old man. Maximilian rushed up the little staircase, while Noirtier's eyes seemed to say,—"Quicker, quicker!"

In a minute the young man darted through several rooms, till at length he reached Valentine's. There was no occasion to push the door, it was wide open. A sob was the only sound he heard. He saw as though in a mist, a black figure kneeling and buried in a confused mass of white drapery. A terrible fear transfixed him. It was then he heard a voice exclaim "Valentine is dead!" and another voice which, like an echo repeated,—"Dead,—dead!"

CHAPTER 103.
MAXIMILIAN.

Villefort rose, half ashamed of being surprised in such a paroxysm of grief. The terrible office he had held for twenty-five years had succeeded in making him more or less than man. His glance, at first wandering, fixed itself upon Morrel. "Who are you, sir," he asked, "that forget that this is not the manner to enter a house stricken with death? Go, sir, go!" But Morrel remained motionless; he could not detach his eyes from that disordered bed, and the pale corpse of the young girl who was lying on it. "Go!—do you hear?" said Villefort, while d'Avrigny advanced to lead Morrel out. Maximilian stared for a moment at the corpse, gazed all around the room, then upon the two men; he opened his mouth to speak, but finding it impossible to give utterance to the innumerable ideas that occupied his brain, he went out, thrusting his hands through his hair in such a manner that Villefort and d'Avrigny, for a moment diverted from the engrossing topic, exchanged glances, which seemed to say,—"He is mad!"

But in less than five minutes the staircase groaned beneath an extraordinary weight. Morrel was seen carrying, with superhuman strength, the arm-chair containing Noirtier up-stairs. When he reached the landing he placed the arm-chair on the floor and rapidly rolled it into Valentine's room. This could only have been accomplished by means of unnatural strength supplied by powerful excitement. But the most fearful spectacle was Noirtier being pushed towards the bed, his face expressing all his meaning, and his eyes supplying the want of every other faculty. That pale face and flaming glance appeared to Villefort like a frightful apparition. Each time he had been brought into contact with his father, something terrible had happened. "See what they have done!" cried Morrel, with one hand leaning on the back of the chair, and the other extended towards Valentine. "See, my father, see!"

Villefort drew back and looked with astonishment on the young man, who, almost a stranger to him, called Noirtier his father. At this moment the whole soul of the old man seemed centred in his eyes which became bloodshot; the veins of the throat swelled; his cheeks and temples became purple, as though he was struck with epilepsy; nothing was wanting to complete this but the utterance of a cry. And the cry issued from his pores, if we may thus speak—a cry frightful in its silence. D'Avrigny rushed towards the old man and made him inhale a powerful restorative.

"Sir," cried Morrel, seizing the moist hand of the paralytic, "they ask me who I am, and what right I have to be here. Oh, you know it, tell them, tell them!" And the young man's voice was choked by sobs. As for the old man, his chest heaved with his panting respiration. One could have thought that he was undergoing the agonies preceding death. At length, happier than the young man, who sobbed without weeping, tears glistened in the eyes of Noirtier. "Tell them," said Morrel in a hoarse voice, "tell them that I am her betrothed. Tell them she was my beloved, my noble girl, my only blessing in the world. Tell them—oh, tell them, that corpse belongs to me!"

The young man overwhelmed by the weight of his anguish, fell heavily on his knees before the bed, which his fingers grasped with convulsive energy. D'Avrigny, unable to bear the sight of this touching emotion, turned away; and Villefort, without seeking any further explanation, and attracted towards him by the irresistible magnetism which draws us towards those who have loved the people for whom we mourn, extended his hand towards the young man. But Morrel saw nothing; he had grasped the hand of Valentine, and unable to weep vented his agony in groans as he bit the sheets. For some time nothing was heard in that chamber but sobs, exclamations, and prayers. At length Villefort, the most composed of all, spoke: "Sir," said he to Maximilian, "you say you loved Valentine, that you were betrothed to her. I knew nothing of this engagement, of this love, yet I, her father, forgive you, for I see that your grief is real and deep; and besides my own sorrow is too great for anger to find a place in my heart. But you see that the angel whom you hoped for has left this earth—she has nothing more to do with the adoration of men. Take a last farewell, sir, of her sad remains; take the hand you expected to possess once more within your own, and then separate yourself from her forever. Valentine now requires only the ministrations of the priest."

"You are mistaken, sir," exclaimed Morrel, raising himself on one knee, his heart pierced by a more acute pang than any he had yet felt—"you are mistaken; Valentine, dying as she has, not only requires a priest, but an avenger. You, M. de Villefort, send for the priest; I will be the avenger."

"What do you mean, sir?" asked Villefort, trembling at the new idea inspired by the delirium of Morrel.

"I tell you, sir, that two persons exist in you; the father has mourned sufficiently, now let the procureur fulfil his office."

The eyes of Noirtier glistened, and d'Avrigny approached.

"Gentlemen," said Morrel, reading all that passed through the minds of the witnesses to the scene, "I know what I am saying, and you know as well as I do what I am about to say—Valentine has been assassinated!" Villefort hung his head, d'Avrigny approached nearer, and Noirtier said "Yes" with his eyes. "Now, sir," continued Morrel, "in these days no one can disappear by violent means without some inquiries being made as to the cause of her disappearance, even were she not a young, beautiful, and adorable creature like Valentine. Mr. Procureur," said Morrel with increasing vehemence, "no mercy is allowed; I denounce the crime; it is your place to seek the assassin." The young man's implacable eyes interrogated Villefort, who, on his side, glanced from Noirtier to d'Avrigny. But instead of finding sympathy in the eyes of the doctor and his father, he only saw an expression as inflexible as that of Maximilian. "Yes," indicated the old man.

"Assuredly," said d'Avrigny.

"Sir," said Villefort, striving to struggle against this triple force and his own emotion,—"sir, you are deceived; no one commits crimes here. I am stricken by fate. It is horrible, indeed, but no one assassinates."

The eyes of Noirtier lighted up with rage, and d'Avrigny prepared to speak. Morrel, however, extended his arm, and commanded silence. "And I say that murders are committed here," said Morrel, whose voice, though lower in tone, lost none of its terrible distinctness: "I tell you that this is the fourth victim within the last four months. I tell you, Valentine's life was attempted by poison four days ago, though she escaped, owing to the precautions of M. Noirtier. I tell you that the dose has been double, the poison changed, and that this time it has succeeded. I tell you that you know these things as well as I do, since this gentleman has forewarned you, both as a doctor and as a friend."

"Oh, you rave, sir," exclaimed Villefort, in vain endeavoring to escape the net in which he was taken.

"I rave?" said Morrel; "well, then, I appeal to M. d'Avrigny himself. Ask him, sir, if he recollects the words he uttered in the garden of this house on the night of Madame de Saint-Meran's death. You thought yourselves alone, and talked about that tragical death, and the fatality you mentioned then is the same which has caused the murder of Valentine." Villefort and d'Avrigny exchanged looks. "Yes, yes," continued Morrel; "recall the scene, for the words you thought were only given to silence and solitude fell into my ears. Certainly, after witnessing the culpable indolence manifested by M. de Villefort towards his own relations, I ought to have denounced him to the authorities; then I should not have been an accomplice to thy death, as I now am, sweet, beloved Valentine; but the accomplice shall become the avenger. This fourth murder is apparent to all, and if thy father abandon thee, Valentine, it is I, and I swear it, that shall pursue the assassin." And this time, as though nature had at least taken compassion on the vigorous frame, nearly bursting with its own strength, the words of Morrel were stifled in his throat; his breast heaved; the tears, so long rebellious, gushed from his eyes; and he threw himself weeping on his knees by the side of the bed.

Then d'Avrigny spoke. "And I, too," he exclaimed in a low voice, "I unite with M. Morrel in demanding justice for crime; my blood boils at the idea of having encouraged a murderer by my cowardly concession."

"Oh, merciful heavens!" murmured Villefort. Morrel raised his head, and reading the eyes of the old man, which gleamed with unnatural lustre,—"Stay," he said, "M. Noirtier wishes to speak."

"Yes," indicated Noirtier, with an expression the more terrible, from all his faculties being centred in his glance.

"Do you know the assassin?" asked Morrel.

"Yes," replied Noirtier.

"And will you direct us?" exclaimed the young man. "Listen, M. d'Avrigny, listen!" Noirtier looked upon Morrel with one of those melancholy smiles which had so often made Valentine happy, and thus fixed his attention. Then, having riveted the eyes of his interlocutor on his own, he glanced towards the door.

"Do you wish me to leave?" said Morrel, sadly.

"Yes," replied Noirtier.

"Alas, alas, sir, have pity on me!"

The old man's eyes remained fixed on the door.

"May I, at least, return?" asked Morrel.

"Yes."

"Must I leave alone?"

"No."

"Whom am I to take with me? The procureur?"

"No."

"The doctor?"

"Yes."

"You wish to remain alone with M. de Villefort?"

"Yes."

"But can he understand you?"

"Yes."

"Oh," said Villefort, inexpressibly delighted to think that the inquiries were to be made by him alone,—"oh, be satisfied, I can understand my father." D'Avrigny took the young man's arm, and led him out of the room. A more than deathlike silence then reigned in the house. At the end of a quarter of an hour a faltering footstep was heard, and Villefort appeared at the door of the apartment where d'Avrigny and Morrel had been staying, one absorbed in meditation, the other in grief. "You can come," he said, and led them back to Noirtier. Morrel looked attentively on Villefort. His face was livid, large drops rolled down his face, and in his fingers he held the fragments of a quill pen which he had torn to atoms.

"Gentlemen," he said in a hoarse voice, "give me your word of honor that this horrible secret shall forever remain buried amongst ourselves!" The two men drew back.

"I entreat you."—continued Villefort.

"But," said Morrel, "the culprit—the murderer—the assassin."

"Do not alarm yourself, sir; justice will be done," said Villefort. "My father has revealed the culprit's name; my father thirsts for revenge as much as you do, yet even he conjures you as I do to keep this secret. Do you not, father?"

"Yes," resolutely replied Noirtier. Morrel suffered an exclamation of horror and surprise to escape him. "Oh, sir," said Villefort, arresting Maximilian by the arm, "if my father, the inflexible man, makes this request, it is because he knows, be assured, that Valentine will be terribly revenged. Is it not so, father?" The old man made a sign in the affirmative. Villefort continued: "He knows me, and I have pledged my word to him. Rest assured, gentlemen, that within three days, in a less time than justice would demand, the revenge I shall have taken for the murder of my child will be such as to make the boldest heart tremble;" and as he spoke these words he ground his teeth, and grasped the old man's senseless hand.

"Will this promise be fulfilled, M. Noirtier?" asked Morrel, while d'Avrigny looked inquiringly.

"Yes," replied Noirtier with an expression of sinister joy.

"Swear, then," said Villefort, joining the hands of Morrel and d'Avrigny, "swear that you will spare the honor of my house, and leave me to avenge my child." D'Avrigny turned round and uttered a very feeble "Yes," but Morrel, disengaging his hand, rushed to the bed, and after having pressed the cold lips of Valentine with his own, hurriedly left, uttering a long, deep groan of despair and anguish. We have before stated that all the servants had fled. M. de Villefort was therefore obliged to request M. d'Avrigny to superintend all the arrangements consequent upon a death in a large city, more especially a death under such suspicious circumstances.

It was something terrible to witness the silent agony, the mute despair of Noirtier, whose tears silently rolled down his cheeks. Villefort retired to his study, and d'Avrigny left to summon the doctor of the mayoralty, whose office it is to examine bodies after decease, and who is expressly named "the doctor of the dead." M. Noirtier could not be persuaded to quit his grandchild. At the end of a quarter of an hour M. d'Avrigny returned with his associate; they found the outer gate closed, and not a servant remaining in the house; Villefort himself was obliged to open to them. But he stopped on the landing; he had not the courage to again visit the death chamber. The two doctors, therefore, entered the room alone. Noirtier was near the bed, pale, motionless, and silent as the corpse. The district doctor approached with the indifference of a man accustomed to spend half his time amongst the dead; he then lifted the sheet which was placed over the face, and just unclosed the lips.

"Alas," said d'Avrigny, "she is indeed dead, poor child!"

"Yes," answered the doctor laconically, dropping the sheet he had raised. Noirtier uttered a kind of hoarse, rattling sound; the old man's eyes sparkled, and the good doctor understood that he wished to behold his child. He therefore approached the bed, and while his companion was dipping the fingers with which he had touched the lips of the corpse in chloride of lime, he uncovered the calm and pale face, which looked like that of a sleeping angel. A tear, which appeared in the old man's eye, expressed his thanks to the doctor. The doctor of the dead then laid his permit on the corner of the table, and having fulfilled his duty, was conducted out by d'Avrigny. Villefort met them at the door of his study; having in a few words thanked the district doctor, he turned to d'Avrigny, and said,—"And now the priest."

"Is there any particular priest you wish to pray with Valentine?" asked d'Avrigny.

"No." said Villefort; "fetch the nearest."

"The nearest," said the district doctor, "is a good Italian abbe, who lives next door to you. Shall I call on him as I pass?"

"D'Avrigny," said Villefort, "be so kind, I beseech you, as to accompany this gentleman. Here is the key of the door, so that you can go in and out as you please; you will bring the priest with you, and will oblige me by introducing him into my child's room."

"Do you wish to see him?"

"I only wish to be alone. You will excuse me, will you not? A priest can understand a father's grief." And M. de Villefort, giving the key to d'Avrigny, again bade farewell to the strange doctor, and retired to his study, where he began to work. For some temperaments work is a remedy for all afflictions. As the doctors entered the street, they saw a man in a cassock standing on the threshold of the next door. "This is the abbe of whom I spoke," said the doctor to d'Avrigny. D'Avrigny accosted the priest. "Sir," he said, "are you disposed to confer a great obligation on an unhappy father who has just lost his daughter? I mean M. de Villefort, the king's attorney."

"Ah," said the priest, in a marked Italian accent; "yes, I have heard that death is in that house."

"Then I need not tell you what kind of service he requires of you."

"I was about to offer myself, sir," said the priest; "it is our mission to forestall our duties."

"It is a young girl."

"I know it, sir; the servants who fled from the house informed me. I also know that her name is Valentine, and I have already prayed for her."

"Thank you, sir," said d'Avrigny; "since you have commenced your sacred office, deign to continue it. Come and watch by the dead, and all the wretched family will be grateful to you."

"I am going, sir; and I do not hesitate to say that no prayers will be more fervent than mine." D'Avrigny took the priest's hand, and without meeting Villefort, who was engaged in his study, they reached Valentine's room, which on the following night was to be occupied by the undertakers. On entering the room, Noirtier's eyes met those of the abbe, and no doubt he read some particular expression in them, for he remained in the room. D'Avrigny recommended the attention of the priest to the living as well as to the dead, and the abbe promised to devote his prayers to Valentine and his attentions to Noirtier. In order, doubtless, that he might not be disturbed while fulfilling his sacred mission, the priest rose as soon as d'Avrigny departed, and not only bolted the door through which the doctor had just left, but also that leading to Madame de Villefort's room.

CHAPTER 104.
DANGLARS SIGNATURE.

The next morning dawned dull and cloudy. During the night the undertakers had executed their melancholy office, and wrapped the corpse in the winding-sheet, which, whatever may be said about the equality of death, is at least a last proof of the luxury so pleasing in life. This winding-sheet was nothing more than a beautiful piece of cambric, which the young girl had bought a fortnight before. During the evening two men, engaged for the purpose, had carried Noirtier from Valentine's room into his own, and contrary to all expectation there was no difficulty in withdrawing him from his child. The Abbe Busoni had watched till daylight, and then left without calling any one. D'Avrigny returned about eight o'clock in the morning; he met Villefort on his way to Noirtier's room, and accompanied him to see how the old man had slept. They found him in the large arm-chair, which served him for a bed, enjoying a calm, nay, almost a smiling sleep. They both stood in amazement at the door.

"See," said d'Avrigny to Villefort, "nature knows how to alleviate the deepest sorrow. No one can say that M. Noirtier did not love his child, and yet he sleeps."

"Yes, you are right," replied Villefort, surprised; "he sleeps, indeed! And this is the more strange, since the least contradiction keeps him awake all night."

"Grief has stunned him," replied d'Avrigny; and they both returned thoughtfully to the procureur's study.

"See, I have not slept," said Villefort, showing his undisturbed bed; "grief does not stun me. I have not been in bed for two nights; but then look at my desk; see what I have written during these two days and nights. I have filled those papers, and have made out the accusation against the assassin Benedetto. Oh, work, work,—my passion, my joy, my delight,—it is for thee to alleviate my sorrows!" and he convulsively grasped the hand of d'Avrigny.

"Do you require my services now?" asked d'Avrigny.

"No," said Villefort; "only return again at eleven o'clock; at twelve the—the—oh, heavens, my poor, poor child!" and the procureur again becoming a man, lifted up his eyes and groaned.

"Shall you be present in the reception room?"

"No; I have a cousin who has undertaken this sad office. I shall work, doctor—when I work I forget everything." And, indeed, no sooner had the doctor left the room, than he was again absorbed in study. On the doorsteps d'Avrigny met the cousin whom Villefort had mentioned, a personage as insignificant in our story as in the world he occupied— one of those beings designed from their birth to make themselves useful to others. He was punctual, dressed in black, with crape around his hat, and presented himself at his cousin's with a face made up for the occasion, and which he could alter as might be required. At twelve o'clock the mourning-coaches rolled into the paved court, and the Rue du Faubourg Saint-Honore was filled with a crowd of idlers, equally pleased to witness the festivities or the mourning of the rich, and who rush with the same avidity to a funeral procession as to the marriage of a duchess.

Gradually the reception-room filled, and some of our old friends made their appearance—we mean Debray, Chateau-Renaud, and Beauchamp, accompanied by all the leading men of the day at the bar, in literature, or the army, for M. de Villefort moved in the first Parisian circles, less owing to his social position than to his personal merit. The cousin standing at the door ushered in the guests, and it was rather a relief to the indifferent to see a person as unmoved as themselves, and who did not exact a mournful face or force tears, as would have been the case with a father, a brother, or a lover. Those who were acquainted soon formed into little groups. One of them was made of Debray, Chateau-Renaud, and Beauchamp.

"Poor girl," said Debray, like the rest, paying an involuntary tribute to the sad event,—"poor girl, so young, so rich, so beautiful! Could you have imagined this scene,

Chateau-Renaud, when we saw her, at the most three weeks ago, about to sign that contract?"

"Indeed, no," said Chateau-Renaud—"Did you know her?"

"I spoke to her once or twice at Madame de Morcerf's, among the rest; she appeared to me charming, though rather melancholy. Where is her stepmother? Do you know?"

"She is spending the day with the wife of the worthy gentleman who is receiving us."

"Who is he?"

"Whom do you mean?"

"The gentleman who receives us? Is he a deputy?"

"Oh, no. I am condemned to witness those gentlemen every day," said Beauchamp; "but he is perfectly unknown to me."

"Have you mentioned this death in your paper?"

"It has been mentioned, but the article is not mine; indeed, I doubt if it will please M. Villefort, for it says that if four successive deaths had happened anywhere else than in the house of the king's attorney, he would have interested himself somewhat more about it."

"Still," said Chateau-Renaud, "Dr. d'Avrigny, who attends my mother, declares he is in despair about it. But whom are you seeking, Debray?"

"I am seeking the Count of Monte Cristo" said the young man.

"I met him on the boulevard, on my way here," said Beauchamp. "I think he is about to leave Paris; he was going to his banker."

"His banker? Danglars is his banker, is he not?" asked Chateau-Renaud of Debray.

"I believe so," replied the secretary with slight uneasiness. "But Monte Cristo is not the only one I miss here; I do not see Morrel."

"Morrel? Do they know him?" asked Chateau-Renaud. "I think he has only been introduced to Madame de Villefort."

"Still, he ought to have been here," said Debray; "I wonder what will be talked about to-night; this funeral is the news of the day. But hush, here comes our minister of justice; he will feel obliged to make some little speech to the cousin," and the three young men drew near to listen. Beauchamp told the truth when he said that on his way to the funeral he had met Monte Cristo, who was directing his steps towards the Rue de la Chausse d'Antin, to M. Danglars'.

The banker saw the carriage of the count enter the court yard, and advanced to meet him with a sad, though affable smile. "Well," said he, extending his hand to Monte Cristo, "I suppose you have come to sympathize with me, for indeed misfortune has taken possession of my house. When I perceived you, I was just asking myself whether I had not wished harm towards those poor Morcerfs, which would have justified the proverb of 'He who wishes misfortunes to happen to others experiences them himself.' Well, on my word of honor, I answered, 'No!' I wished no ill to Morcerf; he was a little proud, perhaps, for a man who like myself has risen from nothing; but we all have our faults. Do you know, count, that persons of our time of life—not that you belong to the class, you are still a young man,—but as I was saying, persons of our time of life have been very unfortunate this year. For example, look at the puritanical procureur, who has just lost his daughter, and in fact nearly all his family, in so singular a manner; Morcerf dishonored and dead; and then myself covered with ridicule through the villany of Benedetto; besides"—

"Besides what?" asked the Count.

"Alas, do you not know?"

"What new calamity?"

"My daughter"—

"Mademoiselle Danglars?"

"Eugenie has left us!"

"Good heavens, what are you telling me?"

"The truth, my dear count. Oh, how happy you must be in not having either wife or children!"

"Do you think so?"

"Indeed I do."

"And so Mademoiselle Danglars"—

"She could not endure the insult offered to us by that wretch, so she asked permission to travel."

"And is she gone?"

"The other night she left."

"With Madame Danglars?"

"No, with a relation. But still, we have quite lost our dear Eugenie; for I doubt whether her pride will ever allow her to return to France."

"Still, baron," said Monte Cristo, "family griefs, or indeed any other affliction which would crush a man whose child was his only treasure, are endurable to a millionaire. Philosophers may well say, and practical men will always support the opinion, that money mitigates many trials; and if you admit the efficacy of this sovereign balm, you ought to be very easily consoled—you, the king of finance, the focus of immeasurable power."

Danglars looked at him askance, as though to ascertain whether he spoke seriously. "Yes," he answered, "if a fortune brings consolation, I ought to be consoled; I am rich."

"So rich, dear sir, that your fortune resembles the pyramids; if you wished to demolish them you could not, and if it were possible, you would not dare!" Danglars smiled at the good-natured pleasantry of the count. "That reminds me," he said, "that when you entered I was on the point of signing five little bonds; I have already signed two: will you allow me to do the same to the others?"

"Pray do so."

There was a moment's silence, during which the noise of the banker's pen was alone heard, while Monte Cristo examined the gilt mouldings on the ceiling. "Are they Spanish, Haitian, or Neapolitan bonds?" said Monte Cristo. "No," said Danglars, smiling, "they are bonds on the bank of France, payable to bearer. Stay, count," he added, "you, who may be called the emperor, if I claim the title of king of finance, have you many pieces of paper of this size, each worth a million?" The count took into his hands the papers, which Danglars had so proudly presented to him, and read:—

"To the Governor of the Bank. Please pay to my order, from the fund deposited by me, the sum of a million, and charge the same to my account.

"Baron Danglars."

"One, two, three, four, five," said Monte Cristo; "five millions—why what a Croesus you are!"

"This is how I transact business," said Danglars.

"It is really wonderful," said the count; "above all, if, as I suppose, it is payable at sight."

"It is, indeed, said Danglars.

"It is a fine thing to have such credit; really, it is only in France these things are done. Five millions on five little scraps of paper!—it must be seen to be believed."

"You do not doubt it?"

"No!"

"You say so with an accent—stay, you shall be convinced; take my clerk to the bank, and you will see him leave it with an order on the Treasury for the same sum."

"No," said Monte Cristo folding the five notes, "most decidedly not; the thing is so curious, I will make the experiment myself. I am credited on you for six millions. I have drawn nine hundred thousand francs, you therefore still owe me five millions and a hundred thousand francs. I will take the five scraps of paper that I now hold as bonds, with your signature alone, and here is a receipt in full for the six millions between us. I had prepared it beforehand, for I am much in want of money to-day." And Monte Cristo placed the bonds in his pocket with one hand, while with the other he held out the receipt to Danglars. If a thunderbolt had fallen at the banker's feet, he could not have experienced greater terror.

"What," he stammered, "do you mean to keep that money? Excuse me, excuse me, but I owe this money to the charity fund,—a deposit which I promised to pay this morning."

"Oh, well, then," said Monte Cristo, "I am not particular about these five notes, pay me in a different form; I wished, from curiosity, to take these, that I might be able to say that without any advice or preparation the house of Danglars had paid me five millions without a minute's delay; it would have been remarkable. But here are your bonds; pay me differently;" and he held the bonds towards Danglars, who seized them like a vulture extending its claws to withhold the food that is being wrested from its grasp. Suddenly he rallied, made a violent effort to restrain himself, and then a smile gradually widened the features of his disturbed countenance.

"Certainly," he said, "your receipt is money."

"Oh dear, yes; and if you were at Rome, the house of Thomson & French would make no more difficulty about paying the money on my receipt than you have just done."

"Pardon me, count, pardon me."

"Then I may keep this money?"

"Yes," said Danglars, while the perspiration started from the roots of his hair. "Yes, keep it—keep it."

Monte Cristo replaced the notes in his pocket with that indescribable expression which seemed to say, "Come, reflect; if you repent there is still time."

"No," said Danglars, "no, decidedly no; keep my signatures. But you know none are so formal as bankers in transacting business; I intended this money for the charity fund, and I seemed to be robbing them if I did not pay them with these precise bonds. How absurd—as if one crown were not as good as another. Excuse me;" and he began to laugh loudly, but nervously.

"Certainly, I excuse you," said Monte Cristo graciously, "and pocket them." And he placed the bonds in his pocketbook.

"But," said Danglars, "there is still a sum of one hundred thousand francs?"

"Oh, a mere nothing," said Monte Cristo. "The balance would come to about that sum; but keep it, and we shall be quits."

"Count," said Danglars, "are you speaking seriously?"

"I never joke with bankers," said Monte Cristo in a freezing manner, which repelled impertinence; and he turned to the door, just as the valet de chambre announced,—"M. de Boville, receiver-general of the charities."

"Ma foi," said Monte Cristo; "I think I arrived just in time to obtain your signatures, or they would have been disputed with me."

Danglars again became pale, and hastened to conduct the count out. Monte Cristo exchanged a ceremonious bow with M. de Boville, who was standing in the waiting-room, and who was introduced into Danglars' room as soon as the count had left. The count's sad face was illumined by a faint smile, as he noticed the portfolio which the receiver-general held in his hand. At the door he found his carriage, and was immediately driven to the bank. Meanwhile Danglars, repressing all emotion, advanced to meet the receiver-general. We need not say that a smile of condescension was stamped upon his lips. "Good-morning, creditor," said he; "for I wager anything it is the creditor who visits me."

"You are right, baron," answered M. de Boville; "the charities present themselves to you through me: the widows and orphans depute me to receive alms to the amount of five millions from you."

"And yet they say orphans are to be pitied," said Danglars, wishing to prolong the jest. "Poor things!"

"Here I am in their name," said M. de Boville; "but did you receive my letter yesterday?"

"Yes."

"I have brought my receipt."

"My dear M. de Boville, your widows and orphans must oblige me by waiting twenty-four hours, since M. de Monte Cristo whom you just saw leaving here—you did see him, I think?"

"Yes; well?"

"Well, M. de Monte Cristo has just carried off their five millions."

"How so?"

"The count has an unlimited credit upon me; a credit opened by Thomson & French, of Rome; he came to demand five millions at once, which I paid him with checks on the bank. My funds are deposited there, and you can understand that if I draw out ten millions on the same day it will appear rather strange to the governor. Two days will be a different thing," said Danglars, smiling.

"Come," said Boville, with a tone of entire incredulity, "five millions to that gentleman who just left, and who bowed to me as though he knew me?"

"Perhaps he knows you, though you do not know him; M. de Monte Cristo knows everybody."

"Five millions!"

"Here is his receipt. Believe your own eyes." M. de Boville took the paper Danglars presented him, and read:—

"Received of Baron Danglars the sum of five million one hundred thousand francs, to be repaid on demand by the house of Thomson & French of Rome."

"It is really true," said M. de Boville.

"Do you know the house of Thomson & French?"

"Yes, I once had business to transact with it to the amount of 200,000 francs; but since then I have not heard it mentioned."

"It is one of the best houses in Europe," said Danglars, carelessly throwing down the receipt on his desk.

"And he had five millions in your hands alone! Why, this Count of Monte Cristo must be a nabob?"

"Indeed I do not know what he is; he has three unlimited credits—one on me, one on Rothschild, one on Lafitte; and, you see," he added carelessly, "he has given me the preference, by leaving a balance of 100,000 francs." M. de Boville manifested signs of extraordinary admiration. "I must visit him," he said, "and obtain some pious grant from him."

"Oh, you may make sure of him; his charities alone amount to 20,000 francs a month."

"It is magnificent! I will set before him the example of Madame de Morcerf and her son."

"What example?"

"They gave all their fortune to the hospitals."

"What fortune?"

"Their own—M. de Morcerf's, who is deceased."

"For what reason?"

"Because they would not spend money so guiltily acquired."

"And what are they to live upon?"

"The mother retires into the country, and the son enters the army."

"Well, I must confess, these are scruples."

"I registered their deed of gift yesterday."

"And how much did they possess?"

"Oh, not much—from twelve to thirteen hundred thousand francs. But to return to our millions."

"Certainly," said Danglars, in the most natural tone in the world. "Are you then pressed for this money?"

"Yes; for the examination of our cash takes place to-morrow."

"To-morrow? Why did you not tell me so before? Why, it is as good as a century! At what hour does the examination take place?"

"At two o'clock."

"Send at twelve," said Danglars, smiling. M. de Boville said nothing, but nodded his head, and took up the portfolio. "Now I think of it, you can do better," said Danglars.

"How do you mean?"

"The receipt of M. de Monte Cristo is as good as money; take it to Rothschild's or Lafitte's, and they will take it off your hands at once."

"What, though payable at Rome?"

"Certainly; it will only cost you a discount of 5,000 or 6,000 francs." The receiver started back. "Ma foi," he said, "I prefer waiting till to-morrow. What a proposition!"

"I thought, perhaps," said Danglars with supreme impertinence, "that you had a deficiency to make up?"

"Indeed," said the receiver.

"And if that were the case it would be worth while to make some sacrifice."

"Thank you, no, sir."

"Then it will be to-morrow."

"Yes; but without fail."

"Ah, you are laughing at me; send to-morrow at twelve, and the bank shall be notified."

"I will come myself."

"Better still, since it will afford me the pleasure of seeing you." They shook hands. "By the way," said M. de Boville, "are you not going to the funeral of poor Mademoiselle de Villefort, which I met on my road here?"

"No," said the banker; "I have appeared rather ridiculous since that affair of Benedetto, so I remain in the background."

"Bah, you are wrong. How were you to blame in that affair?"

"Listen—when one bears an irreproachable name, as I do, one is rather sensitive."

"Everybody pities you, sir; and, above all, Mademoiselle Danglars!"

"Poor Eugenie!" said Danglars; "do you know she is going to embrace a religious life?"

"No."

"Alas, it is unhappily but too true. The day after the event, she decided on leaving Paris with a nun of her acquaintance; they are gone to seek a very strict convent in Italy or Spain."

"Oh, it is terrible!" and M. de Boville retired with this exclamation, after expressing acute sympathy with the father. But he had scarcely left before Danglars, with an energy of action those can alone understand who have seen Robert Macaire represented by Frederic, [*] exclaimed,—"Fool!" Then enclosing Monte Cristo's receipt in a little pocket-book, he added:—"Yes, come at twelve o'clock; I shall then be far away." Then he double-locked his door, emptied all his drawers, collected about fifty thousand francs in bank-notes, burned several papers, left others exposed to view, and then commenced writing a letter which he addressed:

"To Madame la Baronne Danglars."

 * Frederic Lemaitre—French actor (1800-1876). Robert Macaire is the hero of two favorite melodramas—"Chien de Montargis" and "Chien d'Aubry"—and the name is applied to bold criminals as a term of derision.

"I will place it on her table myself to-night," he murmured. Then taking a passport from his drawer he said,—"Good, it is available for two months longer."

CHAPTER 105.
THE CEMETERY OF PERE-LA-CHAISE.

M. de Boville had indeed met the funeral procession which was taking Valentine to her last home on earth. The weather was dull and stormy, a cold wind shook the few remaining yellow leaves from the boughs of the trees, and scattered them among the crowd which filled the boulevards. M. de Villefort, a true Parisian, considered the cemetery of Pere-la-Chaise alone worthy of receiving the mortal remains of a Parisian family; there alone the corpses belonging to him would be surrounded by worthy associates. He had therefore purchased a vault, which was quickly occupied by members of his family. On the front of the monument was inscribed: "The families of Saint-Meran and Villefort," for such had been the last wish expressed by poor Renee, Valentine's mother. The pompous procession therefore wended its way towards Pere-la-Chaise from the Faubourg Saint-Honore. Having crossed Paris, it passed through the Faubourg du Temple, then leaving the exterior boulevards, it reached the cemetery. More than fifty private carriages followed the twenty mourning-coaches, and behind them more than five hundred persons joined in the procession on foot.

These last consisted of all the young people whom Valentine's death had struck like a thunderbolt, and who, notwithstanding the raw chilliness of the season, could not refrain from paying a last tribute to the memory of the beautiful, chaste, and adorable girl, thus cut off in the flower of her youth. As they left Paris, an equipage with four horses, at full speed, was seen to draw up suddenly; it contained Monte Cristo. The count left the carriage and mingled in the crowd who followed on foot. Chateau-Renaud perceived him and immediately alighting from his coupe, joined him.

The count looked attentively through every opening in the crowd; he was evidently watching for some one, but his search ended in disappointment. "Where is Morrel?" he asked; "do either of these gentlemen know where he is?"

"We have already asked that question," said Chateau-Renaud, "for none of us has seen him." The count was silent, but continued to gaze around him. At length they arrived at the cemetery. The piercing eye of Monte Cristo glanced through clusters of bushes and trees, and was soon relieved from all anxiety, for seeing a shadow glide between the yew-trees, Monte Cristo recognized him whom he sought. One funeral is generally very much like another in this magnificent metropolis. Black figures are seen scattered over the long white avenues; the silence of earth and heaven is alone broken by the noise made by the crackling branches of hedges planted around the monuments; then follows the melancholy chant of the priests, mingled now and then with a sob of anguish, escaping from some woman concealed behind a mass of flowers.

The shadow Monte Cristo had noticed passed rapidly behind the tomb of Abelard and Heloise, placed itself close to the heads of the horses belonging to the hearse, and following the undertaker's men, arrived with them at the spot appointed for the burial. Each person's attention was occupied. Monte Cristo saw nothing but the shadow, which no one else observed. Twice the count left the ranks to see whether the object of his interest had any concealed weapon beneath his clothes. When the procession stopped, this shadow was recognized as Morrel, who, with his coat buttoned up to his throat, his face livid, and convulsively crushing his hat between his fingers, leaned against a tree, situated on an elevation commanding the mausoleum, so that none of the funeral details could escape his observation. Everything was conducted in the usual manner. A few men, the least impressed of all by the scene, pronounced a discourse, some deploring this premature death, others expatiating on the grief of the father, and one very ingenious person quoting the fact that Valentine had solicited pardon of her father for criminals on whom the arm of justice was ready to fall—until at length they exhausted their stores of metaphor and mournful speeches.

Monte Cristo heard and saw nothing, or rather he only saw Morrel, whose calmness had a frightful effect on those who knew what was passing in his heart. "See," said Beauchamp, pointing out Morrel to Debray. "What is he doing up there?" And they called Chateau-Renaud's attention to him.

"How pale he is!" said Chateau-Renaud, shuddering.

"He is cold," said Debray.

"Not at all," said Chateau-Renaud, slowly; "I think he is violently agitated. He is very susceptible."

"Bah," said Debray; "he scarcely knew Mademoiselle de Villefort; you said so yourself."

"True. Still I remember he danced three times with her at Madame de Morcerf's. Do you recollect that ball, count, where you produced such an effect?"

"No, I do not," replied Monte Cristo, without even knowing of what or to whom he was speaking, so much was he occupied in watching Morrel, who was holding his breath with emotion. "The discourse is over; farewell, gentlemen," said the count. And he disappeared without anyone seeing whither he went. The funeral being over, the guests returned to Paris. Chateau-Renaud looked for a moment for Morrel; but while they were watching the departure of the count, Morrel had quitted his post, and Chateau-Renaud, failing in his search, joined Debray and Beauchamp.

Monte Cristo concealed himself behind a large tomb and awaited the arrival of Morrel, who by degrees approached the tomb now abandoned by spectators and workmen. Morrel threw a glance around, but before it reached the spot occupied by Monte Cristo the latter had advanced yet nearer, still unperceived. The young man knelt down. The count, with outstretched neck and glaring eyes, stood in an attitude ready to pounce upon Morrel upon the first occasion. Morrel bent his head till it touched the stone, then clutching the grating with both hands, he murmured,—"Oh, Valentine!" The count's heart was pierced by the utterance of these two words; he stepped forward, and touching the young man's shoulder, said,—"I was looking for you, my friend." Monte Cristo expected a burst of passion, but he was deceived, for Morrel turning round, said calmly,—

"You see I was praying." The scrutinizing glance of the count searched the young man from head to foot. He then seemed more easy.

"Shall I drive you back to Paris?" he asked.

"No, thank you."

"Do you wish anything?"

"Leave me to pray." The count withdrew without opposition, but it was only to place himself in a situation where he could watch every movement of Morrel, who at length arose, brushed the dust from his knees, and turned towards Paris, without once looking back. He walked slowly down the Rue de la Roquette. The count, dismissing his carriage, followed him about a hundred paces behind. Maximilian crossed the canal and entered the Rue Meslay by the boulevards. Five minutes after the door had been closed on Morrel's entrance, it was again opened for the count. Julie was at the entrance of the garden, where she was attentively watching Penelon, who, entering with zeal into his profession of gardener, was very busy grafting some Bengal roses. "Ah, count," she exclaimed, with the delight manifested by every member of the family whenever he visited the Rue Meslay.

"Maximilian has just returned, has he not, madame?" asked the count.

"Yes, I think I saw him pass; but pray, call Emmanuel."

"Excuse me, madame, but I must go up to Maximilian's room this instant," replied Monte Cristo, "I have something of the greatest importance to tell him."

"Go, then," she said with a charming smile, which accompanied him until he had disappeared. Monte Cristo soon ran up the staircase conducting from the ground-floor to Maximilian's room; when he reached the landing he listened attentively, but all was still. Like many old houses occupied by a single family, the room door was panelled with glass; but it was locked, Maximilian was shut in, and it was impossible to see what was passing in the room, because a red curtain was drawn before the glass. The count's anxiety was manifested by a bright color which seldom appeared on the face of that imperturbable man.

"What shall I do!" he uttered, and reflected for a moment; "shall I ring? No, the sound of a bell, announcing a visitor, will but accelerate the resolution of one in Maximilian's situation, and then the bell would be followed by a louder noise." Monte Cristo trembled from head to foot and as if his determination had been taken with the rapidity of lightning, he struck one of the panes of glass with his elbow; the glass was shivered to atoms, then withdrawing the curtain he saw Morrel, who had been writing at his desk, bound from his seat at the noise of the broken window.

"I beg a thousand pardons," said the count, "there is nothing the matter, but I slipped down and broke one of your panes of glass with my elbow. Since it is opened, I will take advantage of it to enter your room; do not disturb yourself—do not disturb yourself!" And passing his hand through the broken glass, the count opened the door. Morrel, evidently discomposed, came to meet Monte Cristo less with the intention of receiving him than to exclude his entry. "Ma foi," said Monte Cristo, rubbing his elbow, "it's all your servant's fault; your stairs are so polished, it is like walking on glass."

"Are you hurt, sir?" coldly asked Morrel.

"I believe not. But what are you about there? You were writing."

"I?"

"Your fingers are stained with ink."

"Ah, true, I was writing. I do sometimes, soldier though I am."

Monte Cristo advanced into the room; Maximilian was obliged to let him pass, but he followed him. "You were writing?" said Monte Cristo with a searching look.

"I have already had the honor of telling you I was," said Morrel.

The count looked around him. "Your pistols are beside your desk," said Monte Cristo, pointing with his finger to the pistols on the table.

"I am on the point of starting on a journey," replied Morrel disdainfully.

"My friend," exclaimed Monte Cristo in a tone of exquisite sweetness.

"Sir?"

"My friend, my dear Maximilian, do not make a hasty resolution, I entreat you."

"I make a hasty resolution?" said Morrel, shrugging his shoulders; "is there anything extraordinary in a journey?"

"Maximilian," said the count, "let us both lay aside the mask we have assumed. You no more deceive me with that false calmness than I impose upon you with my frivolous solicitude. You can understand, can you not, that to have acted as I have done, to have broken that glass, to have intruded on the solitude of a friend—you can understand that, to have done all this, I must have been actuated by real uneasiness, or rather by a terrible conviction. Morrel, you are going to destroy yourself!"

"Indeed, count," said Morrel, shuddering; "what has put this into your head?"

"I tell you that you are about to destroy yourself," continued the count, "and here is proof of what I say;" and, approaching the desk, he removed the sheet of paper which Morrel had placed over the letter he had begun, and took the latter in his hands.

Morrel rushed forward to tear it from him, but Monte Cristo perceiving his intention, seized his wrist with his iron grasp. "You wish to destroy yourself," said the count; "you have written it."

"Well," said Morrel, changing his expression of calmness for one of violence—"well, and if I do intend to turn this pistol against myself, who shall prevent me—who will dare prevent me? All my hopes are blighted, my heart is broken, my life a burden, everything around me is sad and mournful; earth has become distasteful to me, and human voices distract me. It is a mercy to let me die, for if I live I shall lose my reason and become mad. When, sir, I tell you all this with tears of heartfelt anguish, can you reply that I am wrong, can you prevent my putting an end to my miserable existence? Tell me, sir, could you have the courage to do so?"

"Yes, Morrel," said Monte Cristo, with a calmness which contrasted strangely with the young man's excitement; "yes, I would do so."

"You?" exclaimed Morrel, with increasing anger and reproach—"you, who have deceived me with false hopes, who have cheered and soothed me with vain promises, when I might, if not have saved her, at least have seen her die in my arms! You, who pretend to understand everything, even the hidden sources of knowledge,—and who enact the part of a guardian angel upon earth, and could not even find an antidote to a poison administered to a young girl! Ah, sir, indeed you would inspire me with pity, were you not hateful in my eyes."

"Morrel"—

"Yes; you tell me to lay aside the mask, and I will do so, be satisfied! When you spoke to me at the cemetery, I answered you—my heart was softened; when you arrived here, I allowed you to enter. But since you abuse my confidence, since you have devised a new torture after I thought I had exhausted them all, then, Count of Monte Cristo my pretended benefactor—then, Count of Monte Cristo, the universal guardian, be satisfied, you shall witness the death of your friend;" and Morrel, with a maniacal laugh, again rushed towards the pistols.

"And I again repeat, you shall not commit suicide."

"Prevent me, then!" replied Morrel, with another struggle, which, like the first, failed in releasing him from the count's iron grasp.

"I will prevent you."

"And who are you, then, that arrogate to yourself this tyrannical right over free and rational beings?"

"Who am I?" repeated Monte Cristo. "Listen; I am the only man in the world having the right to say to you, 'Morrel, your father's son shall not die to-day;'" and Monte Cristo, with an expression of majesty and sublimity, advanced with arms folded toward the young man, who, involuntarily overcome by the commanding manner of this man, recoiled a step.

"Why do you mention my father?" stammered he; "why do you mingle a recollection of him with the affairs of today?"

"Because I am he who saved your father's life when he wished to destroy himself, as you do to-day—because I am the man who sent the purse to your young sister, and the Pharaon to old Morrel—because I am the Edmond Dantes who nursed you, a child, on my knees." Morrel made another step back, staggering, breathless, crushed; then all his strength give way, and he fell prostrate at the feet of Monte Cristo. Then his admirable nature underwent a complete and sudden revulsion; he arose, rushed out of the room and to the stairs, exclaiming energetically, "Julie, Julie—Emmanuel, Emmanuel!"

Monte Cristo endeavored also to leave, but Maximilian would have died rather than relax his hold of the handle of the door, which he closed upon the count. Julie, Emmanuel, and some of the servants, ran up in alarm on hearing the cries of Maximilian. Morrel seized their hands, and opening the door exclaimed in a voice choked with sobs, "On your knees—on your knees—he is our benefactor—the saviour of our father! He is"—

He would have added "Edmond Dantes," but the count seized his arm and prevented him. Julie threw herself into the arms of the count; Emmanuel embraced him as a guardian angel; Morrel again fell on his knees, and struck the ground with his forehead. Then the iron-hearted man felt his heart swell in his breast; a flame seemed to rush from his throat to his eyes, he bent his head and wept. For a while nothing was heard in the room but a succession of sobs, while the incense from their grateful hearts mounted to heaven. Julie had scarcely recovered from her deep emotion when she rushed out of the room, descended to the next floor, ran into the drawing-room with childlike joy and raised the crystal globe which covered the purse given by the unknown of the Allees de Meillan. Meanwhile, Emmanuel in a broken voice said to the count, "Oh, count, how could you, hearing us so often speak of our unknown benefactor, seeing us pay such homage of gratitude and adoration to his memory,—how could you continue so long without discovering yourself to us? Oh, it was cruel to us, and—dare I say it?—to you also."

"Listen, my friends," said the count—"I may call you so since we have really been friends for the last eleven years—the discovery of this secret has been occasioned by a great event which you must never know. I wished to bury it during my whole life in my own bosom, but your brother Maximilian wrested it from me by a violence he repents of now, I am sure." Then turning around, and seeing that Morrel, still on his knees, had thrown himself into an arm-chair, he added in a low voice, pressing Emmanuel's hand significantly, "Watch over him."

"Why so?" asked the young man, surprised.

"I cannot explain myself; but watch over him." Emmanuel looked around the room and caught sight of the pistols; his eyes rested on the weapons, and he pointed to them. Monte Cristo bent his head. Emmanuel went towards the pistols. "Leave them," said Monte Cristo. Then walking towards Morrel, he took his hand; the tumultuous agitation of the young man was succeeded by a profound stupor. Julie returned, holding the silken purse in her hands, while tears of joy rolled down her cheeks, like dewdrops on the rose.

"Here is the relic," she said; "do not think it will be less dear to us now we are acquainted with our benefactor!"

"My child," said Monte Cristo, coloring, "allow me to take back that purse? Since you now know my face, I wish to be remembered alone through the affection I hope you will grant me.

"Oh," said Julie, pressing the purse to her heart, "no, no, I beseech you do not take it, for some unhappy day you will leave us, will you not?"

"You have guessed rightly, madame," replied Monte Cristo, smiling; "in a week I shall have left this country, where so many persons who merit the vengeance of heaven lived happily, while my father perished of hunger and grief." While announcing his departure, the count fixed his eyes on Morrel, and remarked that the words, "I shall have left this country," had failed to rouse him from his lethargy. He then saw that he must make another struggle against the grief of his friend, and taking the hands of Emmanuel and Julie, which he pressed within his own, he said with the mild authority of a father, "My kind friends, leave me alone with Maximilian." Julie saw the means offered of carrying off her precious relic, which Monte Cristo had forgotten. She drew her husband to the door. "Let us leave them," she said. The count was alone with Morrel, who remained motionless as a statue.

"Come," said Monte-Cristo, touching his shoulder with his finger, "are you a man again, Maximilian?"

"Yes; for I begin to suffer again."

The count frowned, apparently in gloomy hesitation.

"Maximilian, Maximilian," he said, "the ideas you yield to are unworthy of a Christian."

"Oh, do not fear, my friend," said Morrel, raising his head, and smiling with a sweet expression on the count; "I shall no longer attempt my life."

"Then we are to have no more pistols—no more despair?"

"No; I have found a better remedy for my grief than either a bullet or a knife."

"Poor fellow, what is it?"

"My grief will kill me of itself."

"My friend," said Monte Cristo, with an expression of melancholy equal to his own, "listen to me. One day, in a moment of despair like yours, since it led to a similar resolution, I also wished to kill myself; one day your father, equally desperate, wished to kill himself too. If any one had said to your father, at the moment he raised the pistol to his head—if any one had told me, when in my prison I pushed back the food I had not tasted for three days—if anyone had said to either of us then, 'Live—the day will come when you will be happy, and will bless life!'—no matter whose voice had spoken, we should have heard him with the smile of doubt, or the anguish of incredulity,—and yet how many times has your father blessed life while embracing you—how often have I myself"—

"Ah," exclaimed Morrel, interrupting the count, "you had only lost your liberty, my father had only lost his fortune, but I have lost Valentine."

"Look at me," said Monte Cristo, with that expression which sometimes made him so eloquent and persuasive—"look at me. There are no tears in my eyes, nor is there fever in my veins, yet I see you suffer—you, Maximilian, whom I love as my own son. Well, does not this tell you that in grief, as in life, there is always something to look forward to beyond? Now, if I entreat, if I order you to live, Morrel, it is in the conviction that one day you will thank me for having preserved your life."

"Oh, heavens," said the young man, "oh, heavens— what are you saying, count? Take care. But perhaps you have never loved!"

"Child!" replied the count.

"I mean, as I love. You see, I have been a soldier ever since I attained manhood. I reached the age of twenty-nine without loving, for none of the feelings I before then experienced merit the appellation of love. Well, at twenty-nine I saw Valentine; for two years I have loved her, for two years I have seen written in her heart, as in a book, all the virtues of a daughter and wife. Count, to possess Valentine would have been a happiness too infinite, too ecstatic, too complete, too divine for this world, since it has been denied me; but without Valentine the earth is desolate."

"I have told you to hope," said the count.

"Then have a care, I repeat, for you seek to persuade me, and if you succeed I should lose my reason, for I should hope that I could again behold Valentine." The count smiled. "My friend, my father," said Morrel with excitement, "have a care, I again repeat, for the power you wield over me alarms me. Weigh your words before you speak, for my eyes have already become brighter, and my heart beats strongly; be cautious, or you will make me believe in supernatural agencies. I must obey you, though you bade me call forth the dead or walk upon the water."

"Hope, my friend," repeated the count.

"Ah," said Morrel, falling from the height of excitement to the abyss of despair—"ah, you are playing with me, like those good, or rather selfish mothers who soothe their children with honeyed words, because their screams annoy them. No, my friend, I was wrong to caution you; do not fear, I will bury my grief so deep in my heart, I will disguise it so, that you shall not even care to sympathize with me. Adieu, my friend, adieu!"

"On the contrary," said the count, "after this time you must live with me—you must not leave me, and in a week we shall have left France behind us."

"And you still bid me hope?"

"I tell you to hope, because I have a method of curing you."

"Count, you render me sadder than before, if it be possible. You think the result of this blow has been to produce an ordinary grief, and you would cure it by an ordinary remedy—change of scene." And Morrel dropped his head with disdainful incredulity. "What can I say more?" asked Monte Cristo. "I have confidence in the remedy I propose, and only ask you to permit me to assure you of its efficacy."

"Count, you prolong my agony."

"Then," said the count, "your feeble spirit will not even grant me the trial I request? Come—do you know of what the Count of Monte Cristo is capable? do you know that he holds terrestrial beings under his control? nay, that he can almost work a miracle? Well, wait for the miracle I hope to accomplish, or"—

"Or?" repeated Morrel.

"Or, take care, Morrel, lest I call you ungrateful."

"Have pity on me, count!"

"I feel so much pity towards you, Maximilian, that— listen to me attentively—if I do not cure you in a month, to the day, to the very hour, mark my words, Morrel, I will place loaded pistols before you, and a cup of the deadliest Italian poison—a poison more sure and prompt than that which has killed Valentine."

"Will you promise me?"

"Yes; for I am a man, and have suffered like yourself, and also contemplated suicide; indeed, often since misfortune has left me I have longed for the delights of an eternal sleep."

"But you are sure you will promise me this?" said Morrel, intoxicated. "I not only promise, but swear it!" said Monte Cristo extending his hand.

"In a month, then, on your honor, if I am not consoled, you will let me take my life into my own hands, and whatever may happen you will not call me ungrateful?"

"In a month, to the day, the very hour and the date are sacred, Maximilian. I do not know whether you remember that this is the 5th of September; it is ten years to-day since I saved your father's life, who wished to die." Morrel seized the count's hand and kissed it; the count allowed him to pay the homage he felt due to him. "In a month you will find on the table, at which we shall be then sitting, good pistols and a delicious draught; but, on the other hand, you must promise me not to attempt your life before that time."

"Oh, I also swear it!" Monte Cristo drew the young man towards him, and pressed him for some time to his heart. "And now," he said, "after to-day, you will come and live with me; you can occupy Haidee's apartment, and my daughter will at least be replaced by my son."

"Haidee?" said Morrel, "what has become of her?"

"She departed last night."

"To leave you?"

"To wait for me. Hold yourself ready then to join me at the Champs Elysees, and lead me out of this house without any one seeing my departure." Maximilian hung his head, and obeyed with childlike reverence.

CHAPTER 106.
DIVIDING THE PROCEEDS.

The apartment on the second floor of the house in the Rue Saint-Germain-des-Pres, where Albert de Morcerf had selected a home for his mother, was let to a very mysterious person. This was a man whose face the concierge himself had never seen, for in the winter his chin was buried in one of the large red handkerchiefs worn by gentlemen's coachmen on a cold night, and in the summer he made a point of always blowing his nose just as he approached the door. Contrary to custom, this gentleman had not been watched, for as the report ran that he was a person of high rank, and one who would allow no impertinent interference, his incognito was strictly respected.

His visits were tolerably regular, though occasionally he appeared a little before or after his time, but generally, both in summer and winter, he took possession of his apartment about four o'clock, though he never spent the night there. At half-past three in the winter the fire was lighted by the discreet servant, who had the superintendence of the little apartment, and in the summer ices were placed on the table at the same hour. At four o'clock, as we have already stated, the mysterious personage arrived. Twenty minutes afterwards a carriage stopped at the house, a lady alighted in a black or dark blue dress, and always thickly veiled; she passed like a shadow through the lodge, and ran up-stairs without a sound escaping under the touch of her light foot. No one ever asked her where she was going. Her face, therefore, like that of the gentleman, was perfectly unknown to the two concierges, who were perhaps unequalled throughout the capital for discretion. We need not say she stopped at the second floor. Then she tapped in a peculiar manner at a door, which after being opened to admit her was again fastened, and curiosity penetrated no farther. They used the same precautions in leaving as in entering the house. The lady always left first, and as soon as she had stepped into her carriage, it drove away, sometimes towards the right hand, sometimes to the left; then about twenty minutes afterwards the gentleman would also leave, buried in his cravat or concealed by his handkerchief.

The day after Monte Cristo had called upon Danglars, the mysterious lodger entered at ten o'clock in the morning instead of four in the afternoon. Almost directly afterwards, without the usual interval of time, a cab arrived, and the veiled lady ran hastily up-stairs. The door opened, but before it could be closed, the lady exclaimed: "Oh, Lucien—oh, my friend!" The concierge therefore heard for the first time that the lodger's name was Lucien; still, as he was the very perfection of a door-keeper, he made up his mind not to tell his wife. "Well, what is the matter, my dear?" asked the gentleman whose name the lady's agitation revealed; "tell me what is the matter."

"Oh, Lucien, can I confide in you?"

"Of course, you know you can do so. But what can be the matter? Your note of this morning has completely bewildered me. This precipitation—this unusual appointment. Come, ease me of my anxiety, or else frighten me at once."

"Lucien, a great event has happened!" said the lady, glancing inquiringly at Lucien,—"M. Danglars left last night!"

"Left?—M. Danglars left? Where has he gone?"

"I do not know."

"What do you mean? Has he gone intending not to return?"

"Undoubtedly;—at ten o'clock at night his horses took him to the barrier of Charenton; there a post-chaise was waiting for him—he entered it with his valet de chambre, saying that he was going to Fontainebleau."

"Then what did you mean"—

"Stay—he left a letter for me."

"A letter?"

"Yes; read it." And the baroness took from her pocket a letter which she gave to Debray. Debray paused a moment before reading, as if trying to guess its contents, or perhaps while making up his mind how to act, whatever it might contain. No doubt his ideas were arranged in a few minutes, for he began reading the letter which caused so much uneasiness in the heart of the baroness, and which ran as follows:—

"Madame and most faithful wife."

Debray mechanically stopped and looked at the baroness, whose face became covered with blushes. "Read," she said.

Debray continued:—

"When you receive this, you will no longer have a husband. Oh, you need not be alarmed, you will only have lost him as you have lost your daughter; I mean that I shall be travelling on one of the thirty or forty roads leading out of France. I owe you some explanations for my conduct, and as you are a woman that can perfectly understand me, I will give them. Listen, then. I received this morning five millions which I paid away; almost directly afterwards another demand for the same sum was presented to me; I put this creditor off till to-morrow and I intend leaving to-day, to escape that to-morrow, which would be rather too unpleasant for me to endure. You understand this, do you not, my most precious wife? I say you understand this, because you are as conversant with my affairs as I am; indeed, I think you understand them better, since I am ignorant of what has become of a considerable portion of my fortune, once very tolerable, while I am sure, madame, that you know perfectly well. For women have infallible instincts; they can even explain the marvellous by an algebraic calculation they have invented; but I, who only understand my own figures, know nothing more than that one day these figures deceived me. Have you admired the rapidity of my fall? Have you been slightly dazzled at the sudden fusion of my ingots? I confess I have seen nothing but the fire; let us hope you have found some gold among the ashes. With this consoling idea, I leave you, madame, and most prudent wife, without any conscientious reproach for abandoning you; you have friends left, and the ashes I have already mentioned, and above all the liberty I hasten to restore to you. And here, madame, I must add another word of explanation. So long as I hoped you were working for the good of our house and for the fortune of our daughter, I philosophically closed my eyes; but as you have transformed that house into a vast ruin I will not be the foundation of another man's fortune. You were rich when I married you, but little respected. Excuse me for speaking so very candidly, but as this is intended only for ourselves, I do not see why I should weigh my words. I have augmented our fortune, and it has continued to increase during the last fifteen years, till extraordinary and unexpected catastrophes have suddenly overturned it,—without any fault of mine, I can honestly declare. You, madame, have only sought to increase your own, and I am convinced that you have succeeded. I leave you, therefore, as I took you,—rich, but little respected. Adieu! I also intend from this time to work on my own account. Accept my acknowledgments for the example you have set me, and which I intend following.

"Your very devoted husband,

"Baron Danglars."

The baroness had watched Debray while he read this long and painful letter, and saw him, notwithstanding his self-control, change color once or twice. When he had ended the perusal, he folded the letter and resumed his pensive attitude. "Well?" asked Madame Danglars, with an anxiety easy to be understood.

"Well, madame?" unhesitatingly repeated Debray.

"With what ideas does that letter inspire you?"

"Oh, it is simple enough, madame; it inspires me with the idea that M. Danglars has left suspiciously."

"Certainly; but is this all you have to say to me?"

"I do not understand you," said Debray with freezing coldness.

"He is gone! Gone, never to return!"

"Oh, madame, do not think that!"

"I tell you he will never return. I know his character; he is inflexible in any resolutions formed for his own interests. If he could have made any use of me, he would have taken me with him; he leaves me in Paris, as our separation will conduce to his benefit;—therefore he has gone, and I am free forever," added Madame Danglars, in the same supplicating tone. Debray, instead of answering, allowed her to remain in an attitude of nervous inquiry. "Well?" she said at length, "do you not answer me?"

"I have but one question to ask you,—what do you intend to do?"

"I was going to ask you," replied the baroness with a beating heart.

"Ah, then, you wish to ask advice of me?"

"Yes; I do wish to ask your advice," said Madame Danglars with anxious expectation.

"Then if you wish to take my advice," said the young man coldly, "I would recommend you to travel."

"To travel!" she murmured.

"Certainly; as M. Danglars says, you are rich, and perfectly free. In my opinion, a withdrawal from Paris is absolutely necessary after the double catastrophe of Mademoiselle Danglars' broken contract and M. Danglars' disappearance. The world will think you abandoned and poor, for the wife of a bankrupt would never be forgiven, were she to keep up an appearance of opulence. You have only to remain in Paris for about a fortnight, telling the world you are abandoned, and relating the details of this desertion to your best friends, who will soon spread the report. Then you can quit your house, leaving your jewels and giving up your jointure, and every one's mouth will be filled with praises of your disinterestedness. They will know you are deserted, and think you also poor, for I alone know your real financial position, and am quite ready to give up my accounts as an honest partner." The dread with which the pale and motionless baroness listened to this, was equalled by the calm indifference with which Debray had spoken. "Deserted?" she repeated; "ah, yes, I am, indeed, deserted! You are right, sir, and no one can doubt my position." These were the only words that this proud and violently enamoured woman could utter in response to Debray.

"But then you are rich,—very rich, indeed," continued Debray, taking out some papers from his pocket-book, which he spread upon the table. Madame Danglars did not see them; she was engaged in stilling the beatings of her heart, and restraining the tears which were ready to gush forth. At length a sense of dignity prevailed, and if she did not entirely master her agitation, she at least succeeded in preventing the fall of a single tear. "Madame," said Debray, "it is nearly six months since we have been associated. You furnished a principal of 100,000 francs. Our partnership began in the month of April. In May we commenced operations, and in the course of the month gained 450,000 francs. In June the profit amounted to 900,000. In July we added 1,700,000 francs,—it was, you know, the month of the Spanish bonds. In August we lost 300,000 francs at the beginning of the month, but on the 13th we made up for it, and we now find that our accounts, reckoning from the first day of partnership up to yesterday, when I closed them, showed a capital of 2,400,000 francs, that is, 1,200,000 for each of us. Now, madame," said Debray, delivering up his accounts in the methodical manner of a stockbroker, "there are still 80,000 francs, the interest of this money, in my hands."

"But," said the baroness, "I thought you never put the money out to interest."

"Excuse me, madame," said Debray coldly, "I had your permission to do so, and I have made use of it. There are, then, 40,000 francs for your share, besides the 100,000 you furnished me to begin with, making in all 1,340,000 francs for your portion. Now, madame, I took the precaution of drawing out your money the day before yesterday; it is not long ago, you see, and I was in continual expectation of being called on to deliver up my accounts. There is your money,—half in bank-notes, the other half in checks payable to bearer. I say there, for as I did not consider my house safe enough, or lawyers sufficiently discreet, and as landed property carries evidence with it, and moreover since you have no right to possess anything independent of your husband, I have kept this sum, now your whole fortune, in a chest concealed under that closet, and for greater security I myself concealed it there.

"Now, madame," continued Debray, first opening the closet, then the chest;—"now, madame, here are 800 notes of 1,000. francs each, resembling, as you see, a large book bound in iron; to this I add a certificate in the funds of 25,000. francs; then, for the odd cash, making I think about 110,000. francs, here is a check upon my banker, who, not being M. Danglars, will pay you the amount, you may rest assured." Madame Danglars mechanically took the check, the bond, and the heap of bank-notes. This enormous fortune made no great appearance on the table. Madame Danglars, with tearless eyes, but with her breast heaving with concealed emotion, placed the bank-notes in her bag, put the certificate and check into her pocket-book, and then, standing pale and mute, awaited one kind word of consolation. But she waited in vain.

"Now, madame," said Debray, "you have a splendid fortune, an income of about 60,000 livres a year, which is enormous for a woman who cannot keep an establishment here for a year, at least. You will be able to indulge all your fancies; besides, should you find your income insufficient, you can, for the sake of the past, madame, make use of mine; and I am ready to offer you all I possess, on loan."

"Thank you, sir—thank you," replied the baroness; "you forget that what you have just paid me is much more than a poor woman requires, who intends for some time, at least, to retire from the world."

Debray was, for a moment, surprised, but immediately recovering himself, he bowed with an air which seemed to say, "As you please, madame."

Madame Danglars had until then, perhaps, hoped for something; but when she saw the careless bow of Debray, and the glance by which it was accompanied, together with his significant silence, she raised her head, and without passion or violence or even hesitation, ran down-stairs, disdaining to address a last farewell to one who could thus part from her. "Bah," said Debray, when she had left, "these are fine projects! She will remain at home, read novels, and speculate at cards, since she can no longer do so on the Bourse." Then taking up his account book, he cancelled with the greatest care all the entries of the amounts he had just paid away. "I have 1,060,000 francs remaining," he said. "What a pity Mademoiselle de Villefort is dead! She suited me in every respect, and I would have married her." And he calmly waited until the twenty minutes had elapsed after Madame Danglars' departure before he left the house. During this time he occupied himself in making figures, with his watch by his side.

Asmodeus—that diabolical personage, who would have been created by every fertile imagination if Le Sage had not acquired the priority in his great masterpiece—would have enjoyed a singular spectacle, if he had lifted up the roof of the little house in the Rue Saint-Germain-des-Pres, while Debray was casting up his figures. Above the room in which Debray had been dividing two millions and a half with Madame Danglars was another, inhabited by persons who have played too prominent a part in the incidents we have related for their appearance not to create some interest. Mercedes and Albert were in that room. Mercedes was much changed within the last few days; not that even in her days of fortune she had ever dressed with the magnificent display which makes us no longer able to recognize a woman when she appears in a plain and simple attire; nor indeed, had she fallen into that state of depression where it is impossible to conceal the garb of misery; no, the change in Mercedes was that her eye no longer sparkled, her lips no longer smiled, and there was now a hesitation in uttering the words which formerly sprang so fluently from her ready wit.

It was not poverty which had broken her spirit; it was not a want of courage which rendered her poverty burdensome. Mercedes, although deposed from the exalted position she had occupied, lost in the sphere she had now chosen, like a person passing from a room splendidly lighted into utter darkness, appeared like a queen, fallen from her palace to a hovel, and who, reduced to strict necessity, could neither become reconciled to the earthen vessels she was herself forced to place upon the table, nor to the humble pallet which had become her bed. The beautiful Catalane and noble countess had lost both her proud glance and charming smile, because she saw nothing but misery around her; the walls were hung with one of the gray papers which economical landlords choose as not likely to show the dirt; the floor was uncarpeted; the furniture attracted the attention to the poor attempt at luxury; indeed, everything offended eyes accustomed to refinement and elegance.

Madame de Morcerf had lived there since leaving her house; the continual silence of the spot oppressed her; still, seeing that Albert continually watched her countenance to judge the state of her feelings, she constrained herself to assume a monotonous smile of the lips alone, which, contrasted with the sweet and beaming expression that usually shone from her eyes, seemed like "moonlight on a statue,"—yielding light without warmth. Albert, too, was ill at ease; the remains of luxury prevented him from sinking into his actual position. If he wished to go out without gloves, his hands appeared too white; if he wished to walk through the town, his boots seemed too highly polished. Yet these two noble and intelligent creatures, united by the indissoluble ties of maternal and filial love, had succeeded in tacitly understanding one another, and economizing their stores, and Albert had been able to tell his mother without extorting a change of countenance,—"Mother, we have no more money."

Mercedes had never known misery; she had often, in her youth, spoken of poverty, but between want and necessity, those synonymous words, there is a wide difference. Amongst the Catalans, Mercedes wished for a thousand things, but still she never really wanted any. So long as the nets were good, they caught fish; and so long as they sold their fish, they were able to buy twine for new nets. And then, shut out from friendship, having but one affection, which could not be mixed up with her ordinary pursuits, she thought of herself—of no one but herself. Upon the little she earned she lived as well as she could; now there were two to be supported, and nothing to live upon.

Winter approached. Mercedes had no fire in that cold and naked room—she, who was accustomed to stoves which heated the house from the hall to the boudoir; she had not even one little flower—she whose apartment had been a conservatory of costly exotics. But she had her son. Hitherto the excitement of fulfilling a duty had sustained them. Excitement, like enthusiasm, sometimes renders us unconscious to the things of earth. But the excitement had calmed down, and they felt themselves obliged to descend from dreams to reality; after having exhausted the ideal, they found they must talk of the actual.

"Mother," exclaimed Albert, just as Madame Danglars was descending the stairs, "let us reckon our riches, if you please; I want capital to build my plans upon."

"Capital—nothing!" replied Mercedes with a mournful smile.

"No, mother,—capital 3,000 francs. And I have an idea of our leading a delightful life upon this 3,000 francs."

"Child!" sighed Mercedes.

"Alas, dear mother," said the young man, "I have unhappily spent too much of your money not to know the value of it. These 3,000 francs are enormous, and I intend building upon this foundation a miraculous certainty for the future."

"You say this, my dear boy; but do you think we ought to accept these 3,000 francs?" said Mercedes, coloring.

"I think so," answered Albert in a firm tone. "We will accept them the more readily, since we have them not here; you know they are buried in the garden of the little house in the Allees de Meillan, at Marseilles. With 200 francs we can reach Marseilles."

"With 200 francs?—are you sure, Albert?"

"Oh, as for that, I have made inquiries respecting the diligences and steamboats, and my calculations are made. You will take your place in the coupe to Chalons. You see, mother, I treat you handsomely for thirty-five francs." Albert then took a pen, and wrote:—

Frs.

Coupe, thirty-five francs...................... 35.

From Chalons to Lyons you will go on by the steamboat.. 6.

From Lyons to Avignon (still by steamboat)............. 16.

From Avignon to Marseilles, seven francs.............. 7.

Expenses on the road, about fifty francs............... 50.

Total.. 114 frs.

"Let us put down 120," added Albert, smiling. "You see I am generous, am I not, mother?"

"But you, my poor child?"

"I? do you not see that I reserve eighty francs for myself? A young man does not require luxuries; besides, I know what travelling is."

"With a post-chaise and valet de chambre?"

"Any way, mother."

"Well, be it so. But these 200 francs?"

"Here they are, and 200 more besides. See, I have sold my watch for 100 francs, and the guard and seals for 300. How fortunate that the ornaments were worth more than the watch. Still the same story of superfluities! Now I think we are rich, since instead of the 114 francs we require for the journey we find ourselves in possession of 250."

"But we owe something in this house?"

"Thirty francs; but I pay that out of my 150 francs,—that is understood,—and as I require only eighty francs for my journey, you see I am overwhelmed with luxury. But that is not all. What do you say to this, mother?"

And Albert took out of a little pocket-book with golden clasps, a remnant of his old fancies, or perhaps a tender souvenir from one of the mysterious and veiled ladies who used to knock at his little door,—Albert took out of this pocket-book a note of 1,000 francs.

"What is this?" asked Mercedes.

"A thousand francs."

"But whence have you obtained them?"

"Listen to me, mother, and do not yield too much to agitation." And Albert, rising, kissed his mother on both cheeks, then stood looking at her. "You cannot imagine, mother, how beautiful I think you!" said the young man, impressed with a profound feeling of filial love. "You are, indeed, the most beautiful and most noble woman I ever saw!"

"Dear child!" said Mercedes, endeavoring in vain to restrain a tear which glistened in the corner of her eye. "Indeed, you only wanted misfortune to change my love for you to admiration. I am not unhappy while I possess my son!"

"Ah, just so," said Albert; "here begins the trial. Do you know the decision we have come to, mother?"

"Have we come to any?"

"Yes; it is decided that you are to live at Marseilles, and that I am to leave for Africa, where I will earn for myself the right to use the name I now bear, instead of the one I have thrown aside." Mercedes sighed. "Well, mother, I yesterday engaged myself as substitute in the Spahis," [*] added the young man, lowering his eyes with a certain feeling of shame, for even he was unconscious of the sublimity of his self- abasement. "I thought my body was my own, and that I might sell it. I yesterday took the place of another. I sold myself for more than I thought I was worth," he added, attempting to smile; "I fetched 2,000 francs."

* The Spahis are French cavalry reserved for service in Africa.

"Then these 1,000 francs"—said Mercedes, shuddering—

"Are the half of the sum, mother; the other will be paid in a year."

Mercedes raised her eyes to heaven with an expression it would be impossible to describe, and tears, which had hitherto been restrained, now yielded to her emotion, and ran down her cheeks.

"The price of his blood!" she murmured.

"Yes, if I am killed," said Albert, laughing. "But I assure you, mother, I have a strong intention of defending my person, and I never felt half so strong an inclination to live as I do now."

"Merciful heavens!"

"Besides, mother, why should you make up your mind that I am to be killed? Has Lamoriciere, that Ney of the South, been killed? Has Changarnier been killed? Has Bedeau been killed? Has Morrel, whom we know, been killed? Think of your joy, mother, when you see me return with an embroidered uniform! I declare, I expect to look magnificent in it, and chose that regiment only from vanity." Mercedes sighed while endeavoring to smile; the devoted mother felt that she ought not to allow the whole weight of the sacrifice to fall upon her son. "Well, now you understand, mother!" continued Albert; "here are more than 4,000 francs settled on you; upon these you can live at least two years."

"Do you think so?" said Mercedes. These words were uttered in so mournful a tone that their real meaning did not escape Albert; he felt his heart beat, and taking his mother's hand within his own he said, tenderly,—

"Yes, you will live!"

"I shall live!—then you will not leave me, Albert?"

"Mother, I must go," said Albert in a firm, calm voice; "you love me too well to wish me to remain useless and idle with you; besides, I have signed."

"You will obey your own wish and the will of heaven!"

"Not my own wish, mother, but reason—necessity. Are we not two despairing creatures? What is life to you?— Nothing. What is life to me?—Very little without you, mother; for believe me, but for you I should have ceased to live on the day I doubted my father and renounced his name. Well, I will live, if you promise me still to hope; and if you grant me the care of your future prospects, you will redouble my strength. Then I will go to the governor of

Algeria; he has a royal heart, and is essentially a soldier; I will tell him my gloomy story. I will beg him to turn his eyes now and then towards me, and if he keep his word and interest himself for me, in six months I shall be an officer, or dead. If I am an officer, your fortune is certain, for I shall have money enough for both, and, moreover, a name we shall both be proud of, since it will be our own. If I am killed—well then mother, you can also die, and there will be an end of our misfortunes."

"It is well," replied Mercedes, with her eloquent glance; "you are right, my love; let us prove to those who are watching our actions that we are worthy of compassion."

"But let us not yield to gloomy apprehensions," said the young man; "I assure you we are, or rather we shall be, very happy. You are a woman at once full of spirit and resignation; I have become simple in my tastes, and am without passion, I hope. Once in service, I shall be rich—once in M. Dantes' house, you will be at rest. Let us strive, I beseech you,—let us strive to be cheerful."

"Yes, let us strive, for you ought to live, and to be happy, Albert."

"And so our division is made, mother," said the young man, affecting ease of mind. "We can now part; come, I shall engage your passage."

"And you, my dear boy?"

"I shall stay here for a few days longer; we must accustom ourselves to parting. I want recommendations and some information relative to Africa. I will join you again at Marseilles."

"Well, be it so—let us part," said Mercedes, folding around her shoulders the only shawl she had taken away, and which accidentally happened to be a valuable black cashmere. Albert gathered up his papers hastily, rang the bell to pay the thirty francs he owed to the landlord, and offering his arm to his mother, they descended the stairs. Some one was walking down before them, and this person, hearing the rustling of a silk dress, turned around. "Debray!" muttered Albert.

"You, Morcerf?" replied the secretary, resting on the stairs. Curiosity had vanquished the desire of preserving his incognito, and he was recognized. It was, indeed, strange in this unknown spot to find the young man whose misfortunes had made so much noise in Paris.

"Morcerf!" repeated Debray. Then noticing in the dim light the still youthful and veiled figure of Madame de Morcerf:—"Pardon me," he added with a smile, "I leave you, Albert." Albert understood his thoughts. "Mother," he said, turning towards Mercedes, "this is M. Debray, secretary of the minister for the interior, once a friend of mine."

"How once?" stammered Debray; "what do you mean?"

"I say so, M. Debray, because I have no friends now, and I ought not to have any. I thank you for having recognized me, sir." Debray stepped forward, and cordially pressed the hand of his interlocutor. "Believe me, dear Albert," he said, with all the emotion he was capable of feeling,—"believe me, I feel deeply for your misfortunes, and if in any way I can serve you, I am yours."

"Thank you, sir," said Albert, smiling. "In the midst of our misfortunes, we are still rich enough not to require assistance from any one. We are leaving Paris, and when our journey is paid, we shall have 5,000 francs left." The blood mounted to the temples of Debray, who held a million in his pocket-book, and unimaginative as he was he could not help reflecting that the same house had contained two women, one of whom, justly dishonored, had left it poor with 1,500,000. francs under her cloak, while the other, unjustly stricken, but sublime in her misfortune, was yet rich with a few deniers. This parallel disturbed his usual politeness, the philosophy he witnessed appalled him, he muttered a few words of general civility and ran down-stairs.

That day the minister's clerks and the subordinates had a great deal to put up with from his ill-humor. But that same night, he found himself the possessor of a fine house, situated on the Boulevard de la Madeleine, and an income of 50,000 livres. The next day, just as Debray was signing the deed, that is about five o'clock in the afternoon, Madame de Morcerf, after having affectionately embraced her son, entered the coupe of the diligence, which closed upon her. A man was hidden in Lafitte's banking-house, behind one of the little arched windows which are placed above each desk; he saw Mercedes enter the diligence, and he also saw Albert withdraw. Then he passed his hand across his forehead, which was clouded with doubt. "Alas," he exclaimed, "how can I restore the happiness I have taken away from these poor innocent creatures? God help me!"

CHAPTER 107.
THE LIONS' DEN.

One division of La Force, in which the most dangerous and desperate prisoners are confined, is called the court of Saint-Bernard. The prisoners, in their expressive language, have named it the "Lions' Den," probably because the captives possess teeth which frequently gnaw the bars, and sometimes the keepers also. It is a prison within a prison; the walls are double the thickness of the rest. The gratings are every day carefully examined by jailers, whose herculean proportions and cold pitiless expression prove them to have been chosen to reign over their subjects for their superior activity and intelligence. The court-yard of this quarter is enclosed by enormous walls, over which the sun glances obliquely, when it deigns to penetrate into this gulf of moral and physical deformity. On this paved yard are to be seen,— pacing to and fro from morning till night, pale, careworn, and haggard, like so many shadows,—the men whom justice holds beneath the steel she is sharpening. There, crouched against the side of the wall which attracts and retains the most heat, they may be seen sometimes talking to one another, but more frequently alone, watching the door, which sometimes opens to call forth one from the gloomy assemblage, or to throw in another outcast from society.

The court of Saint-Bernard has its own particular apartment for the reception of guests; it is a long rectangle, divided by two upright gratings placed at a distance of three feet from one another to prevent a visitor from shaking hands with or passing anything to the prisoners. It is a wretched, damp, nay, even horrible spot, more especially when we consider the agonizing conferences which have taken place between those iron bars. And yet, frightful though this spot may be, it is looked upon as a kind of paradise by the men whose days are numbered; it is so rare for them to leave the Lions' Den for any other place than the barrier Saint-Jacques or the galleys!

In the court which we have attempted to describe, and from which a damp vapor was rising, a young man with his hands in his pockets, who had excited much curiosity among the inhabitants of the "Den," might be seen walking. The cut of his clothes would have made him pass for an elegant man, if those clothes had not been torn to shreds; still they did not show signs of wear, and the fine cloth, beneath the careful hands of the prisoner, soon recovered its gloss in the parts which were still perfect, for the wearer tried his best to make it assume the appearance of a new coat. He bestowed the same attention upon the cambric front of a shirt, which had considerably changed in color since his entrance into the prison, and he polished his varnished boots with the corner of a handkerchief embroidered with initials surmounted by a coronet. Some of the inmates of the "Lions' Den" were watching the operations of the prisoner's toilet with considerable interest. "See, the prince is pluming himself," said one of the thieves. "He's a fine looking fellow," said another; "if he had only a comb and hair-grease, he'd take the shine off the gentlemen in white kids."

"His coat looks almost new, and his boots shine like a nigger's face. It's pleasant to have such well-dressed comrades; but didn't those gendarmes behave shameful?— must 'a been jealous, to tear such clothes!"

"He looks like a big-bug," said another; "dresses in fine style. And, then, to be here so young! Oh, what larks!" Meanwhile the object of this hideous admiration approached the wicket, against which one of the keepers was leaning. "Come, sir," he said, "lend me twenty francs; you will soon be paid; you run no risks with me. Remember, I have relations who possess more millions than you have deniers. Come, I beseech you, lend me twenty francs, so that I may buy a dressing-gown; it is intolerable always to be in a coat and boots! And what a coat, sir, for a prince of the Cavalcanti!" The keeper turned his back, and shrugged his shoulders; he did not even laugh at what would have caused any one else to do so; he had heard so many utter the same things,—indeed, he heard nothing else.

"Come," said Andrea, "you are a man void of compassion; I'll have you turned out." This made the keeper turn around, and he burst into a loud laugh. The prisoners then approached and formed a circle. "I tell you that with that wretched sum," continued Andrea, "I could obtain a coat, and a room in which to receive the illustrious visitor I am daily expecting."

"Of course—of course," said the prisoners;—"any one can see he's a gentleman!"

"Well, then, lend him the twenty francs," said the keeper, leaning on the other shoulder; "surely you will not refuse a comrade!"

"I am no comrade of these people," said the young man, proudly, "you have no right to insult me thus."

The thieves looked at one another with low murmurs, and a storm gathered over the head of the aristocratic prisoner, raised less by his own words than by the manner of the keeper. The latter, sure of quelling the tempest when the waves became too violent, allowed them to rise to a certain pitch that he might be revenged on the importunate Andrea, and besides it would afford him some recreation during the long day. The thieves had already approached Andrea, some screaming, "La savate—La savate!" [*] a cruel operation, which consists in cuffing a comrade who may have fallen into disgrace, not with an old shoe, but with an iron-heeled one. Others proposed the "anguille," another kind of recreation, in which a handkerchief is filled with sand, pebbles, and two-sous pieces, when they have them, which the wretches beat like a flail over the head and shoulders of the unhappy sufferer. "Let us horsewhip the fine gentleman!" said others.

* Savate: an old shoe.

But Andrea, turning towards them, winked his eyes, rolled his tongue around his cheeks, and smacked his lips in a manner equivalent to a hundred words among the bandits when forced to be silent. It was a Masonic sign Caderousse had taught him. He was immediately recognized as one of them; the handkerchief was thrown down, and the iron-heeled shoe replaced on the foot of the wretch to whom it belonged. Some voices were heard to say that the gentleman was right; that he intended to be civil, in his way, and that they would set the example of liberty of conscience,—and the mob retired. The keeper was so stupefied at this scene that he took Andrea by the hands and began examining his person, attributing the sudden submission of the inmates of the Lions' Den to something more substantial than mere fascination. Andrea made no resistance, although he protested against it. Suddenly a voice was heard at the wicket. "Benedetto!" exclaimed an inspector. The keeper relaxed his hold. "I am called," said Andrea. "To the visitors' room!" said the same voice.

"You see some one pays me a visit. Ah, my dear sir, you will see whether a Cavalcanti is to be treated like a common person!" And Andrea, gliding through the court like a black shadow, rushed out through the wicket, leaving his comrades, and even the keeper, lost in wonder. Certainly a call to the visitors' room had scarcely astonished Andrea less than themselves, for the wily youth, instead of making use of his privilege of waiting to be claimed on his entry into La Force, had maintained a rigid silence. "Everything," he said, "proves me to be under the protection of some powerful person,—this sudden fortune, the facility with which I have overcome all obstacles, an unexpected family and an illustrious name awarded to me, gold showered down upon me, and the most splendid alliances about to be entered into. An unhappy lapse of fortune and the absence of my protector have cast me down, certainly, but not forever. The hand which has retreated for a while will be again stretched forth to save me at the very moment when I shall think myself sinking into the abyss. Why should I risk an imprudent step? It might alienate my protector. He has two means of extricating me from this dilemma,—the one by a mysterious escape, managed through bribery; the other by buying off my judges with gold. I will say and do nothing until I am convinced that he has quite abandoned me, and then"—

Andrea had formed a plan which was tolerably clever. The unfortunate youth was intrepid in the attack, and rude in the defence. He had borne with the public prison, and with privations of all sorts; still, by degrees nature, or rather custom, had prevailed, and he suffered from being naked, dirty, and hungry. It was at this moment of discomfort that the inspector's voice called him to the visiting-room. Andrea felt his heart leap with joy. It was too soon for a visit from the examining magistrate, and too late for one from the director of the prison, or the doctor; it must, then, be the visitor he hoped for. Behind the grating of the room into which Andrea had been led, he saw, while his eyes dilated with surprise, the dark and intelligent face of M. Bertuccio, who was also gazing with sad astonishment upon the iron bars, the bolted doors, and the shadow which moved behind the other grating.

"Ah," said Andrea, deeply affected.

"Good morning, Benedetto," said Bertuccio, with his deep, hollow voice.

"You—you?" said the young man, looking fearfully around him.

"Do you not recognize me, unhappy child?"

"Silence,—be silent!" said Andrea, who knew the delicate sense of hearing possessed by the walls; "for heaven's sake, do not speak so loud!"

"You wish to speak with me alone, do you not?" said Bertuccio.

"Oh, yes."

"That is well." And Bertuccio, feeling in his pocket, signed to a keeper whom he saw through the window of the wicket.

"Read?" he said.

"What is that?" asked Andrea.

"An order to conduct you to a room, and to leave you there to talk to me."

"Oh," cried Andrea, leaping with joy. Then he mentally added,—"Still my unknown protector! I am not forgotten. They wish for secrecy, since we are to converse in a private room. I understand, Bertuccio has been sent by my protector."

The keeper spoke for a moment with an official, then opened the iron gates and conducted Andrea to a room on the first floor. The room was whitewashed, as is the custom in prisons, but it looked quite brilliant to a prisoner, though a stove, a bed, a chair, and a table formed the whole of its sumptuous furniture. Bertuccio sat down upon the chair, Andrea threw himself upon the bed; the keeper retired.

"Now," said the steward, "what have you to tell me?"

"And you?" said Andrea.

"You speak first."

"Oh, no. You must have much to tell me, since you have come to seek me."

"Well, be it so. You have continued your course of villany; you have robbed—you have assassinated."

"Well, I should say! If you had me taken to a private room only to tell me this, you might have saved yourself the trouble. I know all these things. But there are some with which, on the contrary, I am not acquainted. Let us talk of those, if you please. Who sent you?"

"Come, come, you are going on quickly, M. Benedetto!"

"Yes, and to the point. Let us dispense with useless words. Who sends you?"

"No one."

"How did you know I was in prison?"

"I recognized you, some time since, as the insolent dandy who so gracefully mounted his horse in the Champs Elysees."

"Oh, the Champs Elysees? Ah, yes; we burn, as they say at the game of pincette. The Champs Elysees? Come, let us talk a little about my father."

"Who, then, am I?"

"You, sir?—you are my adopted father. But it was not you, I presume, who placed at my disposal 100,000 francs, which I spent in four or five months; it was not you who manufactured an Italian gentleman for my father; it was not you who introduced me into the world, and had me invited to a certain dinner at Auteuil, which I fancy I am eating at this moment, in company with the most distinguished people in Paris—amongst the rest with a certain procureur, whose acquaintance I did very wrong not to cultivate, for he would have been very useful to me just now;—it was not you, in fact, who bailed me for one or two millions, when the fatal discovery of my little secret took place. Come, speak, my worthy Corsican, speak!"

"What do you wish me to say?"

"I will help you. You were speaking of the Champs Elysees just now, worthy foster-father."

"Well?"

"Well, in the Champs Elysees there resides a very rich gentleman."

"At whose house you robbed and murdered, did you not?"

"I believe I did."

"The Count of Monte Cristo?"

"'Tis you who have named him, as M. Racine says. Well, am I to rush into his arms, and strain him to my heart, crying, 'My father, my father!' like Monsieur Pixerecourt." [*]

"Do not let us jest," gravely replied Bertuccio, "and dare not to utter that name again as you have pronounced it."

* Guilbert de Pixerecourt, French dramatist (1775-1844).

"Bah," said Andrea, a little overcome, by the solemnity of Bertuccio's manner, "why not?"

"Because the person who bears it is too highly favored by heaven to be the father of such a wretch as you."

"Oh, these are fine words."

"And there will be fine doings, if you do not take care."

"Menaces—I do not fear them. I will say"—

"Do you think you are engaged with a pygmy like yourself?" said Bertuccio, in so calm a tone, and with so steadfast a look, that Andrea was moved to the very soul. "Do you think you have to do with galley-slaves, or novices in the world? Benedetto, you are fallen into terrible hands; they are ready to open for you—make use of them. Do not play with the thunderbolt they have laid aside for a moment, but which they can take up again instantly, if you attempt to intercept their movements."

"My father—I will know who my father is," said the obstinate youth; "I will perish if I must, but I will know it. What does scandal signify to me? What possessions, what reputation, what 'pull,' as Beauchamp says,—have I? You great people always lose something by scandal, notwithstanding your millions. Come, who is my father?"

"I came to tell you."

"Ah," cried Benedetto, his eyes sparkling with joy. Just then the door opened, and the jailer, addressing himself to Bertuccio, said,—"Excuse me, sir, but the examining magistrate is waiting for the prisoner."

"And so closes our interview," said Andrea to the worthy steward; "I wish the troublesome fellow were at the devil!"

"I will return to-morrow," said Bertuccio.

"Good! Gendarmes, I am at your service. Ah, sir, do leave a few crowns for me at the gate that I may have some things I am in need of!"

"It shall be done," replied Bertuccio. Andrea extended his hand; Bertuccio kept his own in his pocket, and merely jingled a few pieces of money. "That's what I mean," said Andrea, endeavoring to smile, quite overcome by the strange tranquillity of Bertuccio. "Can I be deceived?" he murmured, as he stepped into the oblong and grated vehicle which they call "the salad basket." "Never mind, we shall see! To-morrow, then!" he added, turning towards Bertuccio.

"To-morrow!" replied the steward.

CHAPTER 108.
THE JUDGE.

We remember that the Abbe Busoni remained alone with Noirtier in the chamber of death, and that the old man and the priest were the sole guardians of the young girl's body. Perhaps it was the Christian exhortations of the abbe, perhaps his kind charity, perhaps his persuasive words, which had restored the courage of Noirtier, for ever since he had conversed with the priest his violent despair had yielded to a calm resignation which surprised all who knew his excessive affection for Valentine. M. de Villefort had not seen his father since the morning of the death. The whole establishment had been changed; another valet was engaged for himself, a new servant for Noirtier, two women had entered Madame de Villefort's service,—in fact, everywhere, to the concierge and coachmen, new faces were presented to the different masters of the house, thus widening the division which had always existed between the members of the same family.

The assizes, also, were about to begin, and Villefort, shut up in his room, exerted himself with feverish anxiety in drawing up the case against the murderer of Caderousse. This affair, like all those in which the Count of Monte Cristo had interfered, caused a great sensation in Paris. The proofs were certainly not convincing, since they rested upon a few words written by an escaped galley-slave on his death-bed, and who might have been actuated by hatred or revenge in accusing his companion. But the mind of the procureur was made up; he felt assured that Benedetto was guilty, and he hoped by his skill in conducting this aggravated case to flatter his self-love, which was about the only vulnerable point left in his frozen heart.

The case was therefore prepared owing to the incessant labor of Villefort, who wished it to be the first on the list in the coming assizes. He had been obliged to seclude himself more than ever, to evade the enormous number of applications presented to him for the purpose of obtaining tickets of admission to the court on the day of trial. And then so short a time had elapsed since the death of poor Valentine, and the gloom which overshadowed the house was so recent, that no one wondered to see the father so absorbed in his professional duties, which were the only means he had of dissipating his grief.

Once only had Villefort seen his father; it was the day after that upon which Bertuccio had paid his second visit to Benedetto, when the latter was to learn his father's name. The magistrate, harassed and fatigued, had descended to the garden of his house, and in a gloomy mood, similar to that in which Tarquin lopped off the tallest poppies, he began knocking off with his cane the long and dying branches of the rose-trees, which, placed along the avenue, seemed like the spectres of the brilliant flowers which had bloomed in the past season. More than once he had reached that part of the garden where the famous boarded gate stood overlooking the deserted enclosure, always returning by the same path, to begin his walk again, at the same pace and with the same gesture, when he accidentally turned his eyes towards the house, whence he heard the noisy play of his son, who had returned from school to spend the Sunday and Monday with his mother. While doing so, he observed M. Noirtier at one of the open windows, where the old man had been placed that he might enjoy the last rays of the sun which yet yielded some heat, and was now shining upon the dying flowers and red leaves of the creeper which twined around the balcony.

The eye of the old man was riveted upon a spot which Villefort could scarcely distinguish. His glance was so full of hate, of ferocity, and savage impatience, that Villefort turned out of the path he had been pursuing, to see upon what person this dark look was directed. Then he saw beneath a thick clump of linden-trees, which were nearly divested of foliage, Madame de Villefort sitting with a book in her hand, the perusal of which she frequently interrupted to smile upon her son, or to throw back his elastic ball, which he obstinately threw from the drawing-room into the garden. Villefort became pale; he understood the old man's meaning. Noirtier continued to look at the same object, but suddenly his glance was transferred from the wife to the husband, and Villefort himself had to submit to the searching investigation of eyes, which, while changing their direction and even their language, had lost none of their menacing expression. Madame de Villefort, unconscious of the passions that exhausted their fire over her head, at that moment held her son's ball, and was making signs to him to reclaim it with a kiss. Edward begged for a long while, the maternal kiss probably not offering sufficient recompense for the trouble he must take to obtain it; however at length he decided, leaped out of the window into a cluster of heliotropes and daisies, and ran to his mother, his forehead streaming with perspiration. Madame de Villefort wiped his forehead, pressed her lips upon it, and sent him back with the ball in one hand and some bonbons in the other.

Villefort, drawn by an irresistible attraction, like that of the bird to the serpent, walked towards the house. As he approached it, Noirtier's gaze followed him, and his eyes appeared of such a fiery brightness that Villefort felt them pierce to the depths of his heart. In that earnest look might be read a deep reproach, as well as a terrible menace. Then Noirtier raised his eyes to heaven, as though to remind his son of a forgotten oath. "It is well, sir," replied Villefort from below,—"it is well; have patience but one day longer; what I have said I will do." Noirtier seemed to be calmed by these words, and turned his eyes with indifference to the other side. Villefort violently unbuttoned his great-coat, which seemed to strangle him, and passing his livid hand across his forehead, entered his study.

The night was cold and still; the family had all retired to rest but Villefort, who alone remained up, and worked till five o'clock in the morning, reviewing the last interrogatories made the night before by the examining magistrates, compiling the depositions of the witnesses, and putting the finishing stroke to the deed of accusation, which was one of the most energetic and best conceived of any he had yet delivered.

The next day, Monday, was the first sitting of the assizes. The morning dawned dull and gloomy, and Villefort saw the dim gray light shine upon the lines he had traced in red ink. The magistrate had slept for a short time while the lamp sent forth its final struggles; its flickerings awoke him, and he found his fingers as damp and purple as though they had been dipped in blood. He opened the window; a bright yellow streak crossed the sky, and seemed to divide in half the poplars, which stood out in black relief on the horizon. In the clover-fields beyond the chestnut-trees, a lark was mounting up to heaven, while pouring out her clear morning song. The damps of the dew bathed the head of Villefort, and refreshed his memory. "To-day," he said with an effort,—"to-day the man who holds the blade of justice must strike wherever there is guilt." Involuntarily his eyes wandered towards the window of Noirtier's room, where he had seen him the preceding night. The curtain was drawn, and yet the image of his father was so vivid to his mind that he addressed the closed window as though it had been open, and as if through the opening he had beheld the menacing old man. "Yes," he murmured,—"yes, be satisfied."

His head dropped upon his chest, and in this position he paced his study; then he threw himself, dressed as he was, upon a sofa, less to sleep than to rest his limbs, cramped with cold and study. By degrees every one awoke. Villefort, from his study, heard the successive noises which accompany the life of a house,—the opening and shutting of doors, the ringing of Madame de Villefort's bell, to summon the waiting-maid, mingled with the first shouts of the child, who rose full of the enjoyment of his age. Villefort also rang; his new valet brought him the papers, and with them a cup of chocolate.

"What are you bringing me?" said he.

"A cup of chocolate."

"I did not ask for it. Who has paid me this attention?"

"My mistress, sir. She said you would have to speak a great deal in the murder case, and that you should take something to keep up your strength;" and the valet placed the cup on the table nearest to the sofa, which was, like all the rest, covered with papers. The valet then left the room.

Villefort looked for an instant with a gloomy expression, then, suddenly, taking it up with a nervous motion, he swallowed its contents at one draught. It might have been thought that he hoped the beverage would be mortal, and that he sought for death to deliver him from a duty which he would rather die than fulfil. He then rose, and paced his room with a smile it would have been terrible to witness. The chocolate was inoffensive, for M. de Villefort felt no effects. The breakfast-hour arrived, but M. de Villefort was not at table. The valet re-entered.

"Madame de Villefort wishes to remind you, sir," he said, "that eleven o'clock has just struck, and that the trial commences at twelve."

"Well," said Villefort, "what then?"

"Madame de Villefort is dressed; she is quite ready, and wishes to know if she is to accompany you, sir?"

"Where to?"

"To the Palais."

"What to do?"

"My mistress wishes much to be present at the trial."

"Ah," said Villefort, with a startling accent; "does she wish that?"—The man drew back and said, "If you wish to go alone, sir, I will go and tell my mistress." Villefort remained silent for a moment, and dented his pale cheeks with his nails. "Tell your mistress," he at length answered, "that I wish to speak to her, and I beg she will wait for me in her own room."

"Yes, sir."

"Then come to dress and shave me."

"Directly, sir." The valet re-appeared almost instantly, and, having shaved his master, assisted him to dress entirely in black. When he had finished, he said,—

"My mistress said she should expect you, sir, as soon as you had finished dressing."

"I am going to her." And Villefort, with his papers under his arm and hat in hand, directed his steps toward the apartment of his wife. At the door he paused for a moment to wipe his damp, pale brow. He then entered the room. Madame de Villefort was sitting on an ottoman and impatiently turning over the leaves of some newspapers and pamphlets which young Edward, by way of amusing himself, was tearing to pieces before his mother could finish reading them. She was dressed to go out, her bonnet was placed beside her on a chair, and her gloves were on her hands.

"Ah, here you are, monsieur," she said in her naturally calm voice; "but how pale you are! Have you been working all night? Why did you not come down to breakfast? Well, will you take me, or shall I take Edward?" Madame de Villefort had multiplied her questions in order to gain one answer, but to all her inquiries M. de Villefort remained mute and cold as a statue. "Edward," said Villefort, fixing an imperious glance on the child, "go and play in the drawing-room, my dear; I wish to speak to your mamma." Madame de Villefort shuddered at the sight of that cold countenance, that resolute tone, and the awfully strange preliminaries. Edward raised his head, looked at his mother, and then, finding that she did not confirm the order, began cutting off the heads of his leaden soldiers.

"Edward," cried M. de Villefort, so harshly that the child started up from the floor, "do you hear me?—Go!" The child, unaccustomed to such treatment, arose, pale and trembling; it would be difficult to say whether his emotion were caused by fear or passion. His father went up to him, took him in his arms, and kissed his forehead. "Go," he said: "go, my child." Edward ran out. M. de Villefort went to the door, which he closed behind the child, and bolted. "Dear me!" said the young woman, endeavoring to read her husband's inmost thoughts, while a smile passed over her countenance which froze the impassibility of Villefort; "what is the matter?"

"Madame, where do you keep the poison you generally use?" said the magistrate, without any introduction, placing himself between his wife and the door.

Madame de Villefort must have experienced something of the sensation of a bird which, looking up, sees the murderous trap closing over its head. A hoarse, broken tone, which was neither a cry nor a sigh, escaped from her, while she became deadly pale. "Monsieur," she said, "I—I do not understand you." And, in her first paroxysm of terror, she had raised herself from the sofa, in the next, stronger very likely than the other, she fell down again on the cushions. "I asked you," continued Villefort, in a perfectly calm tone, "where you conceal the poison by the aid of which you have killed my father-in-law, M. de Saint-Meran, my mother-in-law, Madame de Saint-Meran, Barrois, and my daughter Valentine."

"Ah, sir," exclaimed Madame de Villefort, clasping her hands, "what do you say?"

"It is not for you to interrogate, but to answer."

"Is it to the judge or to the husband?" stammered Madame de Villefort. "To the judge—to the judge, madame!" It was terrible to behold the frightful pallor of that woman, the anguish of her look, the trembling of her whole frame. "Ah, sir," she muttered, "ah, sir," and this was all.

"You do not answer, madame!" exclaimed the terrible interrogator. Then he added, with a smile yet more terrible than his anger, "It is true, then; you do not deny it!" She moved forward. "And you cannot deny it!" added Villefort, extending his hand toward her, as though to seize her in the name of justice. "You have accomplished these different crimes with impudent address, but which could only deceive those whose affections for you blinded them. Since the death of Madame de Saint-Meran, I have known that a poisoner lived in my house. M. d'Avrigny warned me of it. After the death of Barrois my suspicions were directed towards an angel,—those suspicions which, even when there is no crime, are always alive in my heart; but after the death of Valentine, there has been no doubt in my mind, madame, and not only in mine, but in those of others; thus your crime, known by two persons, suspected by many, will soon become public, and, as I told you just now, you no longer speak to the husband, but to the judge."

The young woman hid her face in her hands. "Oh, sir," she stammered, "I beseech you, do not believe appearances."

"Are you, then, a coward?" cried Villefort, in a contemptuous voice. "But I have always observed that poisoners were cowards. Can you be a coward,—you who have had the courage to witness the death of two old men and a young girl murdered by you?"

"Sir! sir!"

"Can you be a coward?" continued Villefort, with increasing excitement, "you, who could count, one by one, the minutes of four death agonies? You, who have arranged your infernal plans, and removed the beverages with a talent and precision almost miraculous? Have you, then, who have calculated everything with such nicety, have you forgotten to calculate one thing—I mean where the revelation of your crimes will lead you to? Oh, it is impossible—you must have saved some surer, more subtle and deadly poison than any other, that you might escape the punishment that you deserve. You have done this—I hope so, at least." Madame de Villefort stretched out her hands, and fell on her knees.

"I understand," he said, "you confess; but a confession made to the judges, a confession made at the last moment, extorted when the crime cannot be denied, diminishes not the punishment inflicted on the guilty!"

"The punishment?" exclaimed Madame de Villefort, "the punishment, monsieur? Twice you have pronounced that word!"

"Certainly. Did you hope to escape it because you were four times guilty? Did you think the punishment would be withheld because you are the wife of him who pronounces it?—No, madame, no; the scaffold awaits the poisoner, whoever she may be, unless, as I just said, the poisoner has taken the precaution of keeping for herself a few drops of her deadliest potion." Madame de Villefort uttered a wild cry, and a hideous and uncontrollable terror spread over her distorted features. "Oh, do not fear the scaffold, madame," said the magistrate; "I will not dishonor you, since that would be dishonor to myself; no, if you have heard me distinctly, you will understand that you are not to die on the scaffold."

"No, I do not understand; what do you mean?" stammered the unhappy woman, completely overwhelmed.

"I mean that the wife of the first magistrate in the capital shall not, by her infamy, soil an unblemished name; that she shall not, with one blow, dishonor her husband and her child."

"No, no—oh, no!"

"Well, madame, it will be a laudable action on your part, and I will thank you for it!"

"You will thank me—for what?"

"For what you have just said."

"What did I say? Oh, my brain whirls; I no longer understand anything. Oh, my God, my God!" And she rose, with her hair dishevelled, and her lips foaming.

"Have you answered the question I put to you on entering the room?—where do you keep the poison you generally use, madame?" Madame de Villefort raised her arms to heaven, and convulsively struck one hand against the other. "No, no," she vociferated, "no, you cannot wish that!"

"What I do not wish, madame, is that you should perish on the scaffold. Do you understand?" asked Villefort.

"Oh, mercy, mercy, monsieur!"

"What I require is, that justice be done. I am on the earth to punish, madame," he added, with a flaming glance; "any other woman, were it the queen herself, I would send to the executioner; but to you I shall be merciful. To you

I will say, 'Have you not, madame, put aside some of the surest, deadliest, most speedy poison?'"

"Oh, pardon me, sir; let me live!"

"She is cowardly," said Villefort.

"Reflect that I am your wife!"

"You are a poisoner."

"In the name of heaven!"

"No!"

"In the name of the love you once bore me!"

"No, no!"

"In the name of our child! Ah, for the sake of our child, let me live!"

"No, no, no, I tell you; one day, if I allow you to live, you will perhaps kill him, as you have the others!"

"I?—I kill my boy?" cried the distracted mother, rushing toward Villefort; "I kill my son? Ha, ha, ha!" and a frightful, demoniac laugh finished the sentence, which was lost in a hoarse rattle. Madame de Villefort fell at her husband's feet. He approached her. "Think of it, madame," he said; "if, on my return, justice his not been satisfied, I will denounce you with my own mouth, and arrest you with my own hands!" She listened, panting, overwhelmed, crushed; her eye alone lived, and glared horribly. "Do you understand me?" he said. "I am going down there to pronounce the sentence of death against a murderer. If I find you alive on my return, you shall sleep to-night in the conciergerie." Madame de

Villefort sighed; her nerves gave way, and she sunk on the carpet. The king's attorney seemed to experience a sensation of pity; he looked upon her less severely, and, bowing to her, said slowly, "Farewell, madame, farewell!" That farewell struck Madame de Villefort like the executioner's knife. She fainted. The procureur went out, after having double-locked the door.

CHAPTER 109.
THE ASSIZES.

The Benedetto affair, as it was called at the Palais, and by people in general, had produced a tremendous sensation. Frequenting the Cafe de Paris, the Boulevard de Gand, and the Bois de Boulogne, during his brief career of splendor, the false Cavalcanti had formed a host of acquaintances. The papers had related his various adventures, both as the man of fashion and the galley-slave; and as every one who had been personally acquainted with Prince Andrea Cavalcanti experienced a lively curiosity in his fate, they all determined to spare no trouble in endeavoring to witness the trial of M. Benedetto for the murder of his comrade in chains. In the eyes of many, Benedetto appeared, if not a victim to, at least an instance of, the fallibility of the law. M. Cavalcanti, his father, had been seen in Paris, and it was expected that he would re-appear to claim the illustrious outcast. Many, also, who were not aware of the circumstances attending his withdrawal from Paris, were struck with the worthy appearance, the gentlemanly bearing, and the knowledge of the world displayed by the old patrician, who certainly played the nobleman very well, so long as he said nothing, and made no arithmetical calculations. As for the accused himself, many remembered him as being so amiable, so handsome, and so liberal, that they chose to think him the victim of some conspiracy, since in this world large fortunes frequently excite the malevolence and jealousy of some unknown enemy. Every one, therefore, ran to the court; some to witness the sight, others to comment upon it. From seven o'clock in the morning a crowd was stationed at the iron gates, and an hour before the trial commenced the hall was full of the privileged. Before the entrance of the magistrates, and indeed frequently afterwards, a court of justice, on days when some especial trial is to take place, resembles a drawing-room where many persons recognize each other and converse if they can do so without losing their seats; or, if they are separated by too great a number of lawyers, communicate by signs.

It was one of the magnificent autumn days which make amends for a short summer; the clouds which M. de Villefort had perceived at sunrise had all disappeared as if by magic, and one of the softest and most brilliant days of September shone forth in all its splendor.

Beauchamp, one of the kings of the press, and therefore claiming the right of a throne everywhere, was eying everybody through his monocle. He perceived Chateau-Renaud and Debray, who had just gained the good graces of a sergeant-at-arms, and who had persuaded the latter to let them stand before, instead of behind him, as they ought to have done. The worthy sergeant had recognized the minister's secretary and the millionnaire, and, by way of paying extra attention to his noble neighbors, promised to keep their places while they paid a visit to Beauchamp.

"Well," said Beauchamp, "we shall see our friend!"

"Yes, indeed!" replied Debray. "That worthy prince. Deuce take those Italian princes!"

"A man, too, who could boast of Dante for a genealogist, and could reckon back to the 'Divine Comedy.'"

"A nobility of the rope!" said Chateau-Renaud phlegmatically.

"He will be condemned, will he not?" asked Debray of Beauchamp.

"My dear fellow, I think we should ask you that question; you know such news much better than we do. Did you see the president at the minister's last night?"

"Yes."

"What did he say?"

"Something which will surprise you."

"Oh, make haste and tell me, then; it is a long time since that has happened."

"Well, he told me that Benedetto, who is considered a serpent of subtlety and a giant of cunning, is really but a very commonplace, silly rascal, and altogether unworthy of the experiments that will be made on his phrenological organs after his death."

"Bah," said Beauchamp, "he played the prince very well."

"Yes, for you who detest those unhappy princes, Beauchamp, and are always delighted to find fault with them; but not for me, who discover a gentleman by instinct, and who scent out an aristocratic family like a very bloodhound of heraldry."

"Then you never believed in the principality?"

"Yes.—in the principality, but not in the prince."

"Not so bad," said Beauchamp; "still, I assure you, he passed very well with many people; I saw him at the ministers' houses."

"Ah, yes," said Chateau-Renaud. "The idea of thinking ministers understand anything about princes!"

"There is something in what you have just said," said Beauchamp, laughing.

"But," said Debray to Beauchamp, "if I spoke to the president, you must have been with the procureur."

"It was an impossibility; for the last week M. de Villefort has secluded himself. It is natural enough; this strange chain of domestic afflictions, followed by the no less strange death of his daughter"—

"Strange? What do you mean, Beauchamp?"

"Oh, yes; do you pretend that all this has been unobserved at the minister's?" said Beauchamp, placing his eye-glass in his eye, where he tried to make it remain.

"My dear sir," said Chateau-Renaud, "allow me to tell you that you do not understand that manoeuvre with the eye-glass half so well as Debray. Give him a lesson, Debray."

"Stay," said Beauchamp, "surely I am not deceived."

"What is it?"

"It is she!"

"Whom do you mean?"

"They said she had left."

"Mademoiselle Eugenie?" said Chateau-Renaud; "has she returned?"

"No, but her mother."

"Madame Danglars? Nonsense! Impossible!" said Chateau-Renaud; "only ten days after the flight of her daughter, and three days from the bankruptcy of her husband?"

Debray colored slightly, and followed with his eyes the direction of Beauchamp's glance. "Come," he said, "it is only a veiled lady, some foreign princess, perhaps the mother of Cavalcanti. But you were just speaking on a very interesting topic, Beauchamp."

"I?"

"Yes; you were telling us about the extraordinary death of Valentine."

"Ah, yes, so I was. But how is it that Madame de Villefort is not here?"

"Poor, dear woman," said Debray, "she is no doubt occupied in distilling balm for the hospitals, or in making cosmetics for herself or friends. Do you know she spends two or three thousand crowns a year in this amusement? But I wonder she is not here. I should have been pleased to see her, for I like her very much."

"And I hate her," said Chateau-Renaud.

"Why?"

"I do not know. Why do we love? Why do we hate? I detest her, from antipathy."

"Or, rather, by instinct."

"Perhaps so. But to return to what you were saying, Beauchamp."

"Well, do you know why they die so multitudinously at M. de Villefort's?"

"'Multitudinously' is good," said Chateau-Renaud.

"My good fellow, you'll find the word in Saint-Simon."

"But the thing itself is at M. de Villefort's; but let's get back to the subject."

"Talking of that," said Debray, "Madame was making inquiries about that house, which for the last three months has been hung with black."

"Who is Madame?" asked Chateau-Renaud.

"The minister's wife, pardieu!"

"Oh, your pardon! I never visit ministers; I leave that to the princes."

"Really, You were only before sparkling, but now you are brilliant; take compassion on us, or, like Jupiter, you will wither us up."

"I will not speak again," said Chateau-Renaud; "pray have compassion upon me, and do not take up every word I say."

"Come, let us endeavor to get to the end of our story, Beauchamp; I told you that yesterday Madame made inquiries of me upon the subject; enlighten me, and I will then communicate my information to her."

"Well, gentlemen, the reason people die so multitudinously (I like the word) at M. de Villefort's is that there is an assassin in the house!" The two young men shuddered, for the same idea had more than once occurred to them. "And who is the assassin;" they asked together.

"Young Edward!" A burst of laughter from the auditors did not in the least disconcert the speaker, who continued,—"Yes, gentlemen; Edward, the infant phenomenon, who is quite an adept in the art of killing."

"You are jesting."

"Not at all. I yesterday engaged a servant, who had just left M. de Villefort—I intend sending him away to-morrow, for he eats so enormously, to make up for the fast imposed upon him by his terror in that house. Well, now listen."

"We are listening."

"It appears the dear child has obtained possession of a bottle containing some drug, which he every now and then uses against those who have displeased him. First, M. and Madame de Saint-Meran incurred his displeasure, so he poured out three drops of his elixir—three drops were sufficient; then followed Barrois, the old servant of M. Noirtier, who sometimes rebuffed this little wretch—he therefore received the same quantity of the elixir; the same happened to Valentine, of whom he was jealous; he gave her the same dose as the others, and all was over for her as well as the rest."

"Why, what nonsense are you telling us?" said Chateau-Renaud.

"Yes, it is an extraordinary story," said Beauchamp; "is it not?"

"It is absurd," said Debray.

"Ah," said Beauchamp, "you doubt me? Well, you can ask my servant, or rather him who will no longer be my servant to-morrow, it was the talk of the house."

"And this elixir, where is it? what is it?"

"The child conceals it."

"But where did he find it?"

"In his mother's laboratory."

"Does his mother then, keep poisons in her laboratory?"

"How can I tell? You are questioning me like a king's attorney. I only repeat what I have been told, and like my informant I can do no more. The poor devil would eat nothing, from fear."

"It is incredible!"

"No, my dear fellow, it is not at all incredible. You saw the child pass through the Rue Richelieu last year, who amused himself with killing his brothers and sisters by sticking pins in their ears while they slept. The generation who follow us are very precocious."

"Come, Beauchamp," said Chateau-Renaud, "I will bet anything you do not believe a word of all you have been telling us."

"I do not see the Count of Monte Cristo here."

"He is worn out," said Debray; "besides, he could not well appear in public, since he has been the dupe of the Cavalcanti, who, it appears, presented themselves to him with false letters of credit, and cheated him out of 100,000. francs upon the hypothesis of this principality."

"By the way, M. de Chateau-Renaud," asked Beauchamp, "how is Morrel?"

"Ma foi, I have called three times without once seeing him. Still, his sister did not seem uneasy, and told me that though she had not seen him for two or three days, she was sure he was well."

"Ah, now I think of it, the Count of Monte Cristo cannot appear in the hall," said Beauchamp.

"Why not?"

"Because he is an actor in the drama."

"Has he assassinated any one, then?"

"No, on the contrary, they wished to assassinate him. You know that it was in leaving his house that M. de Caderousse was murdered by his friend Benedetto. You know that the famous waistcoat was found in his house, containing the letter which stopped the signature of the marriage-contract. Do you see the waistcoat? There it is, all blood-stained, on the desk, as a testimony of the crime."

"Ah, very good."

"Hush, gentlemen, here is the court; let us go back to our places." A noise was heard in the hall; the sergeant called his two patrons with an energetic "hem!" and the door-keeper appearing, called out with that shrill voice peculiar to his order, ever since the days of Beaumarchais, "The court, gentlemen!"

CHAPTER 110.
THE INDICTMENT.

The judges took their places in the midst of the most profound silence; the jury took their seats; M. de Villefort, the object of unusual attention, and we had almost said of general admiration, sat in the arm-chair and cast a tranquil glance around him. Every one looked with astonishment on that grave and severe face, whose calm expression personal griefs had been unable to disturb, and the aspect of a man who was a stranger to all human emotions excited something very like terror.

"Gendarmes," said the president, "lead in the accused."

At these words the public attention became more intense, and all eyes were turned towards the door through which Benedetto was to enter. The door soon opened and the accused appeared. The same impression was experienced by all present, and no one was deceived by the expression of his countenance. His features bore no sign of that deep emotion which stops the beating of the heart and blanches the cheek. His hands, gracefully placed, one upon his hat, the other in the opening of his white waistcoat, were not at all tremulous; his eye was calm and even brilliant. Scarcely had he entered the hall when he glanced at the whole body of magistrates and assistants; his eye rested longer on the president, and still more so on the king's attorney. By the side of Andrea was stationed the lawyer who was to conduct his defence, and who had been appointed by the court, for Andrea disdained to pay any attention to those details, to which he appeared to attach no importance. The lawyer was a young man with light hair whose face expressed a hundred times more emotion than that which characterized the prisoner.

The president called for the indictment, revised as we know, by the clever and implacable pen of Villefort. During the reading of this, which was long, the public attention was continually drawn towards Andrea, who bore the inspection with Spartan unconcern. Villefort had never been so concise and eloquent. The crime was depicted in the most vivid colors; the former life of the prisoner, his transformation, a review of his life from the earliest period, were set forth with all the talent that a knowledge of human life could furnish to a mind like that of the procureur. Benedetto was thus forever condemned in public opinion before the sentence of the law could be pronounced. Andrea paid no attention to the successive charges which were brought against him. M. de Villefort, who examined him attentively, and who no doubt practiced upon him all the psychological studies he was accustomed to use, in vain endeavored to make him lower his eyes, notwithstanding the depth and profundity of his gaze. At length the reading of the indictment was ended.

"Accused," said the president, "your name and surname?" Andrea arose. "Excuse me, Mr. President," he said, in a clear voice, "but I see you are going to adopt a course of questions through which I cannot follow you. I have an idea, which I will explain by and by, of making an exception to the usual form of accusation. Allow me, then, if you please, to answer in different order, or I will not do so at all." The astonished president looked at the jury, who in turn looked at Villefort. The whole assembly manifested great surprise, but Andrea appeared quite unmoved. "Your age?" said the president; "will you answer that question?"

"I will answer that question, as well as the rest, Mr. President, but in its turn."

"Your age?" repeated the president.

"I am twenty-one years old, or rather I shall be in a few days, as I was born the night of the 27th of September, 1817." M. de Villefort, who was busy taking down some notes, raised his head at the mention of this date. "Where were you born?" continued the president.

"At Auteuil, near Paris." M. de Villefort a second time raised his head, looked at Benedetto as if he had been gazing at the head of Medusa, and became livid. As for Benedetto, he gracefully wiped his lips with a fine cambric pocket-handkerchief. "Your profession?"

"First I was a forger," answered Andrea, as calmly as possible; "then I became a thief, and lately have become an assassin." A murmur, or rather storm, of indignation burst from all parts of the assembly. The judges themselves appeared to be stupefied, and the jury manifested tokens of disgust for cynicism so unexpected in a man of fashion. M. de Villefort pressed his hand upon his brow, which, at first pale, had become red and burning; then he suddenly arose and looked around as though he had lost his senses—he wanted air.

"Are you looking for anything, Mr. Procureur?" asked Benedetto, with his most ingratiating smile. M. de Villefort answered nothing, but sat, or rather threw himself down again upon his chair. "And now, prisoner, will you consent to tell your name?" said the president. "The brutal affectation with which you have enumerated and classified your crimes calls for a severe reprimand on the part of the court, both in the name of morality, and for the respect due to humanity. You appear to consider this a point of honor, and it may be for this reason, that you have delayed acknowledging your name. You wished it to be preceded by all these titles."

"It is quite wonderful, Mr. President, how entirely you have read my thoughts," said Benedetto, in his softest voice and most polite manner. "This is, indeed, the reason why I begged you to alter the order of the questions." The public astonishment had reached its height. There was no longer any deceit or bravado in the manner of the accused. The audience felt that a startling revelation was to follow this ominous prelude.

"Well," said the president; "your name?"

"I cannot tell you my name, since I do not know it; but I know my father's, and can tell it to you."

A painful giddiness overwhelmed Villefort; great drops of acrid sweat fell from his face upon the papers which he held in his convulsed hand.

"Repeat your father's name," said the president. Not a whisper, not a breath, was heard in that vast assembly; every one waited anxiously.

"My father is king's attorney," replied Andrea calmly.

"King's attorney?" said the president, stupefied, and without noticing the agitation which spread over the face of M. de Villefort; "king's attorney?"

"Yes; and if you wish to know his name, I will tell it,— he is named Villefort." The explosion, which had been so long restrained from a feeling of respect to the court of justice, now burst forth like thunder from the breasts of all present; the court itself did not seek to restrain the feelings of the audience. The exclamations, the insults addressed to Benedetto, who remained perfectly unconcerned, the energetic gestures, the movement of the gendarmes, the sneers of the scum of the crowd always sure to rise to the surface in case of any disturbance—all this lasted five minutes, before the door-keepers and magistrates were able to restore silence. In the midst of this tumult the voice of the president was heard to exclaim,—"Are you playing with justice, accused, and do you dare set your fellow-citizens an example of disorder which even in these times has never been equalled?"

Several persons hurried up to M. de Villefort, who sat half bowed over in his chair, offering him consolation, encouragement, and protestations of zeal and sympathy. Order was re-established in the hall, except that a few people still moved about and whispered to one another. A lady, it was said, had just fainted; they had supplied her with a smelling-bottle, and she had recovered. During the scene of tumult, Andrea had turned his smiling face towards the assembly; then, leaning with one hand on the oaken rail of the dock, in the most graceful attitude possible, he said: "Gentlemen, I assure you I had no idea of insulting the court, or of making a useless disturbance in the presence of this honorable assembly. They ask my age; I tell it. They ask where I was born; I answer. They ask my name, I cannot give it, since my parents abandoned me. But though I cannot give my own name, not possessing one, I can tell them my father's. Now I repeat, my father is named M. de Villefort, and I am ready to prove it."

There was an energy, a conviction, and a sincerity in the manner of the young man, which silenced the tumult.

All eyes were turned for a moment towards the procureur, who sat as motionless as though a thunderbolt had changed him into a corpse. "Gentlemen," said Andrea, commanding silence by his voice and manner; "I owe you the proofs and explanations of what I have said."

"But," said the irritated president, "you called yourself Benedetto, declared yourself an orphan, and claimed Corsica as your country."

"I said anything I pleased, in order that the solemn declaration I have just made should not be withheld, which otherwise would certainly have been the case. I now repeat that I was born at Auteuil on the night of the 27th of September, 1817, and that I am the son of the procureur, M. de Villefort. Do you wish for any further details? I will give them. I was born in No. 28, Rue de la Fontaine, in a room hung with red damask; my father took me in his arms, telling my mother I was dead, wrapped me in a napkin marked with an H and an N, and carried me into a garden, where he buried me alive."

A shudder ran through the assembly when they saw that the confidence of the prisoner increased in proportion to the terror of M. de Villefort. "But how have you become acquainted with all these details?" asked the president.

"I will tell you, Mr. President. A man who had sworn vengeance against my father, and had long watched his opportunity to kill him, had introduced himself that night into the garden in which my father buried me. He was concealed in a thicket; he saw my father bury something in the ground, and stabbed him; then thinking the deposit might contain some treasure he turned up the ground, and found me still living. The man carried me to the foundling asylum, where I was registered under the number 37. Three months afterwards, a woman travelled from Rogliano to Paris to fetch me, and having claimed me as her son, carried me away. Thus, you see, though born in Paris, I was brought up in Corsica."

There was a moment's silence, during which one could have fancied the hall empty, so profound was the stillness. "Proceed," said the president.

"Certainly, I might have lived happily amongst those good people, who adored me, but my perverse disposition prevailed over the virtues which my adopted mother endeavored to instil into my heart. I increased in wickedness till I committed crime. One day when I cursed Providence for making me so wicked, and ordaining me to such a fate, my adopted father said to me, 'Do not blaspheme, unhappy child, the crime is that of your father, not yours,—of your father, who consigned you to hell if you died, and to misery if a miracle preserved you alive.' After that I ceased to blaspheme, but I cursed my father. That is why I have uttered the words for which you blame me; that is why I have filled this whole assembly with horror. If I have committed an additional crime, punish me, but if you will allow that ever since the day of my birth my fate has been sad, bitter, and lamentable, then pity me."

"But your mother?" asked the president.

"My mother thought me dead; she is not guilty. I did not even wish to know her name, nor do I know it." Just then a piercing cry, ending in a sob, burst from the centre of the crowd, who encircled the lady who had before fainted, and who now fell into a violent fit of hysterics. She was carried out of the hall, the thick veil which concealed her face dropped off, and Madame Danglars was recognized. Notwithstanding his shattered nerves, the ringing sensation in his ears, and the madness which turned his brain, Villefort rose as he perceived her. "The proofs, the proofs!" said the president; "remember this tissue of horrors must be supported by the clearest proofs."

"The proofs?" said Benedetto, laughing; "do you want proofs?"

"Yes."

"Well, then, look at M. de Villefort, and then ask me for proofs."

Every one turned towards the procureur, who, unable to bear the universal gaze now riveted on him alone, advanced staggering into the midst of the tribunal, with his hair dishevelled and his face indented with the mark of his nails. The whole assembly uttered a long murmur of astonishment. "Father," said Benedetto, "I am asked for proofs, do you wish me to give them?"

"No, no, it is useless," stammered M. de Villefort in a hoarse voice; "no, it is useless!"

"How useless?" cried the president, "what do you mean?"

"I mean that I feel it impossible to struggle against this deadly weight which crushes me. Gentlemen, I know I am in the hands of an avenging God! We need no proofs; everything relating to this young man is true." A dull, gloomy silence, like that which precedes some awful phenomenon of nature, pervaded the assembly, who shuddered in dismay. "What, M. de Villefort," cried the president, "do you yield to an hallucination? What, are you no longer in possession of your senses? This strange, unexpected, terrible accusation has disordered your reason. Come, recover."

The procureur dropped his head; his teeth chattered like those of a man under a violent attack of fever, and yet he was deadly pale.

"I am in possession of all my senses, sir," he said; "my body alone suffers, as you may suppose. I acknowledge myself guilty of all the young man has brought against me, and from this hour hold myself under the authority of the procureur who will succeed me."

And as he spoke these words with a hoarse, choking voice, he staggered towards the door, which was mechanically opened by a door-keeper. The whole assembly were dumb with astonishment at the revelation and confession which had produced a catastrophe so different from that which had been expected during the last fortnight by the Parisian world.

"Well," said Beauchamp, "let them now say that drama is unnatural!"

"Ma foi!" said Chateau-Renaud, "I would rather end my career like M. de Morcerf; a pistol-shot seems quite delightful compared with this catastrophe."

"And moreover, it kills," said Beauchamp.

"And to think that I had an idea of marrying his daughter," said Debray. "She did well to die, poor girl!"

"The sitting is adjourned, gentlemen," said the president; "fresh inquiries will be made, and the case will be tried next session by another magistrate." As for Andrea, who was calm and more interesting than ever, he left the hall, escorted by gendarmes, who involuntarily paid him some attention. "Well, what do you think of this, my fine fellow?" asked Debray of the sergeant-at-arms, slipping a louis into his hand. "There will be extenuating circumstances," he replied.

CHAPTER 111.
EXPIATION.

Notwithstanding the density of the crowd, M. de Villefort saw it open before him. There is something so awe-inspiring in great afflictions that even in the worst times the first emotion of a crowd has generally been to sympathize with the sufferer in a great catastrophe. Many people have been assassinated in a tumult, but even criminals have rarely been insulted during trial. Thus Villefort passed through the mass of spectators and officers of the Palais, and withdrew. Though he had acknowledged his guilt, he was protected by his grief. There are some situations which men understand by instinct, but which reason is powerless to explain; in such cases the greatest poet is he who gives utterance to the most natural and vehement outburst of sorrow. Those who hear the bitter cry are as much impressed as if they listened to an entire poem, and when the sufferer is sincere they are right in regarding his outburst as sublime.

It would be difficult to describe the state of stupor in which Villefort left the Palais. Every pulse beat with feverish excitement, every nerve was strained, every vein swollen, and every part of his body seemed to suffer distinctly from the rest, thus multiplying his agony a thousand-fold. He made his way along the corridors through force of habit; he threw aside his magisterial robe, not out of deference to etiquette, but because it was an unbearable burden, a veritable garb of Nessus, insatiate in torture. Having staggered as far as the Rue Dauphine, he perceived his carriage, awoke his sleeping coachman by opening the door himself, threw himself on the cushions, and pointed towards the Faubourg Saint-Honore; the carriage drove on. The weight of his fallen fortunes seemed suddenly to crush him; he could not foresee the consequences; he could not contemplate the future with the indifference of the hardened criminal who merely faces a contingency already familiar. God was still in his heart. "God," he murmured, not knowing what he said,—"God—God!" Behind the event that had overwhelmed him he saw the hand of God. The carriage rolled rapidly onward. Villefort, while turning restlessly on the cushions, felt something press against him. He put out his hand to remove the object; it was a fan which Madame de Villefort had left in the carriage; this fan awakened a recollection which darted through his mind like lightning. He thought of his wife.

"Oh!" he exclaimed, as though a redhot iron were piercing his heart. During the last hour his own crime had alone been presented to his mind; now another object, not less terrible, suddenly presented itself. His wife! He had just acted the inexorable judge with her, he had condemned her to death, and she, crushed by remorse, struck with terror, covered with the shame inspired by the eloquence of his irreproachable virtue,—she, a poor, weak woman, without help or the power of defending herself against his absolute and supreme will,—she might at that very moment, perhaps, be preparing to die! An hour had elapsed since her condemnation; at that moment, doubtless, she was recalling all her crimes to her memory; she was asking pardon for her sins; perhaps she was even writing a letter imploring forgiveness from her virtuous husband—a forgiveness she was purchasing with her death! Villefort again groaned with anguish and despair. "Ah," he exclaimed, "that woman became criminal only from associating with me! I carried the infection of crime with me, and she has caught it as she would the typhus fever, the cholera, the plague! And yet I have punished her—I have dared to tell her—I have— 'Repent and die!' But no, she must not die; she shall live, and with me. We will flee from Paris and go as far as the earth reaches. I told her of the scaffold; oh, heavens, I forgot that it awaits me also! How could I pronounce that word? Yes, we will fly; I will confess all to her,—I will tell her daily that I also have committed a crime!—Oh, what an alliance—the tiger and the serpent; worthy wife of such as I am! She must live that my infamy may diminish hers." And Villefort dashed open the window in front of the carriage.

"Faster, faster!" he cried, in a tone which electrified the coachman. The horses, impelled by fear, flew towards the house.

"Yes, yes," repeated Villefort, as he approached his home—"yes, that woman must live; she must repent, and educate my son, the sole survivor, with the exception of the indestructible old man, of the wreck of my house. She loves him; it was for his sake she has committed these crimes. We ought never to despair of softening the heart of a mother who loves her child. She will repent, and no one will know that she has been guilty. The events which have taken place in my house, though they now occupy the public mind, will be forgotten in time, or if, indeed, a few enemies should persist in remembering them, why then I will add them to my list of crimes. What will it signify if one, two, or three more are added? My wife and child shall escape from this gulf, carrying treasures with them; she will live and may yet be happy, since her child, in whom all her love is centred, will be with her. I shall have performed a good action, and my heart will be lighter." And the procureur breathed more freely than he had done for some time.

The carriage stopped at the door of the house. Villefort leaped out of the carriage, and saw that his servants were surprised at his early return; he could read no other expression on their features. Neither of them spoke to him; they merely stood aside to let him pass by, as usual, nothing more. As he passed by M. Noirtier's room, he perceived two figures through the half-open door; but he experienced no curiosity to know who was visiting his father: anxiety carried him on further.

"Come," he said, as he ascended the stairs leading to his wife's room, "nothing is changed here." He then closed the door of the landing. "No one must disturb us," he said; "I must speak freely to her, accuse myself, and say"—he approached the door, touched the crystal handle, which yielded to his hand. "Not locked," he cried; "that is well." And he entered the little room in which Edward slept; for though the child went to school during the day, his mother could not allow him to be separated from her at night. With a single glance Villefort's eye ran through the room. "Not here," he said; "doubtless she is in her bedroom." He rushed towards the door, found it bolted, and stopped, shuddering. "Heloise!" he cried. He fancied he heard the sound of a piece of furniture being removed. "Heloise!" he repeated.

"Who is there?" answered the voice of her he sought. He thought that voice more feeble than usual.

"Open the door!" cried Villefort. "Open; it is I." But notwithstanding this request, notwithstanding the tone of anguish in which it was uttered, the door remained closed. Villefort burst it open with a violent blow. At the entrance of the room which led to her boudoir, Madame de Villefort was standing erect, pale, her features contracted, and her eyes glaring horribly. "Heloise, Heloise!" he said, "what is the matter? Speak!" The young woman extended her stiff white hands towards him. "It is done, monsieur," she said with a rattling noise which seemed to tear her throat. "What more do you want?" and she fell full length on the floor. Villefort ran to her and seized her hand, which convulsively clasped a crystal bottle with a golden stopper. Madame de Villefort was dead. Villefort, maddened with horror, stepped back to the threshhold of the door, fixing his eyes on the corpse: "My son!" he exclaimed suddenly, "where is my son?—Edward, Edward!" and he rushed out of the room, still crying, "Edward, Edward!" The name was pronounced in such a tone of anguish that the servants ran up.

"Where is my son?" asked Villefort; "let him be removed from the house, that he may not see"—

"Master Edward is not down-stairs, sir," replied the valet.

"Then he must be playing in the garden; go and see."

"No, sir; Madame de Villefort sent for him half an hour ago; he went into her room, and has not been down-stairs since." A cold perspiration burst out on Villefort's brow; his legs trembled, and his thoughts flew about madly in his brain like the wheels of a disordered watch. "In Madame de Villefort's room?" he murmured and slowly returned, with one hand wiping his forehead, and with the other supporting himself against the wall. To enter the room he must again see the body of his unfortunate wife. To call Edward he must reawaken the echo of that room which now appeared like a sepulchre; to speak seemed like violating the silence of the tomb. His tongue was paralyzed in his mouth.

"Edward!" he stammered—"Edward!" The child did not answer. Where, then, could he be, if he had entered his mother's room and not since returned? He stepped forward. The corpse of Madame de Villefort was stretched across the doorway leading to the room in which Edward must be; those glaring eyes seemed to watch over the threshold, and the lips bore the stamp of a terrible and mysterious irony. Through the open door was visible a portion of the boudoir, containing an upright piano and a blue satin couch. Villefort stepped forward two or three paces, and beheld his child lying—no doubt asleep—on the sofa. The unhappy man uttered an exclamation of joy; a ray of light seemed to penetrate the abyss of despair and darkness. He had only to step over the corpse, enter the boudoir, take the child in his arms, and flee far, far away.

Villefort was no longer the civilized man; he was a tiger hurt unto death, gnashing his teeth in his wound. He no longer feared realities, but phantoms. He leaped over the corpse as if it had been a burning brazier. He took the child in his arms, embraced him, shook him, called him, but the child made no response. He pressed his burning lips to the cheeks, but they were icy cold and pale; he felt the stiffened limbs; he pressed his hand upon the heart, but it no longer beat,—the child was dead. A folded paper fell from Edward's breast. Villefort, thunderstruck, fell upon his knees; the child dropped from his arms, and rolled on the floor by the side of its mother. He picked up the paper, and, recognizing his wife's writing, ran his eyes rapidly over its contents; it ran as follows:—

"You know that I was a good mother, since it was for my son's sake I became criminal. A good mother cannot depart without her son."

Villefort could not believe his eyes,—he could not believe his reason; he dragged himself towards the child's body, and examined it as a lioness contemplates its dead cub. Then a piercing cry escaped from his breast, and he cried, "Still the hand of God." The presence of the two victims alarmed him; he could not bear solitude shared only by two corpses. Until then he had been sustained by rage, by his strength of mind, by despair, by the supreme agony which led the Titans to scale the heavens, and Ajax to defy the gods. He now arose, his head bowed beneath the weight of grief, and, shaking his damp, dishevelled hair, he who had never felt compassion for any one determined to seek his father, that he might have some one to whom he could relate his misfortunes,—some one by whose side he might weep. He descended the little staircase with which we are acquainted, and entered Noirtier's room. The old man appeared to be listening attentively and as affectionately as his infirmities would allow to the Abbe Busoni, who looked cold and calm, as usual. Villefort, perceiving the abbe, passed his hand across his brow. He recollected the call he had made upon him after the dinner at Auteuil, and then the visit the abbe had himself paid to his house on the day of Valentine's death. "You here, sir!" he exclaimed; "do you, then, never appear but to act as an escort to death?"

Busoni turned around, and, perceiving the excitement depicted on the magistrate's face, the savage lustre of his eyes, he understood that the revelation had been made at the assizes; but beyond this he was ignorant. "I came to pray over the body of your daughter."

"And now why are you here?"

"I come to tell you that you have sufficiently repaid your debt, and that from this moment I will pray to God to forgive you, as I do."

"Good heavens!" exclaimed Villefort, stepping back fearfully, "surely that is not the voice of the Abbe Busoni!"

"No!" The abbe threw off his wig, shook his head, and his hair, no longer confined, fell in black masses around his manly face.

"It is the face of the Count of Monte Cristo!" exclaimed the procureur, with a haggard expression.

"You are not exactly right, M. Procureur; you must go farther back."

"That voice, that voice!—where did I first hear it?"

"You heard it for the first time at Marseilles, twenty-three years ago, the day of your marriage with Mademoiselle de Saint-Meran. Refer to your papers."

"You are not Busoni?—you are not Monte Cristo? Oh, heavens—you are, then, some secret, implacable, and mortal enemy! I must have wronged you in some way at Marseilles. Oh, woe to me!"

"Yes; you are now on the right path," said the count, crossing his arms over his broad chest; "search—search!"

"But what have I done to you?" exclaimed Villefort, whose mind was balancing between reason and insanity, in that cloud which is neither a dream nor reality; "what have I done to you? Tell me, then! Speak!"

"You condemned me to a horrible, tedious death; you killed my father; you deprived me of liberty, of love, and happiness."

"Who are you, then? Who are you?"

"I am the spectre of a wretch you buried in the dungeons of the Chateau d'If. God gave that spectre the form of the Count of Monte Cristo when he at length issued from his tomb, enriched him with gold and diamonds, and led him to you!"

"Ah, I recognize you—I recognize you!" exclaimed the king's attorney; "you are"—

"I am Edmond Dantes!"

"You are Edmond Dantes," cried Villefort, seizing the count by the wrist; "then come here!" And up the stairs he dragged Monte Cristo; who, ignorant of what had happened, followed him in astonishment, foreseeing some new catastrophe. "There, Edmond Dantes!" he said, pointing to the bodies of his wife and child, "see, are you well avenged?" Monte Cristo became pale at this horrible sight; he felt that he had passed beyond the bounds of vengeance, and that he could no longer say, "God is for and with me." With an expression of indescribable anguish he threw himself upon the body of the child, reopened its eyes, felt its pulse, and then rushed with him into Valentine's room, of which he double-locked the door. "My child," cried Villefort, "he carries away the body of my child! Oh, curses, woe, death to you!" and he tried to follow Monte Cristo; but as though in a dream he was transfixed to the spot,—his eyes glared as though they were starting through the sockets; he griped the flesh on his chest until his nails were stained with blood; the veins of his temples swelled and boiled as though they would burst their narrow boundary, and deluge his brain with living fire. This lasted several minutes, until the frightful overturn of reason was accomplished; then uttering a loud cry followed by a burst of laughter, he rushed down the stairs.

A quarter of an hour afterwards the door of Valentine's room opened, and Monte Cristo reappeared. Pale, with a dull eye and heavy heart, all the noble features of that face, usually so calm and serene, were overcast by grief. In his arms he held the child, whom no skill had been able to recall to life. Bending on one knee, he placed it reverently by the side of its mother, with its head upon her breast. Then, rising, he went out, and meeting a servant on the stairs, he asked, "Where is M. de Villefort?"

The servant, instead of answering, pointed to the garden. Monte Cristo ran down the steps, and advancing towards the spot designated beheld Villefort, encircled by his servants, with a spade in his hand, and digging the earth with fury. "It is not here!" he cried. "It is not here!" And then he moved farther on, and began again to dig.

Monte Cristo approached him, and said in a low voice, with an expression almost humble, "Sir, you have indeed lost a son; but"—

Villefort interrupted him; he had neither listened nor heard. "Oh, I will find it," he cried; "you may pretend he is not here, but I will find him, though I dig forever!" Monte Cristo drew back in horror. "Oh," he said, "he is mad!" And as though he feared that the walls of the accursed house would crumble around him, he rushed into the street, for the first time doubting whether he had the right to do as he had done. "Oh, enough of this,—enough of this," he cried; "let me save the last." On entering his house, he met Morrel, who wandered about like a ghost awaiting the heavenly mandate for return to the tomb. "Prepare yourself, Maximilian," he said with a smile; "we leave Paris to-morrow."

"Have you nothing more to do there?" asked Morrel.

"No," replied Monte Cristo; "God grant I may not have done too much already."

The next day they indeed left, accompanied only by Baptistin. Haidee had taken away Ali, and Bertuccio remained with Noirtier.

CHAPTER 112.
THE DEPARTURE.

The recent event formed the theme of conversation throughout all Paris. Emmanuel and his wife conversed with natural astonishment in their little apartment in the Rue Meslay upon the three successive, sudden, and most unexpected catastrophes of Morcerf, Danglars, and Villefort. Maximilian, who was paying them a visit, listened to their conversation, or rather was present at it, plunged in his accustomed state of apathy. "Indeed," said Julie, "might we not almost fancy, Emmanuel, that those people, so rich, so happy but yesterday, had forgotten in their prosperity that an evil genius—like the wicked fairies in Perrault's stories who present themselves unbidden at a wedding or baptism—hovered over them, and appeared all at once to revenge himself for their fatal neglect?"

"What a dire misfortune!" said Emmanuel, thinking of Morcerf and Danglars.

"What dreadful sufferings!" said Julie, remembering Valentine, but whom, with a delicacy natural to women, she did not name before her brother.

"If the Supreme Being has directed the fatal blow," said Emmanuel, "it must be that he in his great goodness

227

has perceived nothing in the past lives of these people to merit mitigation of their awful punishment."

"Do you not form a very rash judgment, Emmanuel?" said Julie. "When my father, with a pistol in his hand, was once on the point of committing suicide, had any one then said, 'This man deserves his misery,' would not that person have been deceived?"

"Yes; but your father was not allowed to fall. A being was commissioned to arrest the fatal hand of death about to descend on him."

Emmanuel had scarcely uttered these words when the sound of the bell was heard, the well-known signal given by the porter that a visitor had arrived. Nearly at the same instant the door was opened and the Count of Monte Cristo appeared on the threshold. The young people uttered a cry of joy, while Maximilian raised his head, but let it fall again immediately. "Maximilian," said the count, without appearing to notice the different impressions which his presence produced on the little circle, "I come to seek you."

"To seek me?" repeated Morrel, as if awakening from a dream.

"Yes," said Monte Cristo; "has it not been agreed that I should take you with me, and did I not tell you yesterday to prepare for departure?"

"I am ready," said Maximilian; "I came expressly to wish them farewell."

"Whither are you going, count?" asked Julie.

"In the first instance to Marseilles, madame."

"To Marseilles!" exclaimed the young couple.

"Yes, and I take your brother with me."

"Oh, count." said Julie, "will you restore him to us cured of his melancholy?"—Morrel turned away to conceal the confusion of his countenance.

"You perceive, then, that he is not happy?" said the count. "Yes," replied the young woman; "and fear much that he finds our home but a dull one."

"I will undertake to divert him," replied the count.

"I am ready to accompany you, sir," said Maximilian. "Adieu, my kind friends! Emmanuel—Julie—farewell!"

"How farewell?" exclaimed Julie; "do you leave us thus, so suddenly, without any preparations for your journey, without even a passport?"

"Needless delays but increase the grief of parting," said Monte Cristo, "and Maximilian has doubtless provided himself with everything requisite; at least, I advised him to do so."

"I have a passport, and my clothes are ready packed," said Morrel in his tranquil but mournful manner.

"Good," said Monte Cristo, smiling; "in these prompt arrangements we recognize the order of a well-disciplined soldier."

"And you leave us," said Julie, "at a moment's warning? you do not give us a day—no, not even an hour before your departure?"

"My carriage is at the door, madame, and I must be in Rome in five days."

"But does Maximilian go to Rome?" exclaimed Emmanuel.

"I am going wherever it may please the count to take me," said Morrel, with a smile full of grief; "I am under his orders for the next month."

"Oh, heavens, how strangely he expresses himself, count!" said Julie.

"Maximilian goes with me," said the count, in his kindest and most persuasive manner; "therefore do not make yourself uneasy on your brother's account."

"Once more farewell, my dear sister; Emmanuel, adieu!" Morrel repeated.

"His carelessness and indifference touch me to the heart," said Julie. "Oh, Maximilian, Maximilian, you are certainly concealing something from us."

"Pshaw!" said Monte Cristo, "you will see him return to you gay, smiling, and joyful."

Maximilian cast a look of disdain, almost of anger, on the count.

"We must leave you," said Monte Cristo.

"Before you quit us, count," said Julie, "will you permit us to express to you all that the other day"—

"Madame," interrupted the count, taking her two hands in his, "all that you could say in words would never express what I read in your eyes; the thoughts of your heart are fully understood by mine. Like benefactors in romances, I should have left you without seeing you again, but that would have been a virtue beyond my strength, because I am a weak and vain man, fond of the tender, kind, and thankful glances of my fellow-creatures. On the eve of departure I carry my egotism so far as to say, 'Do not forget me, my kind friends, for probably you will never see me again.'"

"Never see you again?" exclaimed Emmanuel, while two large tears rolled down Julie's cheeks, "never behold you again? It is not a man, then, but some angel that leaves us, and this angel is on the point of returning to heaven after having appeared on earth to do good."

"Say not so," quickly returned Monte Cristo—"say not so, my friends; angels never err, celestial beings remain where they wish to be. Fate is not more powerful than they; it is they who, on the contrary, overcome fate. No, Emmanuel, I am but a man, and your admiration is as unmerited as your words are sacrilegious." And pressing his lips on the hand of Julie, who rushed into his arms, he extended his other hand to Emmanuel; then tearing himself from this abode of peace and happiness, he made a sign to Maximilian, who followed him passively, with the indifference which had been perceptible in him ever since the death of Valentine had so stunned him. "Restore my brother to peace and happiness," whispered Julie to Monte Cristo. And the count pressed her hand in reply, as he had done eleven years before on the staircase leading to Morrel's study.

"You still confide, then, in Sinbad the Sailor?" asked he, smiling.

"Oh, yes," was the ready answer.

"Well, then, sleep in peace, and put your trust in heaven." As we have before said, the postchaise was waiting; four powerful horses were already pawing the ground with impatience, while Ali, apparently just arrived from a long walk, was standing at the foot of the steps, his face bathed in perspiration. "Well," asked the count in Arabic, "have you been to see the old man?" Ali made a sign in the affirmative.

"And have you placed the letter before him, as I ordered you to do?"

The slave respectfully signalized that he had. "And what did he say, or rather do?" Ali placed himself in the light, so that his master might see him distinctly, and then imitating in his intelligent manner the countenance of the old man, he closed his eyes, as Noirtier was in the custom of doing when saying "Yes."

"Good; he accepts," said Monte Cristo. "Now let us go."

These words had scarcely escaped him, when the carriage was on its way, and the feet of the horses struck a shower of sparks from the pavement. Maximilian settled himself in his corner without uttering a word. Half an hour had passed when the carriage stopped suddenly; the count had just pulled the silken check-string, which was fastened to Ali's finger. The Nubian immediately descended and opened the carriage door. It was a lovely starlight night—they had just reached the top of the hill Villejuif, from whence Paris appears like a sombre sea tossing its millions of phosphoric waves into light—waves indeed more noisy, more passionate, more changeable, more furious, more greedy, than those of the tempestuous ocean,—waves which never rest as those of the sea sometimes do,—waves ever dashing, ever foaming, ever ingulfing what falls within their grasp. The count stood alone, and at a sign from his hand, the carriage went on for a short distance. With folded arms, he gazed for some time upon the great city. When he had fixed his piercing look on this modern Babylon, which equally engages the contemplation of the religious enthusiast, the materialist, and the scoffer,—"Great city," murmured he, inclining his head, and joining his hands as if in prayer, "less than six months have elapsed since first I entered thy gates. I believe that the Spirit of God led my steps to thee and that he also enables me to quit thee in triumph; the secret cause of my presence within thy walls I have confided alone to him who only has had the power to read my heart. God only knows that I retire from thee without pride or hatred, but not without many regrets; he only knows that the power confided to me has never been made subservient to my personal good or to any useless cause. Oh, great city, it is in thy palpitating bosom that I have found that which I sought; like a patient miner, I have dug deep into thy very entrails to root out evil thence. Now my work is accomplished, my mission is terminated, now thou canst neither afford me pain nor pleasure. Adieu, Paris, adieu!"

His look wandered over the vast plain like that of some genius of the night; he passed his hand over his brow, got into the carriage, the door was closed on him, and the vehicle quickly disappeared down the other side of the hill in a whirlwind of noise and dust.

Ten leagues were passed and not a single word was uttered.

Morrel was dreaming, and Monte Cristo was looking at the dreamer.

"Morrel," said the count to him at length, "do you repent having followed me?"

"No, count; but to leave Paris"—

"If I thought happiness might await you in Paris, Morrel, I would have left you there."

"Valentine reposes within the walls of Paris, and to leave Paris is like losing her a second time."

"Maximilian," said the count, "the friends that we have lost do not repose in the bosom of the earth, but are buried deep in our hearts, and it has been thus ordained that we may always be accompanied by them. I have two friends, who in this way never depart from me; the one who gave me being, and the other who conferred knowledge and intelligence on me. Their spirits live in me. I consult them when doubtful, and if I ever do any good, it is due to their beneficent counsels. Listen to the voice of your heart, Morrel, and ask it whether you ought to preserve this melancholy exterior towards me."

"My friend," said Maximilian, "the voice of my heart is very sorrowful, and promises me nothing but misfortune."

"It is the way of weakened minds to see everything through a black cloud. The soul forms its own horizons; your soul is darkened, and consequently the sky of the future appears stormy and unpromising."

"That may possibly be true," said Maximilian, and he again subsided into his thoughtful mood.

The journey was performed with that marvellous rapidity which the unlimited power of the count ever commanded. Towns fled from them like shadows on their path, and trees shaken by the first winds of autumn seemed like giants madly rushing on to meet them, and retreating as rapidly when once reached. The following morning they arrived at Chalons, where the count's steamboat waited for them. Without the loss of an instant, the carriage was placed on board and the two travellers embarked without delay. The boat was built for speed; her two paddle-wheels were like two wings with which she skimmed the water like a bird. Morrel was not insensible to that sensation of delight which is generally experienced in passing rapidly through the air, and the wind which occasionally raised the hair from his forehead seemed on the point of dispelling momentarily the clouds collected there.

As the distance increased between the travellers and Paris, almost superhuman serenity appeared to surround the count; he might have been taken for an exile about to revisit his native land. Ere long Marseilles presented herself to view,—Marseilles, white, fervid, full of life and energy,—Marseilles, the younger sister of Tyre and Carthage, the successor to them in the empire of the Mediterranean,—Marseilles, old, yet always young. Powerful memories were stirred within them by the sight of the round tower, Fort Saint-Nicolas, the City Hall designed by Puget, [*] the port with its brick quays, where they had both played in childhood, and it was with one accord that they stopped on the Cannebiere. A vessel was setting sail for Algiers, on board of which the bustle usually attending departure prevailed. The passengers and their relations crowded on the deck, friends taking a tender but sorrowful leave of each other, some weeping, others noisy in their grief, the whole forming a spectacle that might be exciting even to those who witnessed similar sights daily, but which had no power to disturb the current of thought that had taken possession of the mind of Maximilian from the moment he had set foot on the broad pavement of the quay.

* Pierre Puget, the sculptor-architect, was born at Marseilles in 1622.

"Here," said he, leaning heavily on the arm of Monte Cristo,—"here is the spot where my father stopped, when the Pharaon entered the port; it was here that the good old man, whom you saved from death and dishonor, threw himself into my arms. I yet feel his warm tears on my face, and his were not the only tears shed, for many who witnessed our meeting wept also." Monte Cristo gently smiled and said,— "I was there;" at the same time pointing to the corner of a street. As he spoke, and in the very direction he indicated, a groan, expressive of bitter grief, was heard, and a woman was seen waving her hand to a passenger on board the vessel about to sail. Monte Cristo looked at her with an emotion that must have been remarked by Morrel had not his eyes been fixed on the vessel.

"Oh, heavens!" exclaimed Morrel, "I do not deceive myself—that young man who is waving his hat, that youth in the uniform of a lieutenant, is Albert de Morcerf!"

"Yes," said Monte Cristo, "I recognized him."

"How so?—you were looking the other way." the Count smiled, as he was in the habit of doing when he did not want to make any reply, and he again turned towards the veiled woman, who soon disappeared at the corner of the street. Turning to his friend,—"Dear Maximilian," said the count, "have you nothing to do in this land?"

"I have to weep over the grave of my father," replied Morrel in a broken voice.

"Well, then, go,—wait for me there, and I will soon join you."

"You leave me, then?"

"Yes; I also have a pious visit to pay."

Morrel allowed his hand to fall into that which the count extended to him; then with an inexpressibly sorrowful inclination of the head he quitted the count and bent his steps to the east of the city. Monte Cristo remained on the same spot until Maximilian was out of sight; he then walked slowly towards the Allees de Meillan to seek out a small house with which our readers were made familiar at the beginning of this story. It yet stood, under the shade of the fine avenue of lime-trees, which forms one of the most frequent walks of the idlers of Marseilles, covered by an immense vine, which spreads its aged and blackened branches over the stone front, burnt yellow by the ardent sun of the south. Two stone steps worn away by the friction of many feet led to the door, which was made of three planks; the door had never been painted or varnished, so great cracks yawned in it during the dry season to close again when the rains came on. The house, with all its crumbling antiquity and apparent misery, was yet cheerful and picturesque, and was the same that old Dantes formerly inhabited—the only difference being that the old man occupied merely the garret, while the whole house was now placed at the command of Mercedes by the count.

The woman whom the count had seen leave the ship with so much regret entered this house; she had scarcely closed the door after her when Monte Cristo appeared at the corner of a street, so that he found and lost her again almost at the same instant. The worn out steps were old acquaintances of his; he knew better than any one else how to open that weather-beaten door with the large headed nail which served to raise the latch within. He entered without knocking, or giving any other intimation of his presence, as if he had been a friend or the master of the place. At the end of a passage paved with bricks, was a little garden, bathed in sunshine, and rich in warmth and light. In this garden Mercedes had found, at the place indicated by the count, the sum of money which he, through a sense of delicacy, had described as having been placed there twenty-four years previously. The trees of the garden were easily seen from the steps of the street-door. Monte Cristo, on stepping into the house, heard a sigh that was almost a deep sob; he looked in the direction whence it came, and there under an arbor of Virginia jessamine, [*] with its thick foliage and beautiful long purple flowers, he saw Mercedes seated, with her head bowed, and weeping bitterly. She had raised her veil, and with her face hidden by her hands was giving free scope to the sighs and tears which had been so long restrained by the presence of her son. Monte Cristo advanced a few steps, which were heard on the gravel. Mercedes raised her head, and uttered a cry of terror on beholding a man before her.

* The Carolina—not Virginia—jessamine, gelsemium sempervirens (properly speaking not a jessamine at all) has yellow blossoms. The reference is no doubt to the Wistaria frutescens.—Ed.

"Madame," said the count, "it is no longer in my power to restore you to happiness, but I offer you consolation; will you deign to accept it as coming from a friend?"

"I am, indeed, most wretched," replied Mercedes. "Alone in the world, I had but my son, and he has left me!"

"He possesses a noble heart, madame," replied the count, "and he has acted rightly. He feels that every man owes a tribute to his country; some contribute their talents, others their industry; these devote their blood, those their nightly labors, to the same cause. Had he remained with you, his life must have become a hateful burden, nor would he have participated in your griefs. He will increase in strength and honor by struggling with adversity, which he will convert into prosperity. Leave him to build up the future for you, and I venture to say you will confide it to safe hands."

"Oh," replied the wretched woman, mournfully shaking her head, "the prosperity of which you speak, and which, from the bottom of my heart, I pray God in his mercy to grant him, I can never enjoy. The bitter cup of adversity has been drained by me to the very dregs, and I feel that the grave is not far distant. You have acted kindly, count, in bringing me back to the place where I have enjoyed so much bliss. I ought to meet death on the same spot where happiness was once all my own."

"Alas," said Monte Cristo, "your words sear and embitter my heart, the more so as you have every reason to hate me. I have been the cause of all your misfortunes; but why do you pity, instead of blaming me? You render me still more unhappy"—

"Hate you, blame you—you, Edmond! Hate, reproach, the man that has spared my son's life! For was it not your fatal and sanguinary intention to destroy that son of whom M. de Morcerf was so proud? Oh, look at me closely, and discover if you can even the semblance of a reproach in me." The count looked up and fixed his eyes on Mercedes, who arose partly from her seat and extended both her hands towards him. "Oh, look at me," continued she, with a feeling of profound melancholy, "my eyes no longer dazzle by their brilliancy, for the time has long fled since I used to smile on Edmond Dantes, who anxiously looked out for me from the window of yonder garret, then inhabited by his old father. Years of grief have created an abyss between those days and the present. I neither reproach you nor hate you, my friend. Oh, no, Edmond, it is myself that I blame, myself that I hate! Oh, miserable creature that I am!" cried she, clasping her hands, and raising her eyes to heaven. "I once possessed piety, innocence, and love, the three ingredients of the happiness of angels, and now what am I?" Monte Cristo approached her, and silently took her hand. "No," said she, withdrawing it gently—"no, my friend, touch me not. You have spared me, yet of all those who have fallen under your vengeance I was the most guilty. They were influenced by hatred, by avarice, and by self-love; but I was base, and for want of courage acted against my judgment. Nay, do not press my hand, Edmond; you are thinking, I am sure, of some kind speech to console me, but do not utter it to me, reserve it for others more worthy of your kindness. See" (and she exposed her face completely to view)—"see, misfortune has silvered my hair, my eyes have shed so many tears that they are encircled by a rim of purple, and my brow is wrinkled. You, Edmond, on the contrary,—you are still young, handsome, dignified; it is because you have had faith; because you have had strength, because you have had trust in God, and God has sustained you. But as for me, I have been a coward; I have denied God and he has abandoned me."

Mercedes burst into tears; her woman's heart was breaking under its load of memories. Monte Cristo took her hand and imprinted a kiss on it; but she herself felt that it was a kiss of no greater warmth than he would have bestowed on the hand of some marble statue of a saint. "It often happens," continued she, "that a first fault destroys the prospects of a whole life. I believed you dead; why did I survive you? What good has it done me to mourn for you eternally in the secret recesses of my heart?—only to make a woman of thirty-nine look like a woman of fifty. Why, having recognized you, and I the only one to do so—why was I able to save my son alone? Ought I not also to have rescued the man that I had accepted for a husband, guilty though he were? Yet I let him die! What do I say? Oh, merciful heavens, was I not accessory to his death by my supine insensibility, by my contempt for him, not remembering, or not willing to remember, that it was for my sake he had become a traitor and a perjurer? In what am I benefited by accompanying my son so far, since I now abandon him, and allow him to depart alone to the baneful climate of Africa? Oh, I have been base, cowardly, I tell you; I have abjured my affections, and like all renegades I am of evil omen to those who surround me!"

"No, Mercedes," said Monte Cristo, "no; you judge yourself with too much severity. You are a noble-minded woman, and it was your grief that disarmed me. Still I was but an agent, led on by an invisible and offended Deity, who chose not to withhold the fatal blow that I was destined to hurl. I take that God to witness, at whose feet I have prostrated myself daily for the last ten years, that I would have sacrificed my life to you, and with my life the projects that were indissolubly linked with it. But—and I say it with some pride, Mercedes—God needed me, and I lived. Examine the past and the present, and endeavor to dive into futurity, and then say whether I am not a divine instrument. The most dreadful misfortunes, the most frightful sufferings, the abandonment of all those who loved me, the persecution of those who did not know me, formed the trials of my youth; when suddenly, from captivity, solitude, misery, I was restored to light and liberty, and became the possessor of a fortune so brilliant, so unbounded, so unheard-of, that I must have been blind not to be conscious that God had endowed me with it to work out his own great designs. From that time I looked upon this fortune as something confided to me for an especial purpose. Not a thought was given to a life which you once, Mercedes, had the power to render blissful; not one hour of peaceful calm was mine; but I felt myself driven on like an exterminating angel. Like adventurous captains about to embark on some enterprise full of danger, I laid in my provisions, I loaded my weapons, I collected every means of attack and defence; I inured my body to the most violent exercises, my soul to the bitterest trials; I taught my arm to slay, my eyes to behold excruciating sufferings, and my mouth to smile at the most horrid spectacles. Good-natured, confiding, and forgiving as I had been, I became revengeful, cunning, and wicked, or rather, immovable as fate. Then I launched out into the path that was opened to me. I overcame every obstacle, and reached the goal; but woe to those who stood in my pathway!"

"Enough," said Mercedes; "enough, Edmond! Believe me, that she who alone recognized you has been the only one to comprehend you; and had she crossed your path, and you had crushed her like glass, still, Edmond, still she must have admired you! Like the gulf between me and the past, there is an abyss between you, Edmond, and the rest of mankind; and I tell you freely that the comparison I draw between you and other men will ever be one of my greatest tortures. No, there is nothing in the world to resemble you in worth and goodness! But we must say farewell, Edmond, and let us part."

"Before I leave you, Mercedes, have you no request to make?" said the count.

"I desire but one thing in this world, Edmond,—the happiness of my son."

"Pray to the Almighty to spare his life, and I will take upon myself to promote his happiness."

"Thank you, Edmond."

"But have you no request to make for yourself, Mercedes?"

"For myself I want nothing. I live, as it were, between two graves. One is that of Edmond Dantes, lost to me long, long since. He had my love! That word ill becomes my faded lip now, but it is a memory dear to my heart, and one that I would not lose for all that the world contains. The other grave is that of the man who met his death from the hand of Edmond Dantes. I approve of the deed, but I must pray for the dead."

"Your son shall be happy, Mercedes," repeated the count.

"Then I shall enjoy as much happiness as this world can possibly confer."

"But what are your intentions?"

"To say that I shall live here, like the Mercedes of other times, gaining my bread by labor, would not be true, nor would you believe me. I have no longer the strength to do anything but to spend my days in prayer. However, I shall have no occasion to work, for the little sum of money buried by you, and which I found in the place you mentioned, will be sufficient to maintain me. Rumor will probably be busy respecting me, my occupations, my manner of living—that will signify but little."

"Mercedes," said the count, "I do not say it to blame you, but you made an unnecessary sacrifice in relinquishing the whole of the fortune amassed by M. de Morcerf; half of it at least by right belonged to you, in virtue of your vigilance and economy."

"I perceive what you are intending to propose to me; but I cannot accept it, Edmond—my son would not permit it."

"Nothing shall be done without the full approbation of Albert de Morcerf. I will make myself acquainted with his intentions and will submit to them. But if he be willing to accept my offers, will you oppose them?"

"You well know, Edmond, that I am no longer a reasoning creature; I have no will, unless it be the will never to decide. I have been so overwhelmed by the many storms that have broken over my head, that I am become passive in the hands of the Almighty, like a sparrow in the talons of an eagle. I live, because it is not ordained for me to die. If succor be sent to me, I will accept it."

"Ah, madame," said Monte Cristo, "you should not talk thus! It is not so we should evince our resignation to the will of heaven; on the contrary, we are all free agents."

"Alas!" exclaimed Mercedes, "if it were so, if I possessed free-will, but without the power to render that will efficacious, it would drive me to despair." Monte Cristo dropped his head and shrank from the vehemence of her grief. "Will you not even say you will see me again?" he asked.

"On the contrary, we shall meet again," said Mercedes, pointing to heaven with solemnity. "I tell you so to prove to you that I still hope." And after pressing her own trembling hand upon that of the count, Mercedes rushed up the stairs and disappeared. Monte Cristo slowly left the house and turned towards the quay. But Mercedes did not witness his departure, although she was seated at the little window of the room which had been occupied by old Dantes. Her eyes were straining to see the ship which was carrying her son over the vast sea; but still her voice involuntarily murmured softly, "Edmond, Edmond, Edmond!"

CHAPTER 113.
THE PAST.

The count departed with a sad heart from the house in which he had left Mercedes, probably never to behold her again. Since the death of little Edward a great change had taken place in Monte Cristo. Having reached the summit of his vengeance by a long and tortuous path, he saw an abyss of doubt yawning before him. More than this, the conversation which had just taken place between Mercedes and himself had awakened so many recollections in his heart that he felt it necessary to combat with them. A man of the count's temperament could not long indulge in that melancholy which can exist in common minds, but which destroys superior ones. He thought he must have made an error in his calculations if he now found cause to blame himself.

"I cannot have deceived myself," he said; "I must look upon the past in a false light. What!" he continued, "can I have been following a false path?—can the end which I proposed be a mistaken end?—can one hour have sufficed to prove to an architect that the work upon which he founded all his hopes was an impossible, if not a sacrilegious, undertaking? I cannot reconcile myself to this idea—it would madden me. The reason why I am now dissatisfied is that I have not a clear appreciation of the past. The past, like the country through which we walk, becomes indistinct as we advance. My position is like that of a person wounded in a dream; he feels the wound, though he cannot recollect when he received it. Come, then, thou regenerate man, thou extravagant prodigal, thou awakened sleeper, thou all-powerful visionary, thou invincible millionaire,—once again review thy past life of starvation and wretchedness, revisit the scenes where fate and misfortune conducted, and where despair received thee. Too many diamonds, too much gold and splendor, are now reflected by the mirror in which Monte Cristo seeks to behold Dantes. Hide thy diamonds, bury thy gold, shroud thy splendor, exchange riches for poverty, liberty for a prison, a living body for a corpse!" As he thus reasoned, Monte Cristo walked down the Rue de la Caisserie. It was the same through which, twenty-four years ago, he had been conducted by a silent and nocturnal guard; the houses, to-day so smiling and animated, were on that night dark, mute, and closed. "And yet they were the same," murmured Monte Cristo, "only now it is broad daylight instead of night; it is the sun which brightens the place, and makes it appear so cheerful."

He proceeded towards the quay by the Rue Saint-Laurent, and advanced to the Consigne; it was the point where he had embarked. A pleasure-boat with striped awning was going by. Monte Cristo called the owner, who immediately rowed up to him with the eagerness of a boatman hoping for a good fare. The weather was magnificent, and the excursion a treat.

The sun, red and flaming, was sinking into the embrace of the welcoming ocean. The sea, smooth as crystal, was now and then disturbed by the leaping of fish, which were pursued by some unseen enemy and sought for safety in another element; while on the extreme verge of the horizon might be seen the fishermen's boats, white and graceful as the sea-gull, or the merchant vessels bound for Corsica or Spain.

But notwithstanding the serene sky, the gracefully formed boats, and the golden light in which the whole scene was bathed, the Count of Monte Cristo, wrapped in his cloak, could think only of this terrible voyage, the details of which were one by one recalled to his memory. The solitary light burning at the Catalans; that first sight of the Chateau d'If, which told him whither they were leading him; the struggle with the gendarmes when he wished to throw himself overboard; his despair when he found himself vanquished, and the sensation when the muzzle of the carbine touched his forehead—all these were brought before him in vivid and frightful reality. Like the streams which the heat of the summer has dried up, and which after the autumnal storms gradually begin oozing drop by drop, so did the count feel his heart gradually fill with the bitterness which formerly nearly overwhelmed Edmond Dantes. Clear sky, swift-flitting boats, and brilliant sunshine disappeared; the heavens were hung with black, and the gigantic structure of the Chateau d'If seemed like the phantom of a mortal enemy. As they reached the shore, the count instinctively shrunk to the extreme end of the boat, and the owner was obliged to call out, in his sweetest tone of voice, "Sir, we are at the landing."

Monte Cristo remembered that on that very spot, on the same rock, he had been violently dragged by the guards, who forced him to ascend the slope at the points of their bayonets. The journey had seemed very long to Dantes, but Monte Cristo found it equally short. Each stroke of the oar seemed to awaken a new throng of ideas, which sprang up with the flying spray of the sea.

There had been no prisoners confined in the Chateau d'If since the revolution of July; it was only inhabited by a guard, kept there for the prevention of smuggling. A concierge waited at the door to exhibit to visitors this monument of curiosity, once a scene of terror. The count inquired whether any of the ancient jailers were still there; but they had all been pensioned, or had passed on to some other employment. The concierge who attended him had only been there since 1830. He visited his own dungeon. He again beheld the dull light vainly endeavoring to penetrate the narrow opening. His eyes rested upon the spot where had stood his bed, since then removed, and behind the bed the new stones indicated where the breach made by the Abbe Faria had been. Monte Cristo felt his limbs tremble; he seated himself upon a log of wood.

"Are there any stories connected with this prison besides the one relating to the poisoning of Mirabeau?" asked the count; "are there any traditions respecting these dismal abodes,—in which it is difficult to believe men can ever have imprisoned their fellow-creatures?"

"Yes, sir; indeed, the jailer Antoine told me one connected with this very dungeon."

Monte Cristo shuddered; Antoine had been his jailer. He had almost forgotten his name and face, but at the mention of the name he recalled his person as he used to see it, the face encircled by a beard, wearing the brown jacket, the bunch of keys, the jingling of which he still seemed to hear. The count turned around, and fancied he saw him in the corridor, rendered still darker by the torch carried by the concierge. "Would you like to hear the story, sir?"

"Yes; relate it," said Monte Cristo, pressing his hand to his heart to still its violent beatings; he felt afraid of hearing his own history.

"This dungeon," said the concierge, "was, it appears, some time ago occupied by a very dangerous prisoner, the more so since he was full of industry. Another person was confined in the Chateau at the same time, but he was not wicked, he was only a poor mad priest."

"Ah, indeed?—mad!" repeated Monte Cristo; "and what was his mania?"

"He offered millions to any one who would set him at liberty."

Monte Cristo raised his eyes, but he could not see the heavens; there was a stone veil between him and the firmament. He thought that there had been no less thick a veil before the eyes of those to whom Faria offered the treasures. "Could the prisoners see each other?" he asked.

"Oh, no, sir, it was expressly forbidden; but they eluded the vigilance of the guards, and made a passage from one dungeon to the other."

"And which of them made this passage?"

"Oh, it must have been the young man, certainly, for he was strong and industrious, while the abbe was aged and weak; besides, his mind was too vacillating to allow him to carry out an idea."

"Blind fools!" murmured the count.

"However, be that as it may, the young man made a tunnel, how or by what means no one knows; but he made it, and there is the evidence yet remaining of his work. Do you see it?" and the man held the torch to the wall.

"Ah, yes; I see," said the count, in a voice hoarse from emotion.

"The result was that the two men communicated with one another; how long they did so, nobody knows. One day the old man fell ill and died. Now guess what the young one did?"

"Tell me."

"He carried off the corpse, which he placed in his own bed with its face to the wall; then he entered the empty dungeon, closed the entrance, and slipped into the sack which had contained the dead body. Did you ever hear of such an idea?" Monte Cristo closed his eyes, and seemed again to experience all the sensations he had felt when the coarse canvas, yet moist with the cold dews of death, had touched his face. The jailer continued: "Now this was his project. He fancied that they buried the dead at the Chateau d'If, and imagining they would not expend much labor on the grave of a prisoner, he calculated on raising the earth with his shoulders, but unfortunately their arrangements at the Chateau frustrated his projects. They never buried the dead; they merely attached a heavy cannon-ball to the feet, and then threw them into the sea. This is what was done. The young man was thrown from the top of the rock; the corpse was found on the bed next day, and the whole truth was guessed, for the men who performed the office then mentioned what they had not dared to speak of before, that at the moment the corpse was thrown into the deep, they heard a shriek, which was almost immediately stifled by the water in which it disappeared." The count breathed with difficulty; the cold drops ran down his forehead, and his heart was full of anguish.

"No," he muttered, "the doubt I felt was but the commencement of forgetfulness; but here the wound reopens, and the heart again thirsts for vengeance. And the prisoner," he continued aloud, "was he ever heard of afterwards?"

"Oh, no; of course not. You can understand that one of two things must have happened; he must either have fallen flat, in which case the blow, from a height of ninety feet, must have killed him instantly, or he must have fallen upright, and then the weight would have dragged him to the bottom, where he remained—poor fellow!"

"Then you pity him?" said the count.

"Ma foi, yes; though he was in his own element."

"What do you mean?"

"The report was that he had been a naval officer, who had been confined for plotting with the Bonapartists."

"Great is truth," muttered the count, "fire cannot burn, nor water drown it! Thus the poor sailor lives in the recollection of those who narrate his history; his terrible story is recited in the chimney-corner, and a shudder is felt at the description of his transit through the air to be swallowed by the deep." Then, the count added aloud, "Was his name ever known?"

"Oh, yes; but only as No. 34."

"Oh, Villefort, Villefort," murmured the count, "this scene must often have haunted thy sleepless hours!"

"Do you wish to see anything more, sir?" said the concierge.

"Yes, especially if you will show me the poor abbe's room."

"Ah—No. 27."

"Yes; No. 27." repeated the count, who seemed to hear the voice of the abbe answering him in those very words through the wall when asked his name.

"Come, sir."

"Wait," said Monte Cristo, "I wish to take one final glance around this room."

"This is fortunate," said the guide; "I have forgotten the other key."

"Go and fetch it."

"I will leave you the torch, sir."

"No, take it away; I can see in the dark."

"Why, you are like No. 34. They said he was so accustomed to darkness that he could see a pin in the darkest corner of his dungeon."

"He spent fourteen years to arrive at that," muttered the count.

The guide carried away the torch. The count had spoken correctly. Scarcely had a few seconds elapsed, ere he saw everything as distinctly as by daylight. Then he looked around him, and really recognized his dungeon.

"Yes," he said, "there is the stone upon which I used to sit; there is the impression made by my shoulders on the wall; there is the mark of my blood made when one day I dashed my head against the wall. Oh, those figures, how well I remember them! I made them one day to calculate the age of my father, that I might know whether I should find him still living, and that of Mercedes, to know if I should find her still free. After finishing that calculation, I had a minute's hope. I did not reckon upon hunger and infidelity!" and a bitter laugh escaped the count. He saw in fancy the burial of his father, and the marriage of Mercedes. On the other side of the dungeon he perceived an inscription, the white letters of which were still visible on the green wall. "'O God,'" he read, "'preserve my memory!' Oh, yes," he cried, "that was my only prayer at last; I no longer begged for liberty, but memory; I dreaded to become mad and forgetful. O God, thou hast preserved my memory; I thank thee, I thank thee!" At this moment the light of the torch was reflected on the wall; the guide was coming; Monte Cristo went to meet him.

"Follow me, sir;" and without ascending the stairs the guide conducted him by a subterraneous passage to another entrance. There, again, Monte Cristo was assailed by a multitude of thoughts. The first thing that met his eye was the meridian, drawn by the abbe on the wall, by which he calculated the time; then he saw the remains of the bed on which the poor prisoner had died. The sight of this, instead of exciting the anguish experienced by the count in the dungeon, filled his heart with a soft and grateful sentiment, and tears fell from his eyes.

"This is where the mad abbe was kept, sir, and that is where the young man entered;" and the guide pointed to the opening, which had remained unclosed. "From the appearance of the stone," he continued, "a learned gentleman discovered that the prisoners might have communicated together for ten years. Poor things! Those must have been ten weary years."

Dantes took some louis from his pocket, and gave them to the man who had twice unconsciously pitied him. The guide took them, thinking them merely a few pieces of little value; but the light of the torch revealed their true worth. "Sir," he said, "you have made a mistake; you have given me gold."

"I know it." The concierge looked upon the count with surprise. "Sir," he cried, scarcely able to believe his good fortune—"sir, I cannot understand your generosity!"

"Oh, it is very simple, my good fellow; I have been a sailor, and your story touched me more than it would others."

"Then, sir, since you are so liberal, I ought to offer you something."

"What have you to offer to me, my friend? Shells? Straw-work? Thank you!"

"No, sir, neither of those; something connected with this story."

"Really? What is it?"

"Listen," said the guide; "I said to myself, 'Something is always left in a cell inhabited by one prisoner for fifteen years,' so I began to sound the wall."

"Ah," cried Monte Cristo, remembering the abbe's two hiding-places.

"After some search, I found that the floor gave a hollow sound near the head of the bed, and at the hearth."

"Yes," said the count, "yes."

"I raised the stones, and found"—

"A rope-ladder and some tools?"

"How do you know that?" asked the guide in astonishment.

"I do not know—I only guess it, because that sort of thing is generally found in prisoners' cells."

"Yes, sir, a rope-ladder and tools."

"And have you them yet?"

"No, sir; I sold them to visitors, who considered them great curiosities; but I have still something left."

"What is it?" asked the count, impatiently.

"A sort of book, written upon strips of cloth."

"Go and fetch it, my good fellow; and if it be what I hope, you will do well."

"I will run for it, sir;" and the guide went out. Then the count knelt down by the side of the bed, which death had converted into an altar. "Oh, second father," he exclaimed, "thou who hast given me liberty, knowledge, riches; thou who, like beings of a superior order to ourselves, couldst understand the science of good and evil; if in the depths of the tomb there still remain something within us which can respond to the voice of those who are left on earth; if after death the soul ever revisit the places where we have lived and suffered,—then, noble heart, sublime soul, then I conjure thee by the paternal love thou didst bear me, by the filial obedience I vowed to thee, grant me some sign, some revelation! Remove from me the remains of doubt, which, if it change not to conviction, must become remorse!" The count bowed his head, and clasped his hands together.

"Here, sir," said a voice behind him.

Monte Cristo shuddered, and arose. The concierge held out the strips of cloth upon which the Abbe Faria had spread the riches of his mind. The manuscript was the great work by the Abbe Faria upon the kingdoms of Italy. The count seized it hastily, his eyes immediately fell upon the epigraph, and he read, "'Thou shalt tear out the dragons' teeth, and shall trample the lions under foot, saith the Lord.'"

"Ah," he exclaimed, "here is my answer. Thanks, father, thanks." And feeling in his pocket, he took thence a small pocket-book, which contained ten bank-notes, each of 1,000. francs.

"Here," he said, "take this pocket-book."

"Do you give it to me?"

"Yes; but only on condition that you will not open it till I am gone;" and placing in his breast the treasure he had just found, which was more valuable to him than the richest jewel, he rushed out of the corridor, and reaching his boat, cried, "To Marseilles!" Then, as he departed, he fixed his eyes upon the gloomy prison. "Woe," he cried, "to those who confined me in that wretched prison; and woe to those who forgot that I was there!" As he repassed the Catalans, the count turned around and burying his head in his cloak murmured the name of a woman. The victory was complete; twice he had overcome his doubts. The name he pronounced, in a voice of tenderness, amounting almost to love, was that of Haidee.

On landing, the count turned towards the cemetery, where he felt sure of finding Morrel. He, too, ten years ago, had piously sought out a tomb, and sought it vainly. He, who returned to France with millions, had been unable to find the grave of his father, who had perished from hunger. Morrel had indeed placed a cross over the spot, but it had fallen down and the grave-digger had burnt it, as he did all the old wood in the churchyard. The worthy merchant had been more fortunate. Dying in the arms of his children, he had been by them laid by the side of his wife, who had preceded him in eternity by two years. Two large slabs of marble, on which were inscribed their names, were placed on either side of a little enclosure, railed in, and shaded by four cypress-trees. Morrel was leaning against one of these, mechanically fixing his eyes on the graves. His grief was so profound that he was nearly unconscious. "Maximilian," said the count, "you should not look on the graves, but there;" and he pointed upwards.

"The dead are everywhere," said Morrel; "did you not yourself tell me so as we left Paris?"

"Maximilian," said the count, "you asked me during the journey to allow you to remain some days at Marseilles. Do you still wish to do so?"

"I have no wishes, count; only I fancy I could pass the time less painfully here than anywhere else."

"So much the better, for I must leave you; but I carry your word with me, do I not?"

"Ah, count, I shall forget it."

"No, you will not forget it, because you are a man of honor, Morrel, because you have taken an oath, and are about to do so again."

"Oh, count, have pity upon me. I am so unhappy."

"I have known a man much more unfortunate than you, Morrel."

"Impossible!"

"Alas," said Monte Cristo, "it is the infirmity of our nature always to believe ourselves much more unhappy than those who groan by our sides!"

"What can be more wretched than the man who has lost all he loved and desired in the world?"

"Listen, Morrel, and pay attention to what I am about to tell you. I knew a man who like you had fixed all his hopes of happiness upon a woman. He was young, he had an old father whom he loved, a betrothed bride whom he adored. He was about to marry her, when one of the caprices of fate,—which would almost make us doubt the goodness of providence, if that providence did not afterwards reveal itself by proving that all is but a means of conducting to an end,—one of those caprices deprived him of his mistress, of the future of which he had dreamed (for in his blindness he forgot he could only read the present), and cast him into a dungeon."

"Ah," said Morrel, "one quits a dungeon in a week, a month, or a year."

"He remained there fourteen years, Morrel," said the count, placing his hand on the young man's shoulder. Maximilian shuddered.

"Fourteen years!" he muttered—"Fourteen years!" repeated the count. "During that time he had many moments of despair. He also, Morrel, like you, considered himself the unhappiest of men."

"Well?" asked Morrel.

"Well, at the height of his despair God assisted him through human means. At first, perhaps, he did not recognize the infinite mercy of the Lord, but at last he took patience and waited. One day he miraculously left the prison, transformed, rich, powerful. His first cry was for his father; but that father was dead."

"My father, too, is dead," said Morrel.

"Yes; but your father died in your arms, happy, respected, rich, and full of years; his father died poor, despairing, almost doubtful of providence; and when his son sought his grave ten years afterwards, his tomb had disappeared, and no one could say, 'There sleeps the father you so well loved.'"

"Oh!" exclaimed Morrel.

"He was, then, a more unhappy son than you, Morrel, for he could not even find his father's grave."

"But then he had the woman he loved still remaining?"

"You are deceived, Morrel, that woman"—

"She was dead?"

"Worse than that, she was faithless, and had married one of the persecutors of her betrothed. You see, then, Morrel, that he was a more unhappy lover than you."

"And has he found consolation?"

"He has at least found peace."

"And does he ever expect to be happy?"

"He hopes so, Maximilian." The young man's head fell on his breast.

"You have my promise," he said, after a minute's pause, extending his hand to Monte Cristo. "Only remember"—

"On the 5th of October, Morrel, I shall expect you at the Island of Monte Cristo. On the 4th a yacht will wait for you in the port of Bastia, it will be called the Eurus. You will give your name to the captain, who will bring you to me. It is understood—is it not?"

"But, count, do you remember that the 5th of October"—

"Child," replied the count, "not to know the value of a man's word! I have told you twenty times that if you wish to die on that day, I will assist you. Morrel, farewell!"

"Do you leave me?"

"Yes; I have business in Italy. I leave you alone with your misfortunes, and with hope, Maximilian."

"When do you leave?"

"Immediately; the steamer waits, and in an hour I shall be far from you. Will you accompany me to the harbor, Maximilian?"

"I am entirely yours, count." Morrel accompanied the count to the harbor. The white steam was ascending like a plume of feathers from the black chimney. The steamer soon disappeared, and in an hour afterwards, as the count had said, was scarcely distinguishable in the horizon amidst the fogs of the night.

CHAPTER 114.
PEPPINO.

At the same time that the steamer disappeared behind Cape Morgion, a man travelling post on the road from Florence to Rome had just passed the little town of Aquapendente. He was travelling fast enough to cover a great deal of ground without exciting suspicion. This man was dressed in a greatcoat, or rather a surtout, a little worse for the journey, but which exhibited the ribbon of the Legion of Honor still fresh and brilliant, a decoration which also ornamented the under coat. He might be recognized, not only by these signs, but also from the accent with which he spoke to the postilion, as a Frenchman. Another proof that he was a native of the universal country was apparent in the fact of his knowing no other Italian words than the terms used in music, and which like the "goddam" of Figaro, served all possible linguistic requirements. "Allegro!" he called out to the postilions at every ascent. "Moderato!" he cried as they descended. And heaven knows there are hills enough between Rome and Florence by the way of Aquapendente! These two words greatly amused the men to whom they were addressed. On reaching La Storta, the point from whence Rome is first visible, the traveller evinced none of the enthusiastic curiosity which usually leads strangers to stand up and endeavor to catch sight of the dome of St. Peter's, which may be seen long before any other object is distinguishable. No, he merely drew a pocketbook from his pocket, and took from it a paper folded in four, and after having examined it in a manner almost reverential, he said—"Good! I have it still!"

The carriage entered by the Porto del Popolo, turned to the left, and stopped at the Hotel d'Espagne. Old Pastrini, our former acquaintance, received the traveller at the door, hat in hand. The traveller alighted, ordered a good dinner, and inquired the address of the house of Thomson & French, which was immediately given to him, as it was one of the most celebrated in Rome. It was situated in the Via dei Banchi, near St. Peter's. In Rome, as everywhere else, the arrival of a post-chaise is an event. Ten young descendants of Marius and the Gracchi, barefooted and out at elbows, with one hand resting on the hip and the other gracefully curved above the head, stared at the traveller, the post-chaise, and the horses; to these were added about fifty little vagabonds from the Papal States, who earned a pittance by diving into the Tiber at high water from the bridge of St. Angelo. Now, as these street Arabs of Rome, more fortunate than those of Paris, understand every language, more especially the French, they heard the traveller order an apartment, a dinner, and finally inquire the way to the house of Thomson & French. The result was that when the new-comer left the hotel with the cicerone, a man detached himself from the rest of the idlers, and without having been seen by the traveller, and appearing to excite no attention from the guide, followed the stranger with as much skill as a Parisian police agent would have used.

The Frenchman had been so impatient to reach the house of Thomson & French that he would not wait for the horses to be harnessed, but left word for the carriage to overtake him on the road, or to wait for him at the bankers' door. He reached it before the carriage arrived. The Frenchman entered, leaving in the anteroom his guide, who immediately entered into conversation with two or three of the industrious idlers who are always to be found in Rome at the doors of banking-houses, churches, museums, or theatres. With the Frenchman, the man who had followed him entered too; the Frenchman knocked at the inner door, and entered the first room; his shadow did the same.

"Messrs. Thomson & French?" inquired the stranger.

An attendant arose at a sign from a confidential clerk at the first desk. "Whom shall I announce?" said the attendant.

"Baron Danglars."

"Follow me," said the man. A door opened, through which the attendant and the baron disappeared. The man who had followed Danglars sat down on a bench. The clerk continued to write for the next five minutes; the man preserved profound silence, and remained perfectly motionless. Then the pen of the clerk ceased to move over the paper; he raised his head, and appearing to be perfectly sure of privacy,—"Ah, ha," he said, "here you are, Peppino!"

"Yes," was the laconic reply. "You have found out that there is something worth having about this large gentleman?"

"There is no great merit due to me, for we were informed of it."

"You know his business here, then."

"Pardieu, he has come to draw, but I don't know how much!"

"You will know presently, my friend."

"Very well, only do not give me false information as you did the other day."

"What do you mean?—of whom do you speak? Was it the Englishman who carried off 3,000 crowns from here the other day?"

"No; he really had 3,000 crowns, and we found them. I mean the Russian prince, who you said had 30,000 livres, and we only found 22,000."

"You must have searched badly."

"Luigi Vampa himself searched."

"Indeed? But you must let me make my observations, or the Frenchman will transact his business without my knowing the sum." Peppino nodded, and taking a rosary from his pocket began to mutter a few prayers while the clerk disappeared through the same door by which Danglars and the attendant had gone out. At the expiration of ten minutes the clerk returned with a beaming countenance. "Well?" asked Peppino of his friend.

"Joy, joy—the sum is large!"

"Five or six millions, is it not?"

"Yes, you know the amount."

"On the receipt of the Count of Monte Cristo?"

"Why, how came you to be so well acquainted with all this?"

"I told you we were informed beforehand."

"Then why do you apply to me?"

"That I may be sure I have the right man."

"Yes, it is indeed he. Five millions—a pretty sum, eh, Peppino?"

"Hush—here is our man!" The clerk seized his pen, and Peppino his beads; one was writing and the other praying when the door opened. Danglars looked radiant with joy; the banker accompanied him to the door. Peppino followed Danglars.

According to the arrangements, the carriage was waiting at the door. The guide held the door open. Guides are useful people, who will turn their hands to anything. Danglars leaped into the carriage like a young man of twenty. The cicerone reclosed the door, and sprang up by the side of the coachman. Peppino mounted the seat behind.

"Will your excellency visit St. Peter's?" asked the cicerone.

"I did not come to Rome to see," said Danglars aloud; then he added softly, with an avaricious smile, "I came to touch!" and he rapped his pocket-book, in which he had just placed a letter.

"Then your excellency is going"—

"To the hotel."

"Casa Pastrini!" said the cicerone to the coachman, and the carriage drove rapidly on. Ten minutes afterwards the baron entered his apartment, and Peppino stationed himself on the bench outside the door of the hotel, after having whispered something in the ear of one of the descendants of Marius and the Gracchi whom we noticed at the beginning of the chapter, who immediately ran down the road leading to the Capitol at his fullest speed. Danglars was tired and sleepy; he therefore went to bed, placing his pocketbook under his pillow. Peppino had a little spare time, so he had a game of mora with the facchini, lost three crowns, and then to console himself drank a bottle of Orvieto.

The next morning Danglars awoke late, though he went to bed so early; he had not slept well for five or six nights, even if he had slept at all. He breakfasted heartily, and caring little, as he said, for the beauties of the Eternal

City, ordered post-horses at noon. But Danglars had not reckoned upon the formalities of the police and the idleness of the posting-master. The horses only arrived at two o'clock, and the cicerone did not bring the passport till three. All these preparations had collected a number of idlers round the door of Signor Pastrini's; the descendants of Marius and the Gracchi were also not wanting. The baron walked triumphantly through the crowd, who for the sake of gain styled him "your excellency." As Danglars had hitherto contented himself with being called a baron, he felt rather flattered at the title of excellency, and distributed a dozen silver coins among the beggars, who were ready, for twelve more, to call him "your highness."

"Which road?" asked the postilion in Italian. "The Ancona road," replied the baron. Signor Pastrini interpreted the question and answer, and the horses galloped off. Danglars intended travelling to Venice, where he would receive one part of his fortune, and then proceeding to Vienna, where he would find the rest, he meant to take up his residence in the latter town, which he had been told was a city of pleasure.

He had scarcely advanced three leagues out of Rome when daylight began to disappear. Danglars had not intended starting so late, or he would have remained; he put his head out and asked the postilion how long it would be before they reached the next town. "Non capisco" (do not understand), was the reply. Danglars bent his head, which he meant to imply, "Very well." The carriage again moved on. "I will stop at the first posting-house," said Danglars to himself.

He still felt the same self-satisfaction which he had experienced the previous evening, and which had procured him so good a night's rest. He was luxuriously stretched in a good English calash, with double springs; he was drawn by four good horses, at full gallop; he knew the relay to be at a distance of seven leagues. What subject of meditation could present itself to the banker, so fortunately become bankrupt?

Danglars thought for ten minutes about his wife in Paris; another ten minutes about his daughter travelling with Mademoiselle d'Armilly; the same period was given to his creditors, and the manner in which he intended spending their money; and then, having no subject left for contemplation, he shut his eyes, and fell asleep. Now and then a jolt more violent than the rest caused him to open his eyes; then he felt that he was still being carried with great rapidity over the same country, thickly strewn with broken aqueducts, which looked like granite giants petrified while running a race. But the night was cold, dull, and rainy, and it was much more pleasant for a traveller to remain in the warm carriage than to put his head out of the window to make inquiries of a postilion whose only answer was "Non capisco."

Danglars therefore continued to sleep, saying to himself that he would be sure to awake at the posting-house. The carriage stopped. Danglars fancied that they had reached the long-desired point; he opened his eyes and looked through the window, expecting to find himself in the midst of some town, or at least village; but he saw nothing except what seemed like a ruin, where three or four men went and came like shadows. Danglars waited a moment, expecting the postilion to come and demand payment with the termination of his stage. He intended taking advantage of the opportunity to make fresh inquiries of the new conductor; but the horses were unharnessed, and others put in their places, without any one claiming money from the traveller. Danglars, astonished, opened the door; but a strong hand pushed him back, and the carriage rolled on. The baron was completely roused. "Eh?" he said to the postilion, "eh, mio caro?"

This was another little piece of Italian the baron had learned from hearing his daughter sing Italian duets with Cavalcanti. But mio caro did not reply. Danglars then opened the window.

"Come, my friend," he said, thrusting his hand through the opening, "where are we going?"

"Dentro la testa!" answered a solemn and imperious voice, accompanied by a menacing gesture. Danglars thought dentro la testa meant, "Put in your head!" He was making rapid progress in Italian. He obeyed, not without some uneasiness, which, momentarily increasing, caused his mind, instead of being as unoccupied as it was when he began his journey, to fill with ideas which were very likely to keep a traveller awake, more especially one in such a situation as Danglars. His eyes acquired that quality which in the first moment of strong emotion enables them to see distinctly, and which afterwards fails from being too much taxed. Before we are alarmed, we see correctly; when we are alarmed, we see double; and when we have been alarmed, we see nothing but trouble. Danglars observed a man in a cloak galloping at the right hand of the carriage.

"Some gendarme!" he exclaimed. "Can I have been intercepted by French telegrams to the pontifical authorities?" He resolved to end his anxiety. "Where are you taking me?" he asked. "Dentro la testa," replied the same voice, with the same menacing accent.

Danglars turned to the left; another man on horseback was galloping on that side. "Decidedly," said Danglars, with the perspiration on his forehead, "I must be under arrest." And he threw himself back in the calash, not this time to sleep, but to think. Directly afterwards the moon rose. He then saw the great aqueducts, those stone phantoms which he had before remarked, only then they were on the right hand, now they were on the left. He understood that they had described a circle, and were bringing him back to Rome.

"Oh, unfortunate!" he cried, "they must have obtained my arrest." The carriage continued to roll on with frightful speed. An hour of terror elapsed, for every spot they passed showed that they were on the road back. At length he saw a dark mass, against which it seemed as if the carriage was about to dash; but the vehicle turned to one side, leaving the barrier behind and Danglars saw that it was one of the ramparts encircling Rome.

"Mon dieu!" cried Danglars, "we are not returning to Rome; then it is not justice which is pursuing me! Gracious heavens; another idea presents itself—what if they should be"—

His hair stood on end. He remembered those interesting stories, so little believed in Paris, respecting Roman bandits; he remembered the adventures that Albert de Morcerf had related when it was intended that he should marry Mademoiselle Eugenie. "They are robbers, perhaps," he muttered. Just then the carriage rolled on something harder than gravel road. Danglars hazarded a look on both sides of the road, and perceived monuments of a singular form, and his mind now recalled all the details Morcerf had related, and comparing them with his own situation, he felt sure that he must be on the Appian Way. On the left, in a sort of valley, he perceived a circular excavation. It was Caracalla's circus. On a word from the man who rode at the side of the carriage, it stopped. At the same time the door was opened. "Scendi!" exclaimed a commanding voice. Danglars instantly descended; although he did not yet speak Italian, he understood it very well. More dead than alive, he looked around him. Four men surrounded him, besides the postilion.

"Di qua," said one of the men, descending a little path leading out of the Appian Way. Danglars followed his guide without opposition, and had no occasion to turn around to see whether the three others were following him. Still it appeared as though they were stationed at equal distances from one another, like sentinels. After walking for about ten minutes, during which Danglars did not exchange a single word with his guide, he found himself between a hillock and a clump of high weeds; three men, standing silent, formed a triangle, of which he was the centre. He wished to speak, but his tongue refused to move. "Avanti!" said the same sharp and imperative voice.

This time Danglars had double reason to understand, for if the word and gesture had not explained the speaker's meaning, it was clearly expressed by the man walking behind him, who pushed him so rudely that he struck against the guide. This guide was our friend Peppino, who dashed into the thicket of high weeds, through a path which none but lizards or polecats could have imagined to be an open road. Peppino stopped before a pit overhung by thick hedges; the pit, half open, afforded a passage to the young man, who disappeared like the evil spirits in the fairy tales. The voice and gesture of the man who followed Danglars ordered him to do the same. There was no longer any doubt, the bankrupt was in the hands of Roman banditti. Danglars acquitted himself like a man placed between two dangerous positions, and who is rendered brave by fear. Notwithstanding his large stomach, certainly not intended to penetrate the fissures of the Campagna, he slid down like Peppino, and closing his eyes fell upon his feet. As he touched the ground, he opened his eyes. The path was wide, but dark. Peppino, who cared little for being recognized now that he was in his own territories, struck a light and lit a torch. Two other men descended after Danglars forming the rearguard, and pushing Danglars whenever he happened to stop, they came by a gentle declivity to the intersection of two corridors. The walls were hollowed out in sepulchres, one above the other, and which seemed in contrast with the white stones to open their large dark eyes, like those which we see on the faces of the dead. A sentinel struck the rings of his carbine against his left hand. "Who comes there?" he cried.

"A friend, a friend!" said Peppino; "but where is the captain?"

"There," said the sentinel, pointing over his shoulder to a spacious crypt, hollowed out of the rock, the lights from which shone into the passage through the large arched openings. "Fine spoil, captain, fine spoil!" said Peppino in Italian, and taking Danglars by the collar of his coat he dragged him to an opening resembling a door, through which they entered the apartment which the captain appeared to have made his dwelling-place.

"Is this the man?" asked the captain, who was attentively reading Plutarch's "Life of Alexander."

"Himself, captain—himself."

"Very well, show him to me." At this rather impertinent order, Peppino raised his torch to the face of Danglars, who hastily withdrew that he might not have his eyelashes burnt. His agitated features presented the appearance of pale and hideous terror. "The man is tired," said the captain, "conduct him to his bed."

"Oh," murmured Danglars, "that bed is probably one of the coffins hollowed in the wall, and the sleep I shall enjoy will be death from one of the poniards I see glistening in the darkness."

From their beds of dried leaves or wolf-skins at the back of the chamber now arose the companions of the man who had been found by Albert de Morcerf reading "Caesar's Commentaries," and by Danglars studying the "Life of Alexander." The banker uttered a groan and followed his guide; he neither supplicated nor exclaimed. He no longer possessed strength, will, power, or feeling; he followed where they led him. At length he found himself at the foot of a staircase, and he mechanically lifted his foot five or six times. Then a low door was opened before him, and bending his head to avoid striking his forehead he entered a small room cut out of the rock. The cell was clean, though empty, and dry, though situated at an immeasurable distance under the earth. A bed of dried grass covered with goat-skins was placed in one corner. Danglars brightened up on beholding it, fancying that it gave some promise of safety. "Oh, God be praised," he said; "it is a real bed!"

"Ecco!" said the guide, and pushing Danglars into the cell, he closed the door upon him. A bolt grated and Danglars was a prisoner. If there had been no bolt, it would have been impossible for him to pass through the midst of the garrison who held the catacombs of St. Sebastian, encamped round a master whom our readers must have recognized as the famous Luigi Vampa. Danglars, too, had recognized the bandit, whose existence he would not believe when Albert de Morcerf mentioned him in Paris; and not only did he recognize him, but the cell in which Albert had been confined, and which was probably kept for the accommodation of strangers. These recollections were dwelt upon with some pleasure by Danglars, and restored him to some degree of tranquillity. Since the bandits had not despatched him at once, he felt that they would not kill him at all. They had arrested him for the purpose of robbery, and as he had only a few louis about him, he doubted not he would be ransomed. He remembered that Morcerf had been taxed at 4,000 crowns, and as he considered himself of much greater importance than Morcerf he fixed his own price at 8,000 crowns. Eight thousand crowns amounted to 48,000 livres; he would then have about 5,050,000 francs left. With this sum he could manage to keep out of difficulties. Therefore, tolerably secure in being able to extricate himself from his position, provided he were not rated at the unreasonable sum of 5,050,000 francs, he stretched himself on his bed, and after turning over two or three times, fell asleep with the tranquillity of the hero whose life Luigi Vampa was studying.

CHAPTER 115.
LUIGI VAMPA'S BILL OF FARE.

We awake from every sleep except the one dreaded by Danglars. He awoke. To a Parisian accustomed to silken curtains, walls hung with velvet drapery, and the soft perfume of burning wood, the white smoke of which diffuses itself in graceful curves around the room, the appearance of the whitewashed cell which greeted his eyes on awakening seemed like the continuation of some disagreeable dream. But in such a situation a single moment suffices to change the strongest doubt into certainty. "Yes, yes," he murmured, "I am in the hands of the brigands of whom Albert de Morcerf spoke." His first idea was to breathe, that he might know whether he was wounded. He borrowed this from "Don Quixote," the only book he had ever read, but which he still slightly remembered.

"No," he cried, "they have not wounded, but perhaps they have robbed me!" and he thrust his hands into his pockets. They were untouched; the hundred louis he had reserved for his journey from Rome to Venice were in his trousers pocket, and in that of his great-coat he found the little note-case containing his letter of credit for 5,050,000 francs. "Singular bandits!" he exclaimed; "they have left me my purse and pocket-book. As I was saying last night, they

284

intend me to be ransomed. Hallo, here is my watch! Let me see what time it is." Danglars' watch, one of Breguet's repeaters, which he had carefully wound up on the previous night, struck half past five. Without this, Danglars would have been quite ignorant of the time, for daylight did not reach his cell. Should he demand an explanation from the bandits, or should he wait patiently for them to propose it? The last alternative seemed the most prudent, so he waited until twelve o'clock. During all this time a sentinel, who had been relieved at eight o'clock, had been watching his door. Danglars suddenly felt a strong inclination to see the person who kept watch over him. He had noticed that a few rays, not of daylight, but from a lamp, penetrated through the ill-joined planks of the door; he approached just as the brigand was refreshing himself with a mouthful of brandy, which, owing to the leathern bottle containing it, sent forth an odor which was extremely unpleasant to Danglars. "Faugh!" he exclaimed, retreating to the farther corner of his cell.

At twelve this man was replaced by another functionary, and Danglars, wishing to catch sight of his new guardian, approached the door again. He was an athletic, gigantic bandit, with large eyes, thick lips, and a flat nose; his red hair fell in dishevelled masses like snakes around his shoulders. "Ah, ha," cried Danglars, "this fellow is more like an ogre than anything else; however, I am rather too old and tough to be very good eating!" We see that Danglars was collected enough to jest; at the same time, as though to disprove the ogreish propensities, the man took some black bread, cheese, and onions from his wallet, which he began devouring voraciously. "May I be hanged," said Danglars, glancing at the bandit's dinner through the crevices of the door,—"may I be hanged if I can understand how people can eat such filth!" and he withdrew to seat himself upon his goat-skin, which reminded him of the smell of the brandy.

But the mysteries of nature are incomprehensible, and there are certain invitations contained in even the coarsest food which appeal very irresistibly to a fasting stomach. Danglars felt his own not to be very well supplied just then, and gradually the man appeared less ugly, the bread less black, and the cheese more fresh, while those dreadful vulgar onions recalled to his mind certain sauces and side-dishes, which his cook prepared in a very superior manner whenever he said, "Monsieur Deniseau, let me have a nice little fricassee to-day." He got up and knocked on the door; the bandit raised his head. Danglars knew that he was heard, so he redoubled his blows. "Che cosa?" asked the bandit. "Come, come," said Danglars, tapping his fingers against the door, "I think it is quite time to think of giving me something to eat!" But whether he did not understand him, or whether he had received no orders respecting the nourishment of Danglars, the giant, without answering, went on with his dinner. Danglars' feelings were hurt, and not wishing to put himself under obligations to the brute, the banker threw himself down again on his goat-skin and did not breathe another word.

Four hours passed by and the giant was replaced by another bandit. Danglars, who really began to experience sundry gnawings at the stomach, arose softly, again applied his eye to the crack of the door, and recognized the intelligent countenance of his guide. It was, indeed, Peppino who was preparing to mount guard as comfortably as possible by seating himself opposite to the door, and placing between his legs an earthen pan, containing chick-pease stewed with bacon. Near the pan he also placed a pretty little basket of Villetri grapes and a flask of Orvieto. Peppino was decidedly an epicure. Danglars watched these preparations and his mouth watered. "Come," he said to himself, "let me try if he will be more tractable than the other;" and he tapped gently at the door. "On y va," (coming) exclaimed Peppino, who from frequenting the house of Signor Pastrini understood French perfectly in all its idioms.

Danglars immediately recognized him as the man who had called out in such a furious manner, "Put in your head!" But this was not the time for recrimination, so he assumed his most agreeable manner and said with a gracious smile,—"Excuse me, sir, but are they not going to give me any dinner?"

"Does your excellency happen to be hungry?"

"Happen to be hungry,—that's pretty good, when I haven't eaten for twenty-four hours!" muttered Danglars. Then he added aloud, "Yes, sir, I am hungry—very hungry."

"What would your excellency like?" and Peppino placed his pan on the ground, so that the steam rose directly under the nostrils of Danglars. "Give your orders."

"Have you kitchens here?"

"Kitchens?—of course—complete ones."

"And cooks?"

"Excellent!"

"Well, a fowl, fish, game,—it signifies little, so that I eat."

"As your excellency pleases. You mentioned a fowl, I think?"

"Yes, a fowl." Peppino, turning around, shouted, "A fowl for his excellency!" His voice yet echoed in the archway when a handsome, graceful, and half-naked young man appeared, bearing a fowl in a silver dish on his head, without the assistance of his hands. "I could almost believe myself at the Cafe de Paris," murmured Danglars.

"Here, your excellency," said Peppino, taking the fowl from the young bandit and placing it on the worm-eaten table, which with the stool and the goat-skin bed formed the entire furniture of the cell. Danglars asked for a knife and fork. "Here, excellency," said Peppino, offering him a little intend me to be ransomed. Hallo, here is my watch! Let me see what time it is." Danglars' watch, one of Breguet's repeaters, which he had carefully wound up on the previous night, struck half past five. Without this, Danglars would have been quite ignorant of the time, for daylight did not reach his cell. Should he demand an explanation from the bandits, or should he wait patiently for them to propose it? The last alternative seemed the most prudent, so he waited until twelve o'clock. During all this time a sentinel, who had been relieved at eight o'clock, had been watching his door. Danglars suddenly felt a strong inclination to see the person who kept watch over him. He had noticed that a few rays, not of daylight, but from a lamp, penetrated through the ill-joined planks of the door; he approached just as the brigand was refreshing himself with a mouthful of brandy, which, owing to the leathern bottle containing it, sent forth an odor which was extremely unpleasant to Danglars. "Faugh!" he exclaimed, retreating to the farther corner of his cell.

At twelve this man was replaced by another functionary, and Danglars, wishing to catch sight of his new guardian, approached the door again. He was an athletic, gigantic bandit, with large eyes, thick lips, and a flat nose; his red hair fell in dishevelled masses like snakes around his shoulders. "Ah, ha," cried Danglars, "this fellow is more like an ogre than anything else; however, I am rather too old and tough to be very good eating!" We see that Danglars was collected enough to jest; at the same time, as though to disprove the ogreish propensities, the man took some black bread, cheese, and onions from his wallet, which he began devouring voraciously. "May I be hanged," said Danglars, glancing at the bandit's dinner through the crevices of the door,—"may I be hanged if I can understand how people can eat such filth!" and he withdrew to seat himself upon his goat-skin, which reminded him of the smell of the brandy.

But the mysteries of nature are incomprehensible, and there are certain invitations contained in even the coarsest food which appeal very irresistibly to a fasting stomach. Danglars felt his own not to be very well supplied just then, and gradually the man appeared less ugly, the bread less black, and the cheese more fresh, while those dreadful vulgar onions recalled to his mind certain sauces and side-dishes, which his cook prepared in a very superior manner whenever he said, "Monsieur Deniseau, let me have a nice little fricassee to-day." He got up and knocked on the door; the bandit raised his head. Danglars knew that he was heard, so he redoubled his blows. "Che cosa?" asked the bandit. "Come, come," said Danglars, tapping his fingers against the door, "I think it is quite time to think of giving me something to eat!" But whether he did not understand him, or whether he had received no orders respecting the nourishment of Danglars, the giant, without answering, went on with his dinner. Danglars' feelings were hurt, and

"Bread? Very well. Hallo, there, some bread!" he called. The youth brought a small loaf. "How much?" asked Danglars.

"Four thousand nine hundred and ninety-eight louis," said Peppino; "You have paid two louis in advance."

"What? One hundred thousand francs for a loaf?"

"One hundred thousand francs," repeated Peppino.

"But you only asked 100,000 francs for a fowl!"

"We have a fixed price for all our provisions. It signifies nothing whether you eat much or little—whether you have ten dishes or one—it is always the same price."

"What, still keeping up this silly jest? My dear fellow, it is perfectly ridiculous—stupid! You had better tell me at once that you intend starving me to death."

"Oh, dear, no, your excellency, unless you intend to commit suicide. Pay and eat."

"And what am I to pay with, brute?" said Danglars, enraged. "Do you suppose I carry 100,000 francs in my pocket?"

"Your excellency has 5,050,000 francs in your pocket; that will be fifty fowls at 100,000 francs apiece, and half a fowl for the 50,000."

Danglars shuddered. The bandage fell from his eyes, and he understood the joke, which he did not think quite so stupid as he had done just before. "Come," he said, "if I pay you the 100,000 francs, will you be satisfied, and allow me to eat at my ease?"

"Certainly," said Peppino.

"But how can I pay them?"

"Oh, nothing easier; you have an account open with Messrs. Thomson & French, Via dei Banchi, Rome; give me a draft for 4,998 louis on these gentlemen, and our banker shall take it." Danglars thought it as well to comply with a good grace, so he took the pen, ink, and paper Peppino offered him, wrote the draft, and signed it. "Here," he said, "here is a draft at sight."

"And here is your fowl." Danglars sighed while he carved the fowl; it appeared very thin for the price it had cost. As for Peppino, he examined the paper attentively, put it into his pocket, and continued eating his pease.

CHAPTER 116.
THE PARDON.

The next day Danglars was again hungry; certainly the air of that dungeon was very provocative of appetite. The prisoner expected that he would be at no expense that day, for like an economical man he had concealed half of his fowl and a piece of the bread in the corner of his cell. But he had no sooner eaten than he felt thirsty; he had forgotten that. He struggled against his thirst till his tongue clave to the roof of his mouth; then, no longer able to resist, he called out. The sentinel opened the door; it was a new face. He thought it would be better to transact business with his old acquaintance, so he sent for Peppino. "Here I am, your excellency," said Peppino, with an eagerness which Danglars thought favorable to him. "What do you want?"

"Something to drink."

"Your excellency knows that wine is beyond all price near Rome."

"Then give me water," cried Danglars, endeavoring to parry the blow.

"Oh, water is even more scarce than wine, your excellency,—there has been such a drought."

"Come," thought Danglars, "it is the same old story." And while he smiled as he attempted to regard the affair as a joke, he felt his temples get moist with perspiration.

"Come, my friend," said Danglars, seeing that he made no impression on Peppino, "you will not refuse me a glass of wine?"

"I have already told you that we do not sell at retail."

"Well, then, let me have a bottle of the least expensive."

"They are all the same price."

"And what is that?"

"Twenty-five thousand francs a bottle."

"Tell me," cried Danglars, in a tone whose bitterness Harpagon [*] alone has been capable of revealing—"tell me that you wish to despoil me of all; it will be sooner over than devouring me piecemeal."

* The miser in Moliere's comedy of "L'Avare."— Ed.

"It is possible such may be the master's intention."

"The master?—who is he?"

"The person to whom you were conducted yesterday."

"Where is he?"

"Here."

"Let me see him."

"Certainly." And the next moment Luigi Vampa appeared before Danglars.

"You sent for me?" he said to the prisoner.

"Are you, sir, the chief of the people who brought me here?"

"Yes, your excellency. What then?"

"How much do you require for my ransom?"

"Merely the 5,000,000 you have about you." Danglars felt a dreadful spasm dart through his heart. "But this is all I have left in the world," he said, "out of an immense fortune. If you deprive me of that, take away my life also."

"We are forbidden to shed your blood."

"And by whom are you forbidden?"

"By him we obey."

"You do, then, obey some one?"

"Yes, a chief."

"I thought you said you were the chief?"

"So I am of these men; but there is another over me."

"And did your superior order you to treat me in this way?"

"Yes."

"But my purse will be exhausted."

"Probably."

"Come," said Danglars, "will you take a million?"

"No."

"Two millions?—three?—four? Come, four? I will give them to you on condition that you let me go."

"Why do you offer me 4,000,000 for what is worth 5,000,000? This is a kind of usury, banker, that I do not understand."

"Take all, then—take all, I tell you, and kill me!"

"Come, come, calm yourself. You will excite your blood, and that would produce an appetite it would require a million a day to satisfy. Be more economical."

"But when I have no more money left to pay you?" asked the infuriated Danglars.

"Then you must suffer hunger."

"Suffer hunger?" said Danglars, becoming pale.

"Most likely," replied Vampa coolly.

"But you say you do not wish to kill me?"

"No."

"And yet you will let me perish with hunger?"

"Ah, that is a different thing."

"Well, then, wretches," cried Danglars, "I will defy your infamous calculations—I would rather die at once! You may torture, torment, kill me, but you shall not have my signature again!"

"As your excellency pleases," said Vampa, as he left the cell. Danglars, raving, threw himself on the goat-skin. Who could these men be? Who was the invisible chief? What could be his intentions towards him? And why, when every one else was allowed to be ransomed, might he not also be? Oh, yes; certainly a speedy, violent death would be a fine means of deceiving these remorseless enemies, who appeared to pursue him with such incomprehensible vengeance. But to die? For the first time in his life, Danglars contemplated death with a mixture of dread and desire; the time had come when the implacable spectre, which exists in the mind of every human creature, arrested his attention and called out with every pulsation of his heart, "Thou shalt die!"

Danglars resembled a timid animal excited in the chase; first it flies, then despairs, and at last, by the very force of desperation, sometimes succeeds in eluding its pursuers. Danglars meditated an escape; but the walls were solid rock, a man was sitting reading at the only outlet to the cell, and behind that man shapes armed with guns continually passed. His resolution not to sign lasted two days, after which he offered a million for some food. They sent him a magnificent supper, and took his million.

From this time the prisoner resolved to suffer no longer, but to have everything he wanted. At the end of twelve days, after having made a splendid dinner, he reckoned his accounts, and found that he had only 50,000 francs left. Then a strange reaction took place; he who had just abandoned 5,000,000 endeavored to save the 50,000 francs he had left, and sooner than give them up he resolved to enter again upon a life of privation—he was deluded by the hopefulness that is a premonition of madness. He who for so long a time had forgotten God, began to think that miracles were possible—that the accursed cavern might be discovered by the officers of the Papal States, who would release him; that then he would have 50,000 remaining, which would be sufficient to save him from starvation; and finally he prayed that this sum might be preserved to him, and as he prayed he wept. Three days passed thus, during which his prayers were frequent, if not heartfelt. Sometimes he was delirious, and fancied he saw an old man stretched on a pallet; he, also, was dying of hunger.

On the fourth, he was no longer a man, but a living corpse. He had picked up every crumb that had been left from his former meals, and was beginning to eat the matting which covered the floor of his cell. Then he entreated Peppino, as he would a guardian angel, to give him food; he offered him 1,000 francs for a mouthful of bread. But Peppino did not answer. On the fifth day he dragged himself to the door of the cell.

"Are you not a Christian?" he said, falling on his knees. "Do you wish to assassinate a man who, in the eyes of heaven, is a brother? Oh, my former friends, my former friends!" he murmured, and fell with his face to the ground. Then rising in despair, he exclaimed, "The chief, the chief!"

"Here I am," said Vampa, instantly appearing; "what do you want?"

"Take my last gold," muttered Danglars, holding out his pocket-book, "and let me live here; I ask no more for liberty—I only ask to live!"

"Then you suffer a great deal?"

"Oh, yes, yes, cruelly!"

"Still, there have been men who suffered more than you."

"I do not think so."

"Yes; those who have died of hunger."

Danglars thought of the old man whom, in his hours of delirium, he had seen groaning on his bed. He struck his forehead on the ground and groaned. "Yes," he said, "there have been some who have suffered more than I have, but then they must have been martyrs at least."

"Do you repent?" asked a deep, solemn voice, which caused Danglars' hair to stand on end. His feeble eyes endeavored to distinguish objects, and behind the bandit he saw a man enveloped in a cloak, half lost in the shadow of a stone column.

"Of what must I repent?" stammered Danglars.

"Of the evil you have done," said the voice.

"Oh, yes; oh, yes, I do indeed repent." And he struck his breast with his emaciated fist.

"Then I forgive you," said the man, dropping his cloak, and advancing to the light.

"The Count of Monte Cristo!" said Danglars, more pale from terror than he had been just before from hunger and misery.

"You are mistaken—I am not the Count of Monte Cristo."

"Then who are you?"

"I am he whom you sold and dishonored—I am he whose betrothed you prostituted—I am he upon whom you trampled that you might raise yourself to fortune—I am he whose father you condemned to die of hunger—I am he whom you also condemned to starvation, and who yet forgives you, because he hopes to be forgiven—I am Edmond Dantes!" Danglars uttered a cry, and fell prostrate. "Rise," said the count, "your life is safe; the same good fortune has not happened to your accomplices—one is mad, the other dead. Keep the 50,000 francs you have left—I give them to you. The 5,000,000 you stole from the hospitals has been restored to them by an unknown hand. And now eat and drink; I will entertain you to-night. Vampa, when this man is satisfied, let him be free." Danglars remained prostrate while the count withdrew; when he raised his head he saw disappearing down the passage nothing but a shadow, before which the bandits bowed. According to the count's directions, Danglars was waited on by Vampa, who brought him the best wine and fruits of Italy; then, having conducted him to the road, and pointed to the post-chaise, left him leaning against a tree. He remained there all night, not knowing where he was. When daylight dawned he saw that he was near a stream; he was thirsty, and dragged himself towards it. As he stooped down to drink, he saw that his hair had become entirely white.

CHAPTER 117.
THE FIFTH OF OCTOBER.

It was about six o'clock in the evening; an opal-colored light, through which an autumnal sun shed its golden rays, descended on the blue ocean. The heat of the day had gradually decreased, and a light breeze arose, seeming like the respiration of nature on awakening from the burning siesta of the south. A delicious zephyr played along the coasts of the Mediterranean, and wafted from shore to shore the sweet perfume of plants, mingled with the fresh smell of the sea.

A light yacht, chaste and elegant in its form, was gliding amidst the first dews of night over the immense lake, extending from Gibraltar to the Dardanelles, and from Tunis to Venice. The vessel resembled a swan with its wings opened towards the wind, gliding on the water. It advanced swiftly and gracefully, leaving behind it a glittering stretch of foam. By degrees the sun disappeared behind the western horizon; but as though to prove the truth of the fanciful ideas in heathen mythology, its indiscreet rays reappeared on the summit of every wave, as if the god of fire had just sunk upon the bosom of Amphitrite, who in vain endeavored to hide her lover beneath her azure mantle. The yacht moved rapidly on, though there did not appear to be sufficient wind to ruffle the curls on the head of a young girl. Standing on the prow was a tall man, of a dark complexion, who saw with dilating eyes that they were approaching a dark mass of land in the shape of a cone, which rose from the midst of the waves like the hat of a Catalan. "Is that Monte Cristo?" asked the traveller, to whose orders the yacht was for the time submitted, in a melancholy voice.

"Yes, your excellency," said the captain, "we have reached it."

"We have reached it!" repeated the traveller in an accent of indescribable sadness. Then he added, in a low tone, "Yes; that is the haven." And then he again plunged into a train of thought, the character of which was better revealed by a sad smile, than it would have been by tears. A few minutes afterwards a flash of light, which was extinguished instantly, was seen on the land, and the sound of firearms reached the yacht.

"Your excellency," said the captain, "that was the land signal, will you answer yourself?"

"What signal?" The captain pointed towards the island, up the side of which ascended a volume of smoke, increasing as it rose. "Ah, yes," he said, as if awaking from a dream. "Give it to me."

The captain gave him a loaded carbine; the traveller slowly raised it, and fired in the air. Ten minutes afterwards, the sails were furled, and they cast anchor about a hundred fathoms from the little harbor. The gig was already lowered, and in it were four oarsmen and a coxswain. The traveller descended, and instead of sitting down at the stern of the boat, which had been decorated with a blue carpet for his accommodation, stood up with his arms crossed. The rowers waited, their oars half lifted out of the water, like birds drying their wings.

"Give way," said the traveller. The eight oars fell into the sea simultaneously without splashing a drop of water, and the boat, yielding to the impulsion, glided forward. In an instant they found themselves in a little harbor, formed in a natural creek; the boat grounded on the fine sand.

"Will your excellency be so good as to mount the shoulders of two of our men, they will carry you ashore?" The young man answered this invitation with a gesture of indifference, and stepped out of the boat; the sea immediately rose to his waist. "Ah, your excellency," murmured the pilot, "you should not have done so; our master will scold us for it." The young man continued to advance, following the sailors, who chose a firm footing. Thirty strides brought them to dry land; the young man stamped on the ground to shake off the wet, and looked around for some one to show him his road, for it was quite dark. Just as he turned, a hand rested on his shoulder, and a voice which made him shudder exclaimed,—"Good-evening, Maximilian; you are punctual, thank you!"

"Ah, is it you, count?" said the young man, in an almost joyful accent, pressing Monte Cristo's hand with both his own.

"Yes; you see I am as exact as you are. But you are dripping, my dear fellow; you must change your clothes, as Calypso said to Telemachus. Come, I have a habitation prepared for you in which you will soon forget fatigue and cold." Monte Cristo perceived that the young man had turned around; indeed, Morrel saw with surprise that the men who had brought him had left without being paid, or uttering a word. Already the sound of their oars might be heard as they returned to the yacht.

"Oh, yes," said the count, "you are looking for the sailors."

"Yes, I paid them nothing, and yet they are gone."

"Never mind that, Maximilian," said Monte Cristo, smiling. "I have made an agreement with the navy, that the access to my island shall be free of all charge. I have made a bargain." Morrel looked at the count with surprise. "Count," he said, "you are not the same here as in Paris."

"How so?"

"Here you laugh." The count's brow became clouded. "You are right to recall me to myself, Maximilian," he said; "I was delighted to see you again, and forgot for the moment that all happiness is fleeting."

"Oh, no, no, count," cried Maximilian, seizing the count's hands, "pray laugh; be happy, and prove to me, by your indifference, that life is endurable to sufferers. Oh, how charitable, kind, and good you are; you affect this gayety to inspire me with courage."

"You are wrong, Morrel; I was really happy."

"Then you forget me, so much the better."

"How so?"

"Yes; for as the gladiator said to the emperor, when he entered the arena, 'He who is about to die salutes you.'"

"Then you are not consoled?" asked the count, surprised.

"Oh," exclaimed Morrel, with a glance full of bitter reproach, "do you think it possible that I could be?"

"Listen," said the count. "Do you understand the meaning of my words? You cannot take me for a commonplace man, a mere rattle, emitting a vague and senseless noise. When I ask you if you are consoled, I speak to you as a man for whom the human heart has no secrets. Well, Morrel, let us both examine the depths of your heart. Do you still feel the same feverish impatience of grief which made you start like a wounded lion? Have you still that devouring thirst which can only be appeased in the grave? Are you still actuated by the regret which drags the living to the pursuit of death; or are you only suffering from the prostration of fatigue and the weariness of hope deferred? Has the loss of memory rendered it impossible for you to weep? Oh, my dear friend, if this be the case,—if you can no longer weep, if your frozen heart be dead, if you put all your trust in God, then, Maximilian, you are consoled—do not complain."

"Count," said Morrel, in a firm and at the same time soft voice, "listen to me, as to a man whose thoughts are raised to heaven, though he remains on earth; I come to die in the arms of a friend. Certainly, there are people whom I love. I love my sister Julie,—I love her husband Emmanuel; but I require a strong mind to smile on my last moments. My sister would be bathed in tears and fainting; I could not bear to see her suffer. Emmanuel would tear the weapon from my hand, and alarm the house with his cries. You, count, who are more than mortal, will, I am sure, lead me to death by a pleasant path, will you not?"

"My friend," said the count, "I have still one doubt,—are you weak enough to pride yourself upon your sufferings?"

"No, indeed,—I am calm," said Morrel, giving his hand to the count; "my pulse does not beat slower or faster than usual. No, I feel that I have reached the goal, and I will go no farther. You told me to wait and hope; do you know what you did, unfortunate adviser? I waited a month, or rather I suffered for a month! I did hope (man is a poor wretched creature), I did hope. What I cannot tell,—something wonderful, an absurdity, a miracle,—of what nature he alone can tell who has mingled with our reason that folly we call hope. Yes, I did wait—yes, I did hope, count, and during this quarter of an hour we have been talking together, you have unconsciously wounded, tortured my heart, for every word you have uttered proved that there was no hope for me. Oh, count, I shall sleep calmly, deliciously in the arms of death." Morrel uttered these words with an energy which made the count shudder. "My friend," continued Morrel, "you named the fifth of October as the end of the period of waiting,—to-day is the fifth of October," he took out his watch, "it is now nine o'clock,—I have yet three hours to live."

"Be it so," said the count, "come." Morrel mechanically followed the count, and they had entered the grotto before he perceived it. He felt a carpet under his feet, a door opened, perfumes surrounded him, and a brilliant light dazzled his eyes. Morrel hesitated to advance; he dreaded the enervating effect of all that he saw. Monte Cristo drew him in gently. "Why should we not spend the last three hours remaining to us of life, like those ancient Romans, who when condemned by Nero, their emperor and heir, sat down at a table covered with flowers, and gently glided into death, amid the perfume of heliotropes and roses?" Morrel smiled. "As you please," he said; "death is always death,—that is forgetfulness, repose, exclusion from life, and therefore from grief." He sat down, and Monte Cristo placed himself opposite to him. They were in the marvellous dining-room before described, where the statues had baskets on their heads always filled with fruits and flowers. Morrel had looked carelessly around, and had probably noticed nothing.

"Let us talk like men," he said, looking at the count.

"Go on!"

"Count," said Morrel, "you are the epitome of all human knowledge, and you seem like a being descended from a wiser and more advanced world than ours."

"There is something true in what you say," said the count, with that smile which made him so handsome; "I have descended from a planet called grief."

"I believe all you tell me without questioning its meaning; for instance, you told me to live, and I did live; you told me to hope, and I almost did so. I am almost inclined to ask you, as though you had experienced death, 'is it painful to die?'"

Monte Cristo looked upon Morrel with indescribable tenderness. "Yes," he said, "yes, doubtless it is painful, if you violently break the outer covering which obstinately begs for life. If you plunge a dagger into your flesh, if you insinuate a bullet into your brain, which the least shock disorders,—then certainly, you will suffer pain, and you will repent quitting a life for a repose you have bought at so dear a price."

"Yes; I know that there is a secret of luxury and pain in death, as well as in life; the only thing is to understand it."

"You have spoken truly, Maximilian; according to the care we bestow upon it, death is either a friend who rocks us gently as a nurse, or an enemy who violently drags the soul from the body. Some day, when the world is much older, and when mankind will be masters of all the destructive powers in nature, to serve for the general good of humanity; when mankind, as you were just saying, have discovered the secrets of death, then that death will become as sweet and voluptuous as a slumber in the arms of your beloved."

"And if you wished to die, you would choose this death, count?"

"Yes."

Morrel extended his hand. "Now I understand," he said, "why you had me brought here to this desolate spot, in the midst of the ocean, to this subterranean palace; it was because you loved me, was it not, count? It was because you loved me well enough to give me one of those sweet means of death of which we were speaking; a death without agony, a death which allows me to fade away while pronouncing Valentine's name and pressing your hand."

"Yes, you have guessed rightly, Morrel," said the count, "that is what I intended."

"Thanks; the idea that tomorrow I shall no longer suffer, is sweet to my heart."

"Do you then regret nothing?"

"No," replied Morrel.

"Not even me?" asked the count with deep emotion. Morrel's clear eye was for the moment clouded, then it shone with unusual lustre, and a large tear rolled down his cheek.

"What," said the count, "do you still regret anything in the world, and yet die?"

"Oh, I entreat you," exclaimed Morrel in a low voice, "do not speak another word, count; do not prolong my punishment." The count fancied that he was yielding, and this belief revived the horrible doubt that had overwhelmed him at the Chateau d'If. "I am endeavoring," he thought, "to make this man happy; I look upon this restitution as a weight thrown into the scale to balance the evil I have wrought. Now, supposing I am deceived, supposing this man has not been unhappy enough to merit happiness. Alas, what would become of me who can only atone for evil by doing good?" Then he said aloud: "Listen, Morrel, I see your grief is great, but still you do not like to risk your soul." Morrel smiled sadly. "Count," he said, "I swear to you my soul is no longer my own."

"Maximilian, you know I have no relation in the world. I have accustomed myself to regard you as my son: well, then, to save my son, I will sacrifice my life, nay, even my fortune."

"What do you mean?"

"I mean, that you wish to quit life because you do not understand all the enjoyments which are the fruits of a large fortune. Morrel, I possess nearly a hundred millions and I give them to you; with such a fortune you can attain every wish. Are you ambitious? Every career is open to you. Overturn the world, change its character, yield to mad ideas, be even criminal—but live."

"Count, I have your word," said Morrel coldly; then taking out his watch, he added, "It is half-past eleven."

"Morrel, can you intend it in my house, under my very eyes?"

"Then let me go," said Maximilian, "or I shall think you did not love me for my own sake, but for yours;" and he arose.

"It is well," said Monte Cristo whose countenance brightened at these words; "you wish—you are inflexible. Yes, as you said, you are indeed wretched and a miracle alone can cure you. Sit down, Morrel, and wait."

Morrel obeyed; the count arose, and unlocking a closet with a key suspended from his gold chain, took from it a little silver casket, beautifully carved and chased, the corners of which represented four bending figures, similar to the Caryatides, the forms of women, symbols of the angels aspiring to heaven. He placed the casket on the table; then opening it took out a little golden box, the top of which flew open when touched by a secret spring. This box contained an unctuous substance partly solid, of which it was impossible to discover the color, owing to the reflection of the polished gold, sapphires, rubies, emeralds, which ornamented the box. It was a mixed mass of blue, red, and gold. The count took out a small quantity of this with a gilt spoon, and offered it to Morrel, fixing a long steadfast glance upon him. It was then observable that the substance was greenish.

"This is what you asked for," he said, "and what I promised to give you."

"I thank you from the depths of my heart," said the young man, taking the spoon from the hands of Monte Cristo. The count took another spoon, and again dipped it into the golden box. "What are you going to do, my friend?" asked Morrel, arresting his hand.

"Well, the fact is, Morrel, I was thinking that I too am weary of life, and since an opportunity presents itself"—

"Stay!" said the young man. "You who love, and are beloved; you, who have faith and hope,—oh, do not follow my example. In your case it would be a crime. Adieu, my noble and generous friend, adieu; I will go and tell Valentine what you have done for me." And slowly, though without any hesitation, only waiting to press the count's hand fervently, he swallowed the mysterious substance offered by Monte Cristo. Then they were both silent. Ali, mute and attentive, brought the pipes and coffee, and disappeared. By degrees, the light of the lamps gradually faded in the hands of the marble statues which held them, and the perfumes appeared less powerful to Morrel. Seated opposite to him, Monte

Cristo watched him in the shadow, and Morrel saw nothing but the bright eyes of the count. An overpowering sadness took possession of the young man, his hands relaxed their hold, the objects in the room gradually lost their form and color, and his disturbed vision seemed to perceive doors and curtains open in the walls.

"Friend," he cried, "I feel that I am dying; thanks!" He made a last effort to extend his hand, but it fell powerless beside him. Then it appeared to him that Monte Cristo smiled, not with the strange and fearful expression which had sometimes revealed to him the secrets of his heart, but with the benevolent kindness of a father for a child. At the same time the count appeared to increase in stature, his form, nearly double its usual height, stood out in relief against the red tapestry, his black hair was thrown back, and he stood in the attitude of an avenging angel. Morrel, overpowered, turned around in the arm-chair; a delicious torpor permeated every vein. A change of ideas presented themselves to his brain, like a new design on the kaleidoscope. Enervated, prostrate, and breathless, he became unconscious of outward objects; he seemed to be entering that vague delirium preceding death. He wished once again to press the count's hand, but his own was immovable. He wished to articulate a last farewell, but his tongue lay motionless and heavy in his throat, like a stone at the mouth of a sepulchre. Involuntarily his languid eyes closed, and still through his eyelashes a well-known form seemed to move amid the obscurity with which he thought himself enveloped.

The count had just opened a door. Immediately a brilliant light from the next room, or rather from the palace adjoining, shone upon the room in which he was gently gliding into his last sleep. Then he saw a woman of marvellous beauty appear on the threshold of the door separating the two rooms. Pale, and sweetly smiling, she looked like an angel of mercy conjuring the angel of vengeance. "Is it heaven that opens before me?" thought the dying man; "that angel resembles the one I have lost." Monte Cristo pointed out Morrel to the young woman, who advanced towards him with clasped hands and a smile upon her lips.

"Valentine, Valentine!" he mentally ejaculated; but his lips uttered no sound, and as though all his strength were centred in that internal emotion, he sighed and closed his eyes. Valentine rushed towards him; his lips again moved.

"He is calling you," said the count; "he to whom you have confided your destiny—he from whom death would have separated you, calls you to him. Happily, I vanquished death. Henceforth, Valentine, you will never again be separated on earth, since he has rushed into death to find you. Without me, you would both have died. May God accept my atonement in the preservation of these two existences!"

Valentine seized the count's hand, and in her irresistible impulse of joy carried it to her lips.

"Oh, thank me again!" said the count; "tell me till you are weary, that I have restored you to happiness; you do not know how much I require this assurance."

"Oh, yes, yes, I thank you with all my heart," said Valentine; "and if you doubt the sincerity of my gratitude, oh, then, ask Haidee! ask my beloved sister Haidee, who ever since our departure from France, has caused me to wait patiently for this happy day, while talking to me of you."

"You then love Haidee?" asked Monte Cristo with an emotion he in vain endeavored to dissimulate.

"Oh, yes, with all my soul."

"Well, then, listen, Valentine," said the count; "I have a favor to ask of you."

"Of me? Oh, am I happy enough for that?"

"Yes; you have called Haidee your sister,—let her become so indeed, Valentine; render her all the gratitude you fancy that you owe to me; protect her, for" (the count's voice was thick with emotion) "henceforth she will be alone in the world."

"Alone in the world!" repeated a voice behind the count, "and why?"

Monte Cristo turned around; Haidee was standing pale, motionless, looking at the count with an expression of fearful amazement.

"Because to-morrow, Haidee, you will be free; you will then assume your proper position in society, for I will not allow my destiny to overshadow yours. Daughter of a prince, I restore to you the riches and name of your father."

Haidee became pale, and lifting her transparent hands to heaven, exclaimed in a voice stifled with tears, "Then you leave me, my lord?"

"Haidee, Haidee, you are young and beautiful; forget even my name, and be happy."

"It is well," said Haidee; "your order shall be executed, my lord; I will forget even your name, and be happy." And she stepped back to retire.

"Oh, heavens," exclaimed Valentine, who was supporting the head of Morrel on her shoulder, "do you not see how pale she is? Do you not see how she suffers?"

Haidee answered with a heartrending expression, "Why should he understand this, my sister? He is my master, and I am his slave; he has the right to notice nothing."

The count shuddered at the tones of a voice which penetrated the inmost recesses of his heart; his eyes met those of the young girl and he could not bear their brilliancy. "Oh, heavens," exclaimed Monte Cristo, "can my suspicions be correct? Haidee, would it please you not to leave me?"

"I am young," gently replied Haidee; "I love the life you have made so sweet to me, and I should be sorry to die."

"You mean, then, that if I leave you, Haidee"—

"I should die; yes, my lord."

"Do you then love me?"

"Oh, Valentine, he asks if I love him. Valentine, tell him if you love Maximilian." The count felt his heart dilate and throb; he opened his arms, and Haidee, uttering a cry, sprang into them. "Oh, yes," she cried, "I do love you! I love you as one loves a father, brother, husband! I love you as my life, for you are the best, the noblest of created beings!"

"Let it be, then, as you wish, sweet angel; God has sustained me in my struggle with my enemies, and has given me this reward; he will not let me end my triumph in suffering; I wished to punish myself, but he has pardoned me. Love me then, Haidee! Who knows? perhaps your love will make me forget all that I do not wish to remember."

"What do you mean, my lord?"

"I mean that one word from you has enlightened me more than twenty years of slow experience; I have but you in the world, Haidee; through you I again take hold on life, through you I shall suffer, through you rejoice."

"Do you hear him, Valentine?" exclaimed Haidee; "he says that through me he will suffer—through me, who would yield my life for his." The count withdrew for a moment. "Have I discovered the truth?" he said; "but whether it be for recompense or punishment, I accept my fate. Come, Haidee, come!" and throwing his arm around the young girl's waist, he pressed the hand of Valentine, and disappeared.

An hour had nearly passed, during which Valentine, breathless and motionless, watched steadfastly over Morrel.

At length she felt his heart beat, a faint breath played upon his lips, a slight shudder, announcing the return of life, passed through the young man's frame. At length his eyes opened, but they were at first fixed and expressionless; then sight returned, and with it feeling and grief. "Oh," he cried, in an accent of despair, "the count has deceived me; I am yet living;" and extending his hand towards the table, he seized a knife.

"Dearest," exclaimed Valentine, with her adorable smile, "awake, and look at me!" Morrel uttered a loud exclamation, and frantic, doubtful, dazzled, as though by a celestial vision, he fell upon his knees.

The next morning at daybreak, Valentine and Morrel were walking arm-in-arm on the sea-shore, Valentine relating how Monte Cristo had appeared in her room, explained everything, revealed the crime, and, finally, how he had saved her life by enabling her to simulate death. They had found the door of the grotto opened, and gone forth; on the azure dome of heaven still glittered a few remaining stars. Morrel soon perceived a man standing among the rocks, apparently awaiting a sign from them to advance, and pointed him out to Valentine. "Ah, it is Jacopo," she said, "the captain of the yacht;" and she beckoned him towards them.

"Do you wish to speak to us?" asked Morrel.

"I have a letter to give you from the count."

"From the count!" murmured the two young people.

"Yes; read it." Morrel opened the letter, and read:—

"My Dear Maximilian,—

"There is a felucca for you at anchor. Jacopo will carry you to Leghorn, where Monsieur Noirtier awaits his granddaughter, whom he wishes to bless before you lead her to the altar. All that is in this grotto, my friend, my house in the Champs Elysees, and my chateau at Treport, are the marriage gifts bestowed by Edmond Dantes upon the son of his old master, Morrel. Mademoiselle de Villefort will share them with you; for I entreat her to give to the poor the immense fortune reverting to her from her father, now a madman, and her brother who died last September with his mother. Tell the angel who will watch over your future destiny, Morrel, to pray sometimes for a man, who like Satan thought himself for an instant equal to God, but who now acknowledges with Christian humility that God alone possesses supreme power and infinite wisdom. Perhaps those prayers may soften the remorse he feels in his heart. As for you, Morrel, this is the secret of my conduct towards you. There is neither happiness nor misery in the world; there is only the comparison of one state with another, nothing more. He who has felt the deepest grief is best able to experience supreme happiness. We must have felt what it is to die, Morrel, that we may appreciate the enjoyments of living.

"Live, then, and be happy, beloved children of my heart, and never forget that until the day when God shall deign to reveal the future to man, all human wisdom is summed up in these two words,—'*Wait and hope.*'—Your friend,

"Edmond Dantes, Count of Monte Cristo."

During the perusal of this letter, which informed Valentine for the first time of the madness of her father and the death of her brother, she became pale, a heavy sigh escaped from her bosom, and tears, not the less painful because they were silent, ran down her cheeks; her happiness cost her very dear. Morrel looked around uneasily. "But," he said, "the count's generosity is too overwhelming; Valentine will be satisfied with my humble fortune. Where is the count, friend? Lead me to him." Jacopo pointed towards the horizon. "What do you mean?" asked Valentine. "Where is the count?—where is Haidee?"

"Look!" said Jacopo.

The eyes of both were fixed upon the spot indicated by the sailor, and on the blue line separating the sky from the Mediterranean Sea, they perceived a large white sail. "Gone," said Morrel; "gone!—adieu, my friend—adieu, my father!"

"Gone," murmured Valentine; "adieu, my sweet Haidee—adieu, my sister!"

"Who can say whether we shall ever see them again?" said Morrel with tearful eyes.

"Darling," replied Valentine, "has not the count just told us that all human wisdom is summed up in two words?—'*Wait and hope.*'"